The Limbo Stories

Otto Frank Miller

Big Water Press

GRAND HAVEN, MICHIGAN

For Dani

With many thanks to Jeff Dutton and Laura Popelka

Hence thou mayst comprehend that love must be
The seed within yourselves of every virtue,
And every act that merits punishment.

–DANTE ALIGHIERI

CONTENTS

Introduction

Do you believe in God?

It's not necessary that you believe in God for you to enjoy what you are about to read, but be aware that the question is going to come up. It's unavoidable. To be clear, no one is suggesting you will believe in God by the time you are finished with all these stories. That's not the point here.

Do you believe in life after death? There, that's the better question. The "God" question comes loaded with so many other considerations, like "Which God?" or "Whose God?" Let's keep it simple: Once you die, what do you think happens?

Let's suppose you believe that nothing happens. Perhaps you are convinced beyond persuasion that once the flame of life is extinguished and your ashes are blown to the wind, you are simply kaput. If so, please don't be dissuaded because another important question still remains: Do you believe you are living your best life?

The one thing we can all agree on is that, barring some severe medical impairment, at some point everyone alive knows they are alive. There is no debating this one, right? And we can all agree that we are at least trying to live our best lives. Now you may have some habits you wish you could curb, or some people you wish you could forgive, or some regrettable behavior that will haunt you forever, but you definitely strive to make the right decisions as you go about your day. Even if you're a completely self-involved misanthrope, you're still trying to optimize your happiness while you're here, right?

On the next page, you will be introduced to Nick Kraus. Nick Kraus is certain he is living his best life. For the record, Nick is neither completely self-involved nor a misanthrope. Moreover, he is not burdened with any tremendous vices and he is loved by many friends and family. Not only does he have every reason to believe he is living his best life, he is justified in believing he is living a charmed life.

But Nick is wrong. He is not living his best life. Nick is going to die and somehow, someone or something is going to make him go back and try again. Nick will die again. His game piece will be set back on the game board and he will play the game again. And then he will die again. Each time Nick dies he will meet other players on the game board, and they will share their strategies. Each player Nick meets is trying to answer the question, "How do I win this game?" and he is too.

Story 1: Wanderlust

Kansas is featureless. I don't mean to offend, but nothing stands out across the state. To the east there is Missouri with its Ozarks and Mark Twain and a contrived Southern pride, but Kansas seems less interested in drawing attention to itself.

We're heading west and a sign tells me that I have entered Colorado. I slow down to review my map. "I was told there would be mountains," I say to my wife, Lori, in the passenger seat. She is reading a guidebook that tells of free campsites near mountain streams. An index card juts out from between the pages. It reads DUE DATE' across the top.

Lori flips to the front of the book and recites, "The plains rise imperceptibly as you approach the great city of Denver from the east."

"That book has to be a decade out of date."

"Unless it was written before the last tectonic shift in the Earth's crust, I'd say we're fine." The saucer-sized lenses of her sunglasses completely cover her eyes. I cannot read her expression or gauge her mood.

The night before we had slept in our tents on the edge of a farmer's field in central Kansas. We befriended some locals at a produce market we found at the intersection of two state highways. We spoke for an hour after we bought some fruit and told them of our summer journey from Chicago to the West Coast. They were suspicious of our provenance at first.

"Pardon me for saying so, young man, but we don't see a lot of camping types from Chicago passing through here," the gentleman named Earl said. His wife, Ruth, nodded in agreement as she surveyed our left hands.

We explained that we were from central Illinois. We had met in high school and then attended the same university, where we'd both studied to become teachers. We'd enrolled in a government program that would forgive our student loans if we committed to teaching in the ghetto for a few years.

"How were the crops when you set out?" Ruth asked.

They were not interested in hearing about the challenges of the inner city, but we had their trust. Once they knew we were farm people, they felt they understood us. The bed of their truck held dozens of empty harvest baskets. The baskets were made from wide ribbons of shaved cedar that were woven and stapled. They spent their Friday afternoons visiting country markets to provide them their weekend stock.

It was June and there had been scarce rain that spring. I told them that you could tell the corn from the soy but not by much. They had inquired out of genuine interest, as true farmers do. As farmers, they needed to be experts in everything: agriculture, weather, veterinary science, economics, mechanics, law, and accounting. They probably had never taken more than two consecutive days off in their lives. Many farmers had sold out to developers or leased their land to corporate holding companies that worked their land and paid them a dividend. For Earl and Ruth to have thrived on their own for so long meant they were capable and smart. There was a lot I could learn from them and I let them know by asking many questions.

I must have gotten carried away because Lori broke the rhythm of my inquiry. "For how long have you been married?"

"Fifty-two years last week," they answered in unison.

We offered exclamations in response, as we had nothing in our lives that had endured for even half that long.

Ruth surveyed our hands once more. "Is this your honeymoon?"

"No, ma'am. We were married last year right after graduation," Lori answered.

They nodded, again in unison. The trajectory of our life plan met their approval.

"How did you choose this route, Nicholas?" Earl asked.

I had told him my name was Nick, but I enjoyed the way he said the longer version with affection. I was tempted to ask whether he meant marrying at a young age or our route out west but calculated that Earl wasn't one to joke about the Lord's sacraments. I explained that we preferred to take the backroads wherever possible. As teachers, we had the whole summer off. We were in no hurry.

As I spoke, Lori put her hand on my back and poked the nail of her index finger into my skin.

"I better leave you folks to your rounds." I looked at my watch and smiled at the couple. "It was a genuine pleasure to make your acquaintance."

"Where will you stay this evening?" Ruth asked.

"This travel guide says there are some free sites further west down K5, down by the river landing," Lori answered. She began loading our haul of produce into the car.

Earl shook his head. "Those sites are gone I'm afraid. They converted that landing into a pumping station for irrigation."

Ruth looked at Earl. He nodded and then said, "Come stay with us tonight. Our place is down that way."

This was good fortune. I was happy to have more time to talk to the couple.

"We would never impose on you like that. We just met," Lori said.

"Well, we'll need to start looking for another site then," I said to Lori.

I could tell that Ruth and Earl were not the type of people to insist, as well as not the type to interfere in a discussion between man and wife. Earl grabbed the brim of his cap and tipped it at Lori, then he waved goodbye. Ruth smiled and turned.

I pulled Lori closer and brought my mouth to her ear. "Come on, Lor. We don't have to fix supper with them. And you know it could take hours to find another site. Do you want to set up camp in the dark?"

"I don't remember saying I wanted to go camping at all." Lori reviewed her hands and clapped the dust off them. Then she wiped them on her jeans. "Whatever, Nick. Just get me somewhere with a sink please."

I trotted over and waved them down before they pulled away. We followed them down the highway to their land.

I set up our site in a grass yard to the west of their barn while Lori washed up inside. She came out refreshed and sidled up next to me by the fire pit. Earl and Ruth checked on us just before sundown and then went to bed. We stayed up and watched a summer storm roll through to the north. The lightning was red and purple and spread like a web through the clouds. It never seemed to strike the ground. For all the brilliance, the storm was too far away for me to hear the thunder.

***

I'm a big fan of Hunter S. Thompson. He didn't offer much material that was appropriate for my junior high English class, but I peppered in an anecdote whenever possible, a taste of salaciousness to ignite some interest between Jack London stories. The Woody Creek Tavern was Hunter's favorite bar near his home outside Aspen. We arrive in time for a late lunch of chili and beer. A bumper sticker on the wall behind the bar reads COLORADO: I'M NOT FROM HERE BUT I GOT HERE AS FAST AS I COULD.

It's poignant so I point it out to Lori but it doesn't resonate with her.

"Sorry. All that fruit had me up early. I'm not used to drinking at this altitude, either." She puts her forehead in her palm and hoists a spoon into her mouth.

"We budgeted for a few hotel nights," I say. I rub her back with my palm.

"Everything OK sweetheart?" our matronly server asks.

"She'll be OK," I answer as Lori shakes her head no.

Lori puts down her spoon and then cleans her mouth with her napkin. "Our budget is for backcountry motels, not Aspen."

"Good point."

Lori lifts her head. She smacks the table with her left hand and then gives herself a light slap with the same hand. In her right hand, she grips her can of beer and pounds it.

"All right! That's my girl." I love it when she rallies. She is my anchor.

We finish our chili and order pie and coffee. Our late lunch begins to overlap with the early happy hour crowd. Someone turns up the volume on the jukebox. Four cyclists arrive in full touring gear: two men and two women. The clasps of their shoes clack on the floor as the western doors swing behind them.

"This used to be a mining town." I wag my fork toward the new arrivals. "A frontier town."

The two couples find a table. They are middle-aged but in great condition.

"Now it's white collar criminals and their trophy wives on $3,000 ten-speeds," I scoff.

"Why such contempt?" Lori asks. "You'd have us doing the exact same thing if we were in their position."

"Well, I'd never ask you to get that much work done," I joke.

The resting expressions of the women at the biker's table appear fixed to subtle grin. It's unclear whether their dispositions match their amused appearance because they are not saying much at all.

One of them stands to use the powder room. "Order me a spritz," she commands her biker. The zipper of her Lycra top is taxed to the limit by her ample bosom. Her hair is blonde.

The other stands and follows her. Her outfit is head-to-toe black and wetsuit tight. She is tall. "Me too," she says as she slips past.

The men watch their ladies depart. I notice the huskier man hold his stare on Lori before he tracks his gaze back to his tablemates. His black mane throws flashes of silver. I can see the definition of the muscles and veins in his neck as he smiles at his friend.

"The perma-grin sisters have their men in check, huh?" I say. Lori doesn't hear me. She's staring at the huskier biker.

"Let's get some more drinks," she says.

"We just had coffee." I say.

"What, are we in Europe?"

That must have been some coffee. This is quite a rally.

Our server returns. I ask for a couple more beers. Lori interrupts and requests a rum and cola.

"That's the spirit, girl," the server says.

The bikers order some Italian spritz cocktails for their ladies and cans of beer for themselves.

"How far did you folks ride today?" Lori asks as she leans toward their table.

They are eager to engage. The lean one points out that they are neighbors in Red Cliffs, a subdivision up the hills across the highway from Aspen proper. The huskier biker says that's about four kilometers from the tavern. The lean one explains that he does thirty kilometers every day, rain or shine. I puzzle over their choice of units. I don't detect any accents.

"You guys staying in town?" the huskier one asks. He may seem fit now, but I can tell he used to be fat.

Lori tells the men about our camping trip. She seems self-conscious about our frugal itinerary.

"You boys making friends?" the tall wife asks as both women return. They do not look at us as they sit down. They do not wait for a response from their men. There are no introductions.

I had ordered the large chili. My dirty spoon lies abandoned in the deep, scraped-clean cavity of the large bowl. There are some flecks of sauce staining my Key West T-shirt. A portrait of Ernest Hemingway is printed on the front and there is bit of tomato in the middle of his left eye.

"You been to Sloppy Joe's lately?" the lean one asks me. I hear my wife explaining her triathlon training regimen to the husky one.

"Yes. We drove down there last summer for our honeymoon," I say. The shirt is running a little tight. I've fallen into a lifestyle of leisure after busting my tail to drop some pounds for the wedding. It's a cotton shirt so it probably shrunk a little, too.

"Oh, you two are married," the husky man says with surprise. He looks at Lori and she smiles politely. Lori is tall and trim. She would look fit even without exercise but the fact that she was a jock further solidified her sculpted figure.

"Almost a year now," Lori says. She shrugs a little.

The husky man nods at Lori and looks to me. "Good for you," he says.

The drinks arrive. The server places two large goblets in front of the perma-grin wives. Their cocktails are bright orange and bubbles ascend around sparkling ice. They look like two full jars of brand-new pennies. The wives stir their drinks. The men crack their beers.

Lori lifts her drink in salute. I return the gesture along with the other men. The wives ignore us. They talk of patio renovations and hotel suites. Filtered through their artificial smiles, I can't help but think everything they say is pure sarcasm.

Lori is having fun and that's a relief. I stroll to the jukebox and choose a few songs, making sure to select some crowd favorites that folks like to sing along to. I lean against the wall and wait for a couple songs to play before my picks come on. Once they do, I look to Lori hoping she'll affirm my musical taste. Her face brightens and she skips over to me.

"They invited us over for dinner!" she tells me.

"What luck!" I indulge her. I'm happy she's having a good time.

Lori had been talked into enjoying a few of the orange cocktails as my tunes finish playing. Then we hop in the car to head to dinner at the mansion with our new friends.

"What was in those things?" Lori asks. "They were awesome."

Lori had been talked into enjoying a few of the orange cocktails.

"Something called Campari. There was Prosecco, too. Kind of fancy for a tavern in an old mining town, no?" I begin to worry that my boy Hunter Thompson may have been something of a poseur.

"Here, follow this." Lori slaps a napkin on my thigh. It's a scribbled route of switchback roads leading down to the highway and then back up to Red Cliffs. It ends with an address.

"Don't you think we've spent enough time with them?" I take a shot at changing the itinerary. "The wives are completely ignoring us. They might like their husbands back."

"We spent last night in the American Gothic painting. Tonight, I pick the company." She jabs her thumb into her chest for emphasis.

I had switched to soda when I saw Lori switch to cocktails. She's tired and I bet the altitude is getting to her. I'll let her burn bright and flame out early.

She rubs her sternum where she poked herself a little harder than intended. "I don't understand why you're so threatened."

"Who said anything about being threatened?" I laugh. "Should I feel threatened?"

"Well, they're both doctors you know."

"The skinny one is a doctor, a plastic surgeon. The other guy's a PhD," I scoff.

"They're intellectuals," she slurs.

"I wonder if Dr. Schwinn did the professor's liposuction?" I watch the four of them descend the road ahead of me. They take the curves at speed. They cover the terrain like goats.

"Are you mad because Glenn's dad was a doctor?" she jeers.

She's trying to irritate me now. I try not to engage. "Who said anything about Glenn?"

Lori can get feisty when she's drinking. She likes to push my buttons. She likes to challenge me.

"Are you mad that my father is a farmer, like yours? Or that I chose to become an educator, like you?" I ask. This disarms her for a moment.

"Well, what's-his-name there is an educator. Professors teach, you know."

"He's a nutritionist. He got rich selling meal replacements for a bullshit diet program." I land another volley.

I roll down the windows in the car, hoping some fresh air will make her less ornery. A brief shower had passed over while we were in the bar. The smell of fresh rain on the rocky soil soothes me.

I smile in recognition of the majesty before me. The passing shower has left a clean, blue sky. The mountains are alive, and every boulder and bush is vividly defined. We cross a stream that was a dry bed when we passed over it earlier. Before the bar, before the brief shower.

"You'll never forgive me for Glenn," Lori says.

"Where is this coming from?" I lose my cool just a little. "Why do you keep saying his name?"

"I think he was premed," she says.

"Good for him." I pretend to consult the napkin map. "What's our next turn?"

"Hell if I know."

I pull to a cutout on the side of the highway and wait for the peloton of our new friends to pass. They wave us on as they zip by. They commit to a turn on the north side of the highway.

I train my eye on a cluster of mansions tracing the terraced roads winding up the ridges. "Must be up there."

"Oh my," Lori coos and wiggles in her seat a little. It hurts to see her get excited for something I will never be able to give her.

***

It's dark and everyone is drunk except for me. The wives are now sufficiently lubricated to engage in conversation. I perceive what are perhaps sincere smiles struggling through the smirks that are permanently affixed to their faces.

"Isn't this delicious?" the slender brunette says. She brings a bark-hard slice of pesto-slathered crust to her face.

They had pizzas delivered. No chance that meals would be prepared in-house for guests of our standing. They didn't take our requests; they simply ordered ten thin-crust pizzas, personal-sized disks in various states of adornment.

We have an ideal view of Aspen down below. The streets are delineated by yellow orange street lamps that outline the grid of old downtown. The light swells around the hotels, stores, and restaurants. The chairlifts are still yet remain lit. They extend like strands of Christmas lights decorating Ajax Mountain.

There are two bottles of Prosecco in a stainless-steel ice bucket sitting atop a pedestal near the pool. The blonde wife struggles to reach for a bottle. She is waist deep in the pool and her bust knocks over one of the empty bottles at the base of the pedestal. I scurry to retrieve it before it rolls off the patio and onto the rocks.

"Damn these things," the blonde jokes while hoisting her chest in her hands and bouncing her breasts in unison.

I look straight into her chasm of cleavage. She notices and smiles. I look away and she giggles at my bashfulness.

"Jump in, sweetheart. It's plenty warm," the blonde says. She smiles, I think. She dunks herself below the water, then surfaces with back arched and head tilted to the sky. She looks forward enticingly with her long blonde hair slicked across her head and down her back.

The water rinses the makeup from her face. I notice her wax-paper skin and the crow's feet around her eyes that her husband somehow missed. "My trunks are in the car," I say.

"Fetch a pair from the pool house." She nods her head towards the shed. "Or don't."

I look over at Lori, who is flanked by Dr. Schwinn and the dietician. All three of them have glasses of brown liquor in their palms. The men are in robes. They were making noise about going for a dip with their wives but never made it past the bar. It occurs to me that they just wanted a reason to show their bare chests.

"Maybe in a minute. I just ate," I nod toward the husbands and my wife. "I might go see how everything's holding up at the bar."

"That's probably a good idea," the fit brunette says. There is a sincere warning behind her fake smile.

I walk over to the bar, where I hear the dietician is explaining his novel to Lori. "The protagonist is a cop, but he's done playing by the rules. The mafia types are threatening his family and he decides to go straight vigilante on them."

"Sounds like a meaningful contribution to the annals of American literature," I quip. I look to Lori for a reassuring laugh, but she sneers at me.

"So, what are you writing?" she swirls the liquor in her rocks glass.

"Care for a Scotch?" Dr. Schwinn jiggles the bottle in his hand. "It's fifteen years old."

"It looks like she's had my share," I say.

"Shut up, fatty." Lori downs the remainder and extends the empty glass to Dr. Schwinn.

He looks to me and I shake my head no. Lori turns to me and glares.

"Three years of crummy road trips and I've finally found some classy folks to spend an evening with." Lori leans forward and points at me. "I'm going to have some fun tonight."

I look toward the pool and see the blonde stuffing a water-logged slice of pizza in her mouth. Dr. Schwinn and the brunette are exchanging signals. The nutritionist is patting my wife's hand.

"Fuck it, pour me one of those," I say. I'll show her that I can be a good sport.

The conversation seems to have stalled with me in the mix. Dr. Schwinn fills the void by telling us about every ascent he's made up every French mountain on his bike. I time my drinking so I finish my glass at the same time as Lori finishes hers.

"All right, that should do it for us. We've got a big day tomorrow." I clap my hands.

"You can't drive," the nutritionist asserts.

"I had just one. We will be leaving," I say with resolve.

"I'm staying here." Lori has met her quotient. She begins to fall from her stool.

"Lori, it's time to go." I grab her by her wrist to steady her. She pulls her arm away and her momentum takes her to the ground. She sits there and laughs.

Dr. Schwinn lifts her with an arm around her waist. The nutritionist hands her another whiskey as soon as she's on her feet. As I begin to interject, he raises his hand to block my protest.

"Just one more for the road."

"Just one for the road, honey," Lori giggles. There are three full fingers of booze in the glass and she drops the whole measure straight down her throat in one spill. Lori laughs. The men are stunned. My eyes widen.

She laughs so hard she loses her breath. She gags, vomits, and gags again. Her body spasms as she voids her gut.

***

Our hosts give us a bedroom on the main floor. Lori is sitting in the shower of the en-suite bathroom. She's been in there for a half hour. The last time I checked on her it looked like she had been crying. That's just the boo-hoos from the booze, though.

I left the puke for someone else to clean up. It was their fault for putting her in that state. What were they trying to achieve anyway? I'm angry but I have no choice but to stay here at this point. It's too late to find a room and making camp in the dark is a pain, especially with an incapacitated wife.

I hear her strain to lift her herself and then the shower shuts off. A moment later she is standing before me. Her arms are crossed tightly across her chest to close a robe around herself. She is hunched over in a self-embrace.

"I need air," she says. She registers my look of protest and repeats, "I need air."

I abandon the protest. A single serving of good whiskey has a pleasant, somnolent effect and I'm rather comfy in bed with the guidebooks. I'm planning for a day of hiking in the mountains tomorrow.

Our room looks onto the patio and down the valley to Aspen below. After some time, I get up to check on Lori. She is hunched over near the fire pit in the same self-embrace. Dr. Schwinn is lounging next to the nutritionist's fit wife. The damp blonde is passed out in a chaise lounge next to the pool. Someone has placed two beach towels over her as blankets. The husky dietician is not in sight.

I trace my route for tomorrow morning on the map. There are many spurs off the main road leading to the backside of Ajax. Each spur is a head road that starts a little higher up the mountain than the previous. If I had a Jeep with a split differential, I would shoot the whole trail, but I have to respect the limits of my little Subaru. The thought of a hungover wife on the bumpy road settles the decision for me. We'll head to the highest spur, take it for as long as she can handle it and then hike.

With our route decided, I switch books to one about the trees and plants of the American Rocky Mountains. I'm interested in the edible weeds but am distracted by the illustrated pages of wildflowers. The centerfold is a two-page spread of a mountain grove filled with yellow and blue blossoms. I close my eyes and picture the surface of the field undulating hypnotically in the breeze. I awaken when the book topples from my hands onto my chest.

I walk to the bathroom and step over Lori's sopping wet garments. I had put her in the shower fully clothed. I notice her underwear are included in the heap. I better check on her. Evenings at this altitude are cool, even in June.

I look out the bedroom window. The blonde still sleeps in her chair, but the others are gone. I leave the bedroom and find my way to the back patio. I see the husky nutritionist. He is in the hot tub. Lori is in the hot tub. Her robe is on the ground.

***

The early June dawn awakens me. Morning sunbeams dissipate the slick of condensation on the car windows. Lori sleeps next to me and I imagine she will stay asleep for some time. I located the public campsite that I had seen just off the highway after leaving the tavern. It was the type of camper's rest stop you find out west. The few neighbors we have are already awake and breaking camp to continue on their quests.

I pop the rear hatch and squirm out the back of the car. I set to pulling our packs and gear from atop the car. I place them back in the rear on the side where I had slept, being mindful not to disturb Lori.

I head west on the highway away from Aspen, toward Basalt. There's a billboard sign that tells me THE CHALET CAFE' will be one mile up the road on the right. I continue on the road and see a two-story Alpine style cottage with a gang of pickup trucks parked out front.

The place smells like the Saturday mornings of my childhood. Bacon dominates but a bouquet of strong coffee, fried eggs, and maple syrup adds to the tapestry. A petite waitress carrying someone's order makes eye contact with me. I raise my index finger and mouth the word "one" without actually saying it. She smiles and nods.

My coffee cup has been topped off three times before the food comes. I've overcome the haze of my night of poor sleep. My food arrives.

"Thanks."

"You got it. Are you having anything else or do you want this now?" The waitress puts her thumb on a scribbled note card that is my check. Her name tag reads SUSANNE'.

"I'll take it now. Thanks, Susanne," I answer.

"I'm a Suzy." She winks and sets the bill down.

The last patrons of the late morning are gone and I'm alone in the diner with the staff. When Suzy comes back for the check, she sits with me and chats for a bit. She's pretty in a plain way. She's brassy and fun to talk to.

"It's a long drive from Chicago to the coast but it's worth it from here on out," she tells me. "I did it a few years back, from Michigan to L.A."

She tells me about her recent journey. She had followed a boy out west to L.A., a musician. He found some success and that was it for his interest in Suzy. She was working her way back east when she fell in love with Colorado and decided to stick around for a little while.

I'm reclined in my booth with one leg stretched out on the bench seat. Suzy mirrors me from her side of the booth. We are the only people left on the floor until Lori walks through the door. She is wearing a T-shirt, flannel pajama bottoms and gym shoes. I wave her over to sit with me. Suzy abandons her spot in the booth and looks at Lori.

"Can I sit down?" she asks, ignoring Suzy.

"Of course," I say. "Suzy, this is my wife, Lori."

"Pleasure," Suzy says, but her spunk is gone. "Do you want to order something?"

"I wouldn't dare." She rests her elbow on the table and rests her head in her hand. "Maybe a coffee. And a water."

We sit in silence long after she is served her coffee and water. She orders plain toast, too.

"I'm sorry," she says.

"For what?" I look over her head and out the window.

"Don't do me like that."

"It's my fault really," I say. "I'm sorry."

"I show my naked body to another man and you're apologizing to me?"

"Wouldn't be the first time," I reply. We return to silence.

I pull out one of the guidebooks that I have commandeered from her and pretend to look for trails.

"I'm sorry I can't give you a big house with a pool." I assault her with insincere apologies. "I'm sorry I can't give you fancy booze and pesto pizza. I'm sorry I'm not fit."

"I'm sorry I have to endure these fucking road trips," she replies.

***

The Colorado River cuts a deep gorge out near Glenwood Springs. I take my pick of trailheads from the map and make my way with no help from my passenger.

"You never told me you didn't like these trips," I say.

"You choose to not hear it."

Lori sometimes invents her own narratives. I indulge her anyway. "Please tell me what was so bad about hiking up Mount Washington or kayaking the Outer Banks?"

"Listen to yourself, you selfish asshole! How about this question: What was so bad about the trip I wanted to take?"

"Which trip?" I fall for it.

"Exactly." She is satisfied with herself. I let her have her victory.

We follow the map off the highway and then follow the street signs to the parking lot for the trail. From the lot, we walk down to a landing that extends beyond the ridge of the gorge. The view to the bottom is bewildering for a Midwestern boy like me. I see tiny objects moving along the surface of the river below, but I can't figure out what they are. My perspective is warped by the enormity of the chasm.

"Oh my God, those are rafts. How do you think they got down there?" I'm delighted. I've never seen anything like this. The view from the top of a skyscraper just isn't the same. "Can you imagine what the Grand Canyon must be like?"

"I guess I'm going to have to find out now, huh?" Lori huffs.

I put my hands on her shoulders and turn her to face me. "We had a bad day. I know you're sorry. I know you're dragging, but let's not let one bad day ruin another, OK?"

Lori rolls her eyes and snatches her trail book back from me. "How far do you want to go today?"

The irony is that she can outlast me on the trails even when sporting a fierce hangover. She's probably metabolized all the residue of last night by now.

"It's about eight miles down to Glenwood Springs from here. We can make it there for a late lunch and be back here by evening. Sound good?" I tuck my shirt into my shorts but the edge sneaks back out on the right side.

"Sure, honey. Sounds grand." She adjusts her enormous sunglasses.

The rocks and walls of the canyon out here are orange. The color reflects the minerals in the rocks and soil. The book describes it as an earthy red, but it looks positively Martian to me. Vegetation is sparse. One plant that seems to thrive is a small shrub that grows out from between the rocks where sediment has blown in and compounded. The plant looks like rosemary.

From a distance, it looks like the rocks are sprouting wispy mustaches.

Extended periods of the trail curve down and away from the rim of the gorge and then return us to spectacular vistas as the path leads us back up to the edge. As we reach one such crest, I hear a dull horn.

"What was that?" I ask.

"Probably a train," she answers dryly.

"Where is there a train around here?" I spread my arms and turn like a dervish.

Lori cocks her head as if to pity me. The horn sounds again and it echoes off the walls of the canyon. She points down.

I race to the rim and fall to my belly. My body is over the edge all the way to my armpits. The river makes a dogleg turn right from my perspective. There is another long blast from the horn and the nose of the engine emerges from around the turn on the far side of the river. It's an Amtrak train heading back east. The carriages flash as sunshine bounces off their silver skin and sky-light windows. I behold the entire length of the train as it reaches a long, straight stretch of the river.

"You don't see that every day," I say from the ground.

"A train? We live in Chicago," Lori is standing over me with her hands on her hips.

"I mean the whole length of it. All at once, you know?" I continue to marvel. "I wonder what it's like to be down there."

"Me, too. I wish I was on it."

"I do, too. Can you imagine seeing the country like that?" I stand up and dust myself off.

Lori is staring down at the train as it proceeds around the next bend and out of sight.

"I want to go back," she says.

"Back where, honey?"

"All the way back." She refuses to look in my direction. I can only see her profile. A single tear escapes down the side of her cheek from behind her glasses.

I approach her and bring her square by her shoulders. "What is this?"

She begins to sob and heave. I bring her close and she surrenders herself to me. She sobs and heaves rhythmically on my chest.

"I'm sorry," she says between fits of tears.

"For what? Are we still talking about that? I forgot about it already."

"I should have never agreed. It's my fault. I'm sorry," she says into my chest. "I want to go back and start over."

"But we still have the whole summer." I try to pull her away a little bit to look at her, but she resists. "We have all school year to spend in Chicago. Let's see the country while we can."

"Nick, I don't want to see the country with you. I'm sorry. I don't want to." She begins to compose herself. "I want to go back. Before I hurt you again."

"You could never hurt me so bad I would stop loving you." I squeeze her. From the river below, we hear the distant hoots and cheers of rafters as they shoot a set of rapids.

"I know. That's why I have to do this." She begins to weep again. "It's not right."

"What's not right?" I try again to pull her away and, again, she resists. She is strong.

"I'm going to keep hurting you until you resent me. I know it." She cries harder. She's burst the levee holding back her emotions.

The episode weakens her clutch. I remove the sunglasses from her bloodshot eyes. They are blue with streaks of gold and I love her even at her worst. I can fix this. I will fix this.

Lori catches her breath. "Let's go home. We'll talk to someone. We'll try. OK?"

"No, I can fix this," I declare. "I know what you need."

"No, you don't." She pounds my body with her hands.

"We need to move forward. We don't go back, we never go back." I pull her close to my chest. I am looking upriver. Her chin is on my shoulder. She has stopped crying. I've reached her.

"Nick, listen to me. Whatever damage that's been done is small potatoes right now," she says. "Let's be smart. Let's work through this so we still like each other in the end."

"What end?" I say.

"There are no kids. We rent our place."

I pull her away from my chest and grip her firmly by her shoulders. I look straight into her eyes. "There is no end, there is no back. We move forward. Today, tomorrow, and every day after that. Forward. Together. Forever."

She pushes into my chest with both hands to clear herself from me. The force sends me beyond the edge of the rim. One foot is on the rock while the other dangles above the chasm below. I reach out for Lori to save me. She does not reach back.

Interlude 1: Welcome to Limbo

"And that's it. Those are the last few days of my life," I say to my strange new friend.

"So you say," Andres replies.

"Why are we holding hands, by the way?"

"That's how it works here. We walk together and share our stories," Andres says.

"Until when? Until what?" I look around at a legion of souls wandering about.

Andres starts laughing. He skips like a child although he looks to be in his early thirties. I survey the folks nearest us, and everyone looks to be in their early thirties.

"What's so amusing?"

Andres returns to a normal gait. "I've been here a long time, although not as long as others." He points to a line of people leaning along a pasture fence that stretches to eternity. "I've met several lifetime's worth of folks but it's always a delight to have a virgin. Your stories are so fresh and vivid."

"So, you're my first?" I play along. I have a vague notion of where I am. It looks like the featureless plains of Kansas that I just saw but I know I am no longer among the living. "This isn't a dream. I'm not in a coma." I accept the realization aloud.

"You're in purgatory, Nick." Andres shows a sympathetic smile but starts to laugh again. "God's waiting room."

"What does it look like to you?" Andres asks eagerly.

"Endless, flat fields of wheat under a cloudy sky," I respond. "Isn't it the same to you?"

"Not at all. For me, it started as a wide empty beach at low tide, but now my world is a tapestry of Dali paintings. Do you know Dali?"

"So, you see flaming giraffes and stuff like that?" I ask.

"Ah yes, you're familiar with his work. That's good," he says. "Don't worry, you will add your own details if you stay long enough."

"How long will I stay, do you think?"

"That's impossible to say." Andres hesitates to ponder my question. "Let's just say that I am really fortunate to snag a new-comer like you. Virgins are often here and gone in a flash. Sometimes you guys have just a few things to straighten out, which means you got it mostly right, which means you have a lot of valuable lessons to share with the rest of us if we can get our hands on you."

"How does one go anywhere?" I have so many questions.

Andres sweeps his free arm across the horizon. "What about people? Do you see other people?"

"There's lots of folks walking around holding hands. Some are chatting like us, but most are just walking together quietly. And then there's those guys of course." I point to the forlorn looking folks on the fence. "What are they up to?"

"They're going to be here for a while. Already have been here for a while, in fact." He shrugs.

"Why aren't they pairing off?" I ask.

Andres stops and lets my momentum swing me around to face him. He holds both my hands now. "As I already told you, the point of all this is for us to share our stories. Not just you and me, but all of us. For the time being, I'm your guide and you're mine. But you can let go and grab another free hand an-ytime you like."

"No that's fine. I'm fine with you right now," I say to my first. "I'm really curious about those guys along the fence. They're un-nerving."

"What you see as a fence I see as a jetty heading into the sea," Andres says.

"That, too. How do you get a surrealist painting and I'm beaming in the featureless plains of Kansas?"

"It's such a delight to have a virgin. Have I told you that?"

"Twice now," I reply. "Please help me."

"Relax, Nick, be patient. The Lord knows we have time." Andres laughs. "I told you, your details will come with time."

We walk near another pair of people, a man and woman. He is gesturing with his free hand to signal his conviction. They are so wrapped in conversation that they do not notice when I wave hello.

Andres watches me watch them as they pass by. "All you need to understand right now is that all we have here is each other. There is literally nothing else here. There is no food, no shelter, no sleep. Your purpose is to share and accept the stories of the people you meet. To learn and impart your own wisdom."

"To what end?" I ask.

"We will stay here until we get it right," Andes says.

"How does one get anything right in this void?" I whine.

He has pulled me square again. He is holding both my hands. "Do you see anyone else besides the pairings and the lonely souls on your fence?"

I look away from Andres and cast my sight around the horizon. "I see a man on a horse."

"You see them on horses. Very good. That's very American of you." Andres swings my arm in measure with his. "The rider you see is a steward, Nick."

"Is he an angel?" I ask.

Andres shakes his head. "There are no angels here, Nick. They are simply stewards, like ushers at the theater. They move you from row to row."

I watch the rider in the distance interrupt a pairing. He pulls one of them onto the horse behind him. They ride bareback. Now that I have noticed one, I notice others. There is one rider trotting slowly along the fence line with an arm outstretched. Each loner cowers with both hands clutching the fence as the steward nears him.

"Do they take you somewhere bad?" I ask while watching the steward sweep the fence line in vain.

"They take you back to relive the scenes of your life," Andres says.

"Look at that one on the Appaloosa along the fence." I urge him as I point. "He's not getting any takers."

"It's not just any horse but an Appaloosa now. Very good. You are embracing your circumstances," he says.

"What's it look like to you?" I am curious.

"I see a matador riding a dolphin. He is sitting on a silver saddle that is made from melted coins. The dolphin has the head of lion. The lion's face bears a grotesque grin like one of the statues you would see guarding the gates of an Eastern palace." He gesticulates as he talks. He touches his finger to the puffy part of cheek below his eye. "The eyes are black and upon closer inspection, I see they comprise a concentration of ants entangled around a decaying ort of food."

"You're not in Kansas," I say.

"Never been."

"Please tell me where the stewards take you." I squeeze his hand. As I do so, I see a seaside concourse on a coastal town. I quickly release his hand and look at him with surprise.

"Eventually you will learn to share without speaking." He assesses my stunned face. "But I don't think you're ready for that quite yet."

I nod my head in agreement.

"Have you ever had déjà vu?" Andres asks me.

"Of course."

"That's real, Nick. It's not just a feeling. You really are experiencing those things over again." Andres clearly enjoys sharing this revelation with me. He swings our arms in unison.

I try to remember all the times I had felt déjà vu. I can't recall anything in particular. This doesn't make sense. "How can I relive something before I was dead?"

"Forget what you know about time, Nick," he urges me. "Just as you are right here with me, you may be graduating school down there and taking your first steps below that."

"Below what?" I ask.

Andres takes both of my hands. "Look down."

The firmament below my feet is translucent. There is another plain resembling ours with the same cast of characters teeming about. I can make out another stratum below that one and some details from one below that.

I put my hand to my forehead. "This is too much."

"You're right, it is," Andre says. "Would you like me to share a story."

"That might be a nice distraction." I nod and exhale. "Tell me about this thing you have for Dali. Were you a collector? Did you study him?"

"I knew him."

Story 2: Carnevale

My father was a sea merchant from Catalonia. His true origins were in Andorra, but he left there forever upon finding his trade in Cadaqués. He learned the coastal routes along the French Riviera, Liguria, Tuscany, and down past Napoli when he was still a teenager. He was an apprentice carpenter as a boy in the mountains and this was a valued skill to have amongst a wooden vessel's complement.

Because a carpenter's skills are not in constant demand, my father learned other roles on the ship. My father was smart and industrious. He gained the trust of the crew and was highly regarded for his abilities. He settled into the role of purser. He eventually earned the rank of chief purser for the full fleet of shipping vessels owned by the company.

As a purser, my father was responsible for outfitting the fleet with all food and supplies. He did not get paid for this role; his compensation came from profits earned by procuring goods below market rate and then charging the shipping company full fare. My father established a network of suppliers and fixers in every port of call along the routes. He was the first off the vessel and the last one back on in every port. His efforts led to great financial success for our family.

Although my father was not yet thirty, he could boast of his small villa and garden in Cadaqués. I was the eldest of his four boys. He was devoted to us during the brief times we had him home. We pounced on him as soon as he arrived, and he would give us exotic gifts from his travels. We would follow him into the garden and help him pick the high-hanging fruit we had left for him. He would lift us above his head to reach them.

Cadaqués became popular as a resort town just before the Great War. That was when I met Salvador. He was playing football with some friends. He stood out, foremost for the fact that he was the worst player on the pitch but also for the fact that he wore a silk scarf around his neck as he played. The other boys were ruthless, and they would grab the scarf and pull him to the ground whenever he was within reach.

"Dori, you're off," his friend Emilio yelled and gestured for Dali to get off the pitch. The young Emilio waved my cousin Jose onto the field.

I sat cross legged under a tree, eating an orange. Dali sat next down to me in the same manner. He gathered my discarded peels and arranged them in a pattern on the ground, overlapping the peels to form a nautilus before kicking the sculpture away with his boot.

"Why do you play with that scarf on?" I asked. I split the orange in half and handed a share to him.

He accepted the offering. "My notoriety will not be cultivated through athletic endeavor but the image you have of me shall endure beyond this meaningless contest."

"You talk strange," I said without malice.

"Thank you for the orange." He smiled. "My name is Salvador."

"I'm Andres."

"Do you live here, Andres, in Cadaqués, or are you here seeking refuge in one of the resorts?" he asked.

"We live here," I answered. "Where are you from?"

"Figueras, but my family has a residence here." Dali savored a segment of the orange. "What is your father's business?"

"My father is the chief purser for a fleet of merchant vessels surveying the seas from Barcelona to Bari," I said. "As for you?"

"My father practices law, as a profession and at home." Dali spit a seed on the ground.

Establishing your bona fides was a tiresome but necessary exercise. The rigid class system that fomented the anarchist sentiments leading to the war was still on full display in places like Cadaqués. Carousing on the football pitch with a cohort of lesser breeding was tolerated but cultivating a friendship with a boy from the plebiscite was discouraged. It was the best use of everyone's time that it was determined immediately whether future encounters with a particular individual in the small port town held the potential for further interaction or if one party would need to be publicly ignored.

"You're not one of those fucking snobs, are you?" Dali asked.

I appreciated his candor. "No. Are you some kind of dandy?"

"Perhaps, but I am not a *froccio* if that's what you mean." He stroked his scarf.

With that, it was settled. We could be friends.

***

Dali stopped coming to the pitch each morning once his father had arranged for a professional artist to train him. Instead, I would meet him on the shoreline concourse. It was a ribbon of pavement that traced the division between the buildings and the sea itself. Cadaqués is composed of whitewashed homes, churches, and stores. The town is spread across a delta-shaped piedmont that descends at a mild grade down from two short, green mountains. From the sea it looks like a litter of white blocks that a child has stacked against a green background.

Dali was sitting within a cloister that looked out toward the bay through three arched gateways. Inside the courtyard it was shady and cool, at least compared to the sun-scorched concourse outside. He had a piece of paper clipped to an easel and a set of charcoals.

"Am I disturbing you, Dori?" I asked. I would often seek him out along the concourse after lunch. Most folks were at home avoiding the afternoon sun. He liked to sketch and paint along the concourse when there were no crowds to disturb the vistas. This afternoon was bright and clear. We had a splendid view of the idle fishing boats moored in the harbor. Beyond the harbor we could see the closed shutters of the sun-drenched homes lining the concourse on the north side of the bay.

Dali sketched with his chalk in silence. He continued to make subtle strokes. "You're always welcome. You know that."

We did not speak much as he worked. I kneeled behind him to gain his perspective. I watched him create a perfect portrait of the brilliantly lit panorama using only black, grey, and white. He continued to sketch past the point I would have declared the work complete. With a whisper's subtlety, he accentuated the shutters on the homes across the bay. He conjured a railing to run along the concourse in front of those homes and added more shadowing to the curves of the arches.

I didn't understand what he was doing and said so. "It was perfect. Why did you add those things?"

"You're just like Ramon." Dali shook his head. "Why must I tell you that which is plain to see?" Dali unclipped the paper from the easel and handed it to me.

I pinched the top corners of the paper and held it up before myself. "Fascinating."

He had imposed three skulls over his perfect rendering of the scene. The darkened shutters were the vacant eye sockets and the concourse railing delineated the top rows of teeth. By shading the tops of the three arches, he created the curvature of the domes of the skulls.

"It's yours," he said. "Ramon would never accept it anyway."

It was the first of many pieces that he would give me. Unfortunately, it was destroyed in the fire along with everything else.

***

My father and our family flourished during the war decade. By the early 1920s, my father had quit his duties as the chief purser for the fleet and had gone into business for himself. He had organized all his connections in each port into his own system of guilds. He had multiple suppliers of similar goods in each place so he could establish competitive market prices as well as have backup suppliers in case of shortages. My father enjoyed unilateral control of the regional market for several items, including certain textiles and olive oil.

My father sent my three brothers and me to work as foreman of the warehouses he established near the docks of each chief port. I had oversight of Livorno, while my brothers held the outposts in La Spezia, Genoa, and Marseille.

We were among the richest of the young men in our respective ports and enjoyed a playboy lifestyle along our Riviera. Indeed, it did feel like it belonged to us. We had frequent and free passage to visit each other by way of any merchant vessel with which we did business. Payment, if even necessary, was covered by an extra demijohn of wine or perhaps an evening with a lady.

In addition to our warehouse duties, my brothers and I were purveyors of all manner of goods and services in demand by the herds of elite gentry cavorting about the summer resorts. Our faces were familiar in every beach club and summer villa along the Riviera. While the elite had ample means to obtain the best local finery for their galas, the Aragon brothers were renowned for providing the exotic.

The professional women from Southern Italy tended to require some coaxing by their clients, notwithstanding the nature of their business. This challenge appealed to the French men, while the Italian men preferred their ladies from Marseille because they were exactly the opposite. I would often meet my youngest brother, Luis, in Bastia to exchange merchandise.

"Did you bring the resin?" I inquired as I hugged my brother on the dock.

"Yes, the flora, too." Luis raised a leather satchel and handed it to me. "Why so much this time?"

"Both Miguel and Manuel asked for it. Good smoke is a must at every party on the coast it seems."

"This stuff's from Algeria. It's good smoke," Luis assured me. The rocky crags of Corsica's savage interior peaked out from above the cliffs around the port.

"How many ladies made the trip?" I asked.

"I brought three. They're in the cafe on the quay." He pointed toward land as the men unloaded crates from the boat behind us. "I had room for a fourth but an old friend of yours asked to tag along with me."

"Who might that be?" I asked.

"A venerable celebrity. Señor Dali himself graced me with his presence for the passage." Luis beamed a silly smile. "He is so very strange. How are you able to even converse with him?"

"Dear brother, he's refreshing." I palmed my kid brother's blonde head and ruffled his hair. "Let's go see him right away."

"Wait, what girls did you bring for me?"

"Of course, sorry." I turned and waved to two women standing beyond the stacks of crates on the dock. They had dark hair and squinty light eyes. Their plump lips tightened as they moved forward. They were short, like most girls from Calabria, and well endowed.

"Just two?" he asked. We began walking from the dock. The water in the port was calm and azure blue. In the light, one could see ten meters clear to the white, rocky bottom.

"I'm sorry, but it's a hard to get these girls to leave their mothers," I said. "I don't think they care much for Frenchmen either."

"Indeed. One of my three is a return trip. She begged me to send her home." Luis shook his head.

"Well, we'll see if Genoa is close enough to home for her then." I walked with my arm across my brother's back. The two Calabrese girls walked behind us.

***

The homesick girl bolted into the arms of the girls I had brought for Luis as soon as we entered the cafe. They escaped to a far corner and the agitated girl launched into an animated tirade. I could not hear her voice, but her vigorous gestures told a story of their own.

Dali sat with a girl on his lap. He had arranged her chestnut-colored hair in a fantastic manner, with nine small buns circling her head like a crown. The other girl was sitting in a chair directly in front of Dali but facing away. He was reaching around the girl with the buns to put the finishing touches on the backside of the other girl, whose hair was festooned into a blonde blossom that erupted from the top of her head. Dali was extracting melted wax from the candle on the table to reinforce his sculpture.

"Very impressive, Dori," I said. "They look like chess pieces."

Dali offered me no salutation. He cast an objective eye on his creation and nodded to acknowledge my insight.

"They very well may be," he said. He whispered in the ear of the girl on his lap and she rose to sit in an adjacent chair. With the manner of a diplomat, Dali stood and extended his hand. When I reached out, he took my hand and drew me closer. With our hands clenched between our chests, we embraced with our free hands.

"Andres, I require passage to Tuscany." Dali pulled away from me. " I must meet a patron who wishes to commission an extravagant exhibition."

"Certainly, but we must make a call in La Spezia first." I raised my satchel. "I have goods that I must deliver to Miguel and Manuel myself."

"Splendid, a wonderful opportunity for you to recount your adventures along the sea."

"Likewise."

The two French girls marveled at what Dali had done to their hair. In the background, the Italian girl continued to make vigorous gestures as she told her stories. She altered between pumping and sweeping motions and then looked scornfully at Luis. She broke into tears. The new girls abandoned her to her weeping and strode in unison to our table.

"We will not go to Marseille," one of the short girls asserted. " We will take our *paesana* home."

"I'm afraid there are not enough berths on the vessel for all of you." I sipped my coffee and shrugged.

"You can leave the French whores here," the other said in her Calabrese dialect.

One of the chess pieces summoned her best Italian. "If I'm a whore, you're a moaning dog."

"*Filles de salope, voi!*" The first Calabrian returned. She formed bull's horns with her fingers and thrust her hands at the French girls.

"Such impressive tongues on these girls." Dali smiled and looked to the French girls for their return volley.

The girl with the erupting quaff could not be bothered. She was content with her station in life and would ply her trade in any geography. She moved to Dali's lap and nestled herself in his welcoming embrace. The top of her hair tickled his ear and they giggled. The other French girl watched them like a jealous puppy. She drew closer and stroked the back of his purple, suede shirt.

"These two may share my berth." Dali smiled.

"It is a mere night's trip," I conceded.

"Alas," Dali sighed. The three of them flirted like adolescents.

"And what of me?" Luis extended his empty hands. "What of my stock?"

I spoke to my brother in Catalan, doubting it would be understood by all our company. "I will trade them for girls from Manuel's stable in La Spezia and send them your way immediately."

The Italian girls frowned and looked to the veteran making her return trip for guidance. She nodded and they silently agreed that not going to Marseille was concession enough for now.

***

Our vessel made a call in Viareggio as we skipped our way down the coast from Genoa, La Spezia, and Carrara toward Livorno. My father established an outpost there, where we kept a warehouse of overstocked, non-perishable items. Happily, this gave us cause to make frequent visits to the festive town.

Dali and I walked the Via al Mare. I pointed to the new Art Deco buildings lining the boulevard. "Look at this style they import from America. It's all so contrived to me. I hate illusions." I caught myself as I considered my company.

"Andres, even I am an illusion—a clone of my namesake, my dead brother before me."

Shops and bars lined one side of the boulevard; grand hotels lined the other.

"You use your illusions, Dori. You give them value. But I am tortured by the prospect of accomplishing nothing."

"Woe is thee!" He mocked me. "How are you able to feed yourself with such sparse accomplishments? Do your house servants gather scraps from the streets for you?"

We walked until the boulevard ended at the Burlamacca channel. Beyond the channel were the shipyards with massive nautical hangars sheltering the artisans who crafted and constructed seafaring ships. The shipyards were located within a deep, protected harbor and the neighborhood around the harbor was called Darsena. Darsena was home to the nautical industry of Viareggio and all that could be expected to come with it. Warehouses, whorehouses, markets, outfitters, and bars were abundant.

"You are the supplier of the finest goods in all of the Riviera," Dali said. "The Aragon brothers are sought after for every festival from here to Valencia."

"We are sought for what we provide, not for what we produce . . . certainly not for who we are." My crisis of conscious was at full pique.

"You produce the fabric of haute couture," he said.

"We source it from the sail makers. Whatever additional value the designers assign to it is their invention."

"Then what of the comfort you provide?" Dali pointed over his shoulder to the two French girls skipping behind them. They were eating ice cream. The small buns on the taller girl were fraying and strands of single hairs shot loose like sparks. The palm fronds on the shorter girl had begun to droop as the wax adhesive dried. If they noticed, they did not seem to care

"They're the biggest farce of all. For a fee, they let a man feel loved, or powerful, or attractive. It's an act," I scoffed. "Their purpose, just as mine, is to foster lies."

"Is it dishonest to conjure illusions for those who do not want to accept their reality?" he asked.

The four of us walked down the jetty that ran along the channel. There was large signal light at the end of the jetty that sat upon a bright red standard. Across the water from that light was another that sat upon a bright green standard. That one was set at the end of a wide, concrete breaker. Together the lights signaled the open gate to the harbor.

We walked until we reached the statue of St. Nicola at the midpoint of the jetty. We turned and faced the town. There were myriad beach establishments lining the shore as far as the eye could see. Each beach club had different colored umbrellas and heraldry.

"A man is entitled to foster his own reality, Andres," Dali said.

"How can you call it reality if it is not based in truth?"

"What is this truth you speak of?"

"Truth, Dori. Don't play dense. Facts."

"What are facts?" he said sincerely.

"A fact is something that is always true. No matter who you are or where you are, it is always true. Now and forever."

"Nothing lasts forever, Andres."

We could see men in white coats walking from the promenade to their clients on the beach. They carried trays of drinks above their heads. The name of this beach club was Eden. Many fine parties were hosted there.

"We should return here in the spring for Carnevale," Dali suggested. "It is the most spectacular affair of the season."

"Better than in Venice?" I had attended many of the pre-Lent bacchanal festivals of the Riviera, but none here.

"Yes, and by a wide margin. The artisans work all winter on the floats. They are as tall as the Hotel Principe." Dali pointed to the Principe di Piemonte hotel on the Via al Mare. It was five stories tall.

"Yes, I've heard, but what of the pageantry?"

"Well, there is the normal masquerade but here there are the bands and choreography as well. And the dozens of floats and the processions that last all day. And in the evening, the neighborhoods compete to throw the best party."

"It just doesn't sound as elegant as Venice." I dismissed him with a wave of my hand.

"What happened to your contempt for illusions, Andres?" Dali said. "Your arrogance I can tolerate, but hypocrisy is another matter."

We did return in the spring. And we returned every spring after that with my three brothers and father as well. Eventually,

I moved my residence there to a villa I had built on land adjoining the warehouse in Darsena.

I came to think of the Viareggio Carnevale as the marquee event of the Riviera; it served a practical business purpose as well. Our annual reunion in Tuscany became something of a business convention for the Aragon family. We invited the leaders of the trading guilds to join us in the revelry, lubricating them with spirits, smoke, and women before stamping out agreements for the year to come.

***

It was the Spring of 1936 and Darsena was awarded the honor of hosting the final night's celebration of Carnevale. The Via al Mare of Darsena extended several miles south from the shipyards. This area was less developed. The side of the street that ran along the beach was devoid of structures and the other side held only bars. Behind the bars and extending to the end of the boulevard was a pine forest and sand dunes.

The final parade began at sundown at the south end of the boulevard and proceeded north toward the shipyard where we kept our warehouse. Our full entourage marched in the parade, but various parts of our complement peeled off as we passed certain bars. Some men met women we had arranged for them. The men would discretely disappear with them into the pines behind the bars. It was barely sunset when the first of our contingent snuck from the group and advanced to a rendezvous point.

"Monsieur Leclerc rather enjoys the spring rut, I must say," Luis leaned over to say.

"Don't be uncouth," our brother, Miguel, scolded him.

My brothers and I comprised the final line of our formation. Our father marched at the front alongside members of the Livorno guild. In front of them was a troop of black-shirted, fascist soldiers. They were a group of local, young auxiliaries.

The parade procession ended where the Via al Mare turned inland toward the residential area of Darsena. At that point, the floats were wheeled left onto a service road that led past several blocks of warehouses and to the sea. As each float reached the end of its run, it was carried onto the beach, all the way to the shoreline.

The culmination of the month-long festival was marked by a cacophony of horns and drums beating out of rhythm. All the floats assembled on the beach were set ablaze and the crowd was whipped into a lather of dancing, carousing and debauchery. Guns fired in the air to match the random explosions of fireworks.

Along with my father, my brothers and I retreated from the heart of the festivities to our warehouse. Our warehouse sat on the service road leading to the beach where the party culminated, so we didn't feel like we were missing anything. The warehouse had two hangar doors on the roadside that slid open in opposing directions. We opened both doors and a bottle of Lambrusco to toast the end of another festival together.

"To you, Father." Luis said as he raised his glass and bowed his head.

Miguel, Manuel, and I nodded and raised our elbows in unison.

Each of us had established our own families in our respective locales so opportunities for all five of us to meet had become rare. The annual Viareggio reunion was ever more so cherished for this reason.

"I think our associates had an optimal experience this year, judging by the fact that none of them is here to join us for your toast." Manuel smiled.

"I hope our friends from home come meet us soon," Father said. There was concern in his voice. "The stock we hold for them would not react well if it were to meet a stray ember."

Newly sewn sails were draped over reams of fabric stacked on the warehouse floor behind us.

Luis filled his glass and tilted to return to the party. "I will be your shepherd, Father. Wait just a moment."

"No, no, Luis. Relax here with us." My father held him by his shoulder. He smiled at his youngest son and fixed the wayward blonde bangs atop his head with a gentle sweep of his hand.

The fascist youths lined up on the shoreline. They aimed their rifles over the sea and fired on command from their lieutenant. The crowd howled in approval with each volley. They continued until their six-shot magazines were spent.

Some folks in the crowd snapped off fascist salutes as the young men returned to formation. Some were mocking and some were sincere; all were sloppy.

"Pray for them," my father said.

"Pray for us," I replied.

Someone pounded on the harbor side doors to the warehouse.

"Wonderful. Let's handle this business and get back to the party," Luis said.

The stevedores from the awaiting ship rushed in aggressively when my brothers opened the doors. They were not Catalonians. I recognized them from the docks of Livorno. As these men arrived from the harbor side, the fascist youths arrived from the beach. They held their rifles with both hands across their chests. They had affixed bayonets, the blades old and rusted orange.

I made an attempt at levity. "Patience, gents. These goods don't spoil." The armed boys shut the sliding doors behind them.

Our colleagues from the Livorno guild followed their stevedores into the warehouse. They pointed to where the crates of munitions were hidden beneath the sails and the fabric.

"You told us these materials were destined for our fellow patriots in the south," our colleague said to my father.

"Why should you think otherwise?" my father assured him.

The man turned to the ship and addressed his crew in Livornese. "You are certain?"

Two of his men looked at each other and then they looked at someone outside of my view. I advanced toward the dockside door and saw two short Calabrian women cowering on the deck.

"What would these whores know of our stock?" I shouted.

The most assertive of the young men in black shirts stepped forward. "We claim these arms in the name of the cause of the National Party of Italy."

There was a good chance that the rifle he swung at us had passed through this very warehouse a decade earlier. Along with this boy's father it had helped bring the fascists to power.

My father remained calm. He reasoned with the men from Livorno. "We have always been advocates of your cause. Let's resolve this calmly and return to the festival."

The leader of the Livorno guild spoke with an imperious tone. "These munitions were destined for the enemies of our cause in Spain," he said as though reading a verdict.

We were to be robbed of our goods. The stevedores loaded the munitions on their ship while the youths held us at gunpoint. The deal they had made with the Livorno guild would garner them great recognition. They were earning their rightful spots on the frontline of some future battle.

Luis recognized one of the boys and sought to embarrass him. "Oh, Simone, why are you out playing boy soldier with your classmates?"

The boy ignored him and Manuel nudged Luis in the ribs. The Livorno men and the fascist boys were looking for profit and praise, not blood. They would need us for future deals as well. Father would play along with the charade and then place a debit in the ledger he kept for the Livorno guild.

"Simone, a girl from Marseille told me you were the fastest date she ever had," Luis said.

Luis had the boy's attention now. The loose fixtures on his rifle rattled as his hands quaked. Manuel jabbed his elbow into

Luis' ribs with enough force to make him groan. Father looked at Luis and pursed his lips. Luis nodded obediently.

The Livorno crew removed all the crates of rifles, grenades, shells, and other ammunition from the warehouse. With their ship fully laden, the head of the guild addressed the boys. "Remember, wait until we are out of the harbor to arrest them."

The men departed and we were left facing the boys. As the ship left with our goods, the sound of the festival reentered. Pressure left the room.

"Do you really intend to arrest us?" I asked. "I am a resident here. I know your fathers well."

"Why should that matter?" the assertive one asked.

"He may find it hard to believe the charges you bring against us. We have a long history of fair deals. We have many common business partners." I pled with his reason.

"You will be arrested for attempting to smuggle arms to the enemy." The boy shrugged me off.

"You are Stefano from Croce Verde, correct? Your father, Giovanni, will also attest that I am a patriot of the fascist movement." I clicked my heels and saluted the boys crisply.

The boys conferred. My father saw an opportunity to offer a mutually beneficial alternative. "Men, I would like to offer you an award for your assistance this evening," he said. The boy soldiers stopped talking and everyone looked at our father with surprise. His statement confused us all.

"Your response when those Catalonians came to boost the shipment was most impressive," my father said. "Your vigilance even during the peak of the festival is commendable."

"We will definitely tell your fathers of your wise decision to have the arms immediately sent to Livorno under the care of our trusted colleagues," I added while nodding to my father.

Stefano contemplated the development. "You speak of an award?"

"One hundred grams of gold for your men, two hundred for you as the commanding officer," my father promised.

One of the boy soldiers was unconvinced. He whined to Stefano, "The men are gone with the shipment, what will they say?"

My father smiled and assured the boy. "They will say that they confiscated weapons that a bunch of Catalonians had intention to send to the Republicans in Spain."

The boys conferred and Stefano gave his orders. They broke their huddle and Stefano announced, "Fetch the gold and then prepare to leave Viareggio. You must leave tonight."

"*Avec plaisir,*" Luis said with a roll of his eyes

"I've made my home here, Stefano. My family resides in the adjoining apartments as we speak," I pled.

"I know who you are, Señor Aragon, just as you know me," Stefano replied. "Your normal course of business takes you away from home for extended periods of time. I suggest you inform Señora Aragon that duty calls and you will see her for Ferr'Agosto."

"We will send for Sara and the girls, Andres," Manuel said. "Let's not linger."

Father worked a safe hidden beneath a heavy marble tile in the floor of the office. Manuel watched over him. Miguel, Luis, and I remained in the warehouse to distract the boys and make sure they didn't get greedy.

"Simone, you sure do look handsome in that uniform." Luis began anew with his target.

Simone smiled in appreciation. He was insecure and a little dim.

"That rifle really completes the look," Luis said. "I think I understand what Marie saw about you."

Simone beamed.

"She said she was just tickled when you first approached her."

"What else did she say about me?" Simone drew closer to Luis. The rifle relaxed across his shoulder.

"She said you were tender and sweet," Luis answered. Some of the other boys chuckled and whistled at Simone but he did not care.

"Tell me more."

"She asked me if she could stay here after the festival," Luis said. "I think she may have wanted to spend more time with you."

"Oh please, Luis. Please let her stay longer." Simone placed his hands together as if to pray. The other boys groaned at their friend's pathetic display.

"I would, Simone, but I am fairly certain that her mission would be for naught."

"Her mission?"

Luis chuckled. Poor Simone had fallen right into his trap. "She was hoping you could service her like a man, but she says the hardest wood you could ever muster was that rifle!"

The troop of boys erupted in laughter. Luis bent over in spasms of appreciation for his own cleverness.

Simone trembled. He dropped the rifle from his shoulder into his palms. A brutal scowl transfigured his red face like a growling dog.

As Luis stood to catch his breath, Simone charged with the tip of his bayonet pointed at his throat. Miguel noticed before Luis and he slammed into him with a lowered shoulder.

The forced knocked Luis clear of the blade, which lodged into a stack of sails. The other boys tackled Simone and threw him to the ground. The weight of his friends was barely enough to stem his fit. He kicked, bit and spit in a hurricane of embarrassment and anger.

"Are you OK?" I asked Luis, lying prone on the floor of the warehouse.

Luis nodded. I turned to Miguel. Miguel was silent; his face, pale and desperate. He held a palm over the right side of his neck. Blood oozed from around the edges of his hand, then ribbons of blood shot from between his fingers onto the floor. He leaned his back against the stack of sails and then slid to the floor and onto his butt.

"Father!" I screamed. I grabbed the loose edge of a sail and pressed it against Miguel's artery as hard as I could. A crimson cloud spread across the white fabric and wet my hand in moments.

Father arrived from the kitchen. He dropped to his knees and threw his hands atop his head. Manuel was behind him and when he saw the blood, he dropped the gold coins from his hands.

The coins rang out as they bounced across the floor. They twirled in the air and then rolled in circles on the floor until they lost their momentum. Five of them rolled through blood and then traced red spirals on the floor before settling back in Miguel's thick pool. One coin showed heads, the other four were tails.

Miguel died quickly, yet Luis insisted that he was OK and tried to revive him. Father wailed in agony. The soldier boys watched. Stefano looked at me with the same recognition as when I first said his father's name.

"He killed him," I said.

"He killed all of you," he replied.

Interlude 2: It's So Easy

"**W**ere your wife and daughters home?" I ask Andres.

"Yes, Nick, supposing they obeyed me," he answers.

"Were they harmed?"

"In the least, they were harmed by the loss of their husband and father. They must have also lost their home, the support of my livelihood and of course the love of my father and brothers. Yes, I'd say they were harmed, Nick."

"Did they . . . did they die?" I ask.

"Everyone dies, Nick."

I stop walking but still hold his hand. "I'm not trying to bother you. You told me our purpose was to share our stories. You chose to tell the story you did."

Tears quiver on his lower lashes. "I want you to understand that it always hurts, Nick. The sadness stays with you just as at the moment it happened. The pain never dulls."

"I'm sorry, but how could I have known?" I am not completely contrite.

"You couldn't have, but you will," he says. He wipes his tears with the back of his hand. "You should know that you have no future. Your life ended when your wife let you fall into that chasm. My life ended when they lined us up and shot us after setting fire to the warehouse. Whether my wife and daughters died in the inferno, I do not know. Everyone I knew was taken from me that night and I have never seen them again. The only thing I know of life after that moment is what I learn here."

"Your wife and daughters . . . do you think you could ever see them again, here?" I ask.

"This isn't heaven, Nick."

I notice our shadows as we walk. My new reality is developing more context. The sun that I added to my tapestry is slowly falling into the infinite horizon behind us.

"Why did you tell me that story if it you knew it would be so painful?" I ask.

"Do you see the pairs holding hands without speaking?"

"Yes," I say. In fact, we are among the rare pairings that is speaking.

"They are sharing of themselves freely. The problem is that you're so damn green, you couldn't handle that right now," he says.

We pass a man and a woman silently walking hand in hand. Her face is pensive while his is anguished.

"You pulled that story out of me, Nick. And, when I shared it with you, I relived every moment as I did that day," he says.

"I'm sorry," I say. I am contrite.

"You took what you needed from me. Just as I will take what I need when the time is right."

"This really is like losing your virginity, isn't it?" I joke. He does not laugh.

"I want to prepare you." His tone is serious. "That which you share may bring you despair. You may suffer by telling it."

"Don't I have any choice in the matter?"

"Only the choices you made when you were alive."

"But how will I know what to tell you?" I ask.

"You will share with me what I need to learn, a lesson that I am supposed to learn from your life."

"Why must it be so distressing for me?" I ask.

"It may not be. Some stories are lovely parables of encouragement to model one's life after. But usually it's people's mistakes that we get the most from."

I ponder all my regrets. I wince as I remember humiliating myself in front of my fellow teachers. My mind scans a log of every awkward moment and every time I disappointed my parents and Lori.

"Are you ready?" Andres asks.

"No, tell me something."

Andres nods.

"You said that you will learn something from my life, but we haven't talked about what I was supposed to learn from your story."

"You need to draw your own conclusions, Nick. If I knew the lesson, I wouldn't be damned to keep reliving it, would I?" Andres says.

"It seems so obvious," I say, "which makes me think it must not be."

"What seems so obvious?" he asks.

"The lessons from that story. What you should have done differently," I say.

Andres laughs and shakes his head. He mocks me, "Oh, Nick, tell me the error of my ways."

"Well, I did say I must be wrong since it seems too obvious."

"Please, indulge me then," Andres says.

I hesitate. I'm whip shy.

"Come on now. Out with it. Don't be afraid to be direct," he stops and looks straight into my eyes.

"Forgive me for saying so, Andres, but in modern terms you'd be called a pimp, a pusher, a gun runner," I say.

"You make me sound so dangerous, Nick." He seems to admire my description.

"Do you disagree?"

"No, I love it." He smiles, stretches out his free arm, and exclaims, "Behold Andres Aragon, *bon vivant* pirate of the Riviera."

He really is tickled by my characterization.

"To think, I never even mentioned all the mafia types I had to deal with," he says. "For the record, the Corsicans and Sardinians were the most vicious. I attribute it to all that Saracene blood, of course."

"Why didn't you walk away from it all? Take a different path?" I ask. I recognize my naïveté even as the words leave my lips.

"Tell me, Nick, at what point do I spit on the plate that my father set before me?" He becomes pedantic. "And once he set me to work, do you think he had me peddling flesh and smoke right out of the gate?"

"But eventually you learned what it entailed. And then you mentored your younger brothers as well."

"Which of my brothers would you have me disavow?"

"You could have found another trade once they were established. It seems to me that they would have supported you."

"So, according to you, it's OK to sponge off my family as long as I'm not engaged in ill repute myself?" he asks incredulously. "Wouldn't that make me the ultimate pimp?"

"You make a strong point, but what of the women then, since you mention pimp?"

"Professional women have migrated the Riviera since the Romans, Nick. Do you think they walked?" Andres shakes his head. "Those are willing women providing a needed service to willing men. A legal service I will add."

I begin to speak but he interrupts me.

"The drugs, as you call them, that's next on the list, right?" he says. "Completely harmless. Never once did I see a man harm another or disgrace himself while smoking. Now, shall we discuss the impact that alcohol had on your life, dear Nick?"

He stings me with his words. I knew it was too easy. We walk and I notice that our shadows have grown darker. I feel intense heat on my shoulders from the sun I have concocted.

"Are you satisfied, Nick? May we begin now?" Andres asks.

"No, the guns. The weapons." I am not ready to reveal my own story, whatever it may be. "How can you justify profiteering? Your family armed the protagonists of the bloodiest conflicts in human history."

"And yet I never pulled a trigger in my life," Andre replies.

"That doesn't matter. That's not the point." I point at him with my free hand. "You poured the powder in their barrels."

"We didn't make the rifles, Nick. We simply brought them from point A to point B, just as though they were wine or fabric." He smirks and shakes his head.

I try again to seize a point. "You put the guns in the hands of maniac fascists."

"And they pointed them at maniac communists. I never lost any sleep," he says.

"How could you support their cause?" I ask.

"The cause of megalomaniac dictators or the cause of the businessmen trying to preserve their livelihood? We knew nothing of the former but everything of the latter!" Andres yells. "I was denied the chance to see history unfold but I have since heard that the whole communist idea turned out badly for many millions of folks across the globe. Or am I mistaken, Nick?"

I drop my shoulders and my righteous pose.

"Let me ask you. For which of the great causes of American history would you have denied your fellow man his weapon? I bet the old farmer you so admire enlisted before the last ship sank in Hawaii. What would you have told him?" Andres stares me down again.

I am perturbed by the whole exercise. "This can't be the purpose. To sit here and argue the details of our stories. Your impressive moral gymnastics aside, there is clearly something to be done differently."

"Don't hesitate to tell me when it comes to you," Andres says.

"You said I have no future, but I won't believe that." I am frustrated. "Your friend was right; you didn't know how good you had it. Typical of all the rich folks I've met in my life."

Andres rolls his eyes.

"You had all the comforts of the material world and still couldn't be happy," I say. "You weep as you tell the story of your extravagance."

"I weep for the life I lost too soon, not for the content of it. Let's be clear on that."

"Didn't you have your fill of life? I bet you and your brothers were legends in those parts for a long time after you passed," I say.

"And yet I'm still hungry," Andres sighs.

He has grown tired of my critique. He squeezes my hand and I am taken back to my childhood in central Illinois.

Story 3: Turkey Day

"Janice, get my snifter," Uncle Chuck yelled to my aunt as I walked in the door with my sister, Louisa, and parents.

The arrival of the first guests signaled that Uncle Chuck could commence to drinking. Uncle Chuck and Aunt Jan had reached numerous accords for the sake of his health and her sanity. Such concessions were considered monk-like self-discipline on the part of Uncle Chuck. We had arrived before 11 a.m.

My mother hugged her sister. "Happy Thanksgiving, Janice."

"Happy Thanksgiving, Sissie."

My father was besotted with casserole trays and I carried boxes of bakery cakes and pies. The twine used to tie off the boxes cut into the skin between my knuckles.

"Hi, Aunt Jan. Happy turkey day," I said.

"Gobble, gobble," Louisa giggled.

"Oh, my treasures." Aunt Jan caressed our cheeks. "Thank you for coming. My dear treasures."

As she came in for a hug, I set my boxes on the floor and squeezed her around the waist while my sister grabbed a thigh. Aunt Jan had only one child and he was close to college age by then. He dwelled in the basement. I never remembered him being very interested in me, but I didn't take it personally because he didn't seem interested in anyone.

Uncle Chuck was reclined in his leisure chair. He did not stir to help us. "Rich, come sit down." He pointed to indicate the location of another chair that my father might slide over next to him in front of the TV. "Janice, about that snifter. A deal's a deal."

"Yes, dear."

Aunt Jan took the boxes from my hands and retreated to the kitchen. My mother and father followed her. Louisa and I stood in silence in the front room while Uncle Chuck flipped through the channels, waiting for football to start.

"Oh, ooooh, the parade," Louisa said.

"Only for a little bit, sweet pea. The pregame starts in five minutes." He set the remote down on the table next to his chair.

Aunt Jan arrived with a snifter of brandy. My dad pulled a chair from the dining room into the front room next to Uncle Chuck.

"Care for a cognac, Rich? It's an XO." Uncle Chuck tippled the snifter toward my father.

***

Aunt Jan's first husband, Uncle Paul, died in a work accident seventeen years earlier. He was a foreman at the grain mill and his manager had ordered him to send one of his summer helpers into the silo to break down some clumps of moist corn that were clogging up the flow. This was called "walking down the grain" and it was fraught with hazard. Clogs in the flow could be caused by damp corn but also by cavities of air below the surface. It was one of these pockets of air that Uncle Paul stepped into after refusing to risk the life of a teenager to satisfy an impatient boss. Uncle Paul's steps loosened the corn and the vortex pulled him under. He drowned in kernels before they could shut the flow to save him.

Aunt Jan was pregnant at the time of the accident. After the Mondemon company agreed to a multimillion-dollar settlement, Aunt Jan and her infant son became the second richest family in Monticello, Illinois. The richest was the Altgeld family who lived on an estate west of town. They made their money in the cattle trade back in the day when Chicago was meat butcher to the world and Monticello was a weigh station on the rail route up from Kansas.

Aunt Jan refused to let the money change her lifestyle. She raised her son in the house that she and Uncle Paul bought as newlyweds and that's where she remained. She continued to teach elementary school.

Aunt Jan was not a lonely widow. She filled her free time with charity. At first, she worked with clergy at local churches to help identify families in need. She would treat them on a case-by-case basis and provide them with what she felt they needed. In some cases, that was a babysitter for a teenage mother's child so she could finish high school, and sometimes it was a car, so the breadwinner didn't have to pass up a good job across the county. Her diligence made sure that her efforts were never wasted; she rarely refused anyone. Her generous ventures became well known by charity cases and kind-hearted contributors alike. Before long she was the director of a newly formed charitable foundation called Heartland Helpers. It was just the type of charity to attract the attention of the socialite philanthropist crowd. And that is how my Aunt Janice met Charlie Aloysius Altgeld III, the man whom I call Uncle Chuck.

To be sure, Uncle Chuck was no socialite. He was no anything. The pinnacle of his life achievements was a high school diploma. His mother, Margaret Radcliffe-Altgeld, still held out hope that even if he wouldn't turn out as a successful businessman like his father or brothers, he could make a respectable gentleman if she groomed him as a philanthropist.

"You've already given her a hearty sum from my inheritance. Why did you promise her my time as well?" Charlie whined to his mother.

"You may grow to admire this woman, Charles. I certainly do. She came from nothing and was handed a terrible misfortune. Many people would quit on life, but she picked up the pieces and chose to make life better for others."

"These pieces you speak of, you refer to the millions of dollars she got from Mondemon, Daddy's biggest client, correct?" Charlie said.

"Regardless of the provenance of her capital, she has won my respect and admiration. You could learn from her example." Mrs. Radcliffe-Altgeld extended an index finger below her son's chin and raised his face to meet her gaze. "You may not be suited to a life of toil or industry, but I will see you choose a path. This is a chance for you to do something virtuous with your life."

"Fine. Am I expected to bring my own ladle or will one be provided for me?" Charlie joked.

"Don't be a wisenheimer," she admonished. "You are going to help Miss Schmidt evaluate cases. From what I hear about the crowd you run with, you probably have a nice head start."

***

"Scotchtober runs all the way through Thanksgiving. After that it's cognac time all the way until New Year, which gives way to Ginuary, of course," Uncle Chuck explained to my dad.

Uncle Chuck enjoyed my dad's company because my dad would indulge Uncle Chuck in his favorite topic, which was Uncle Chuck himself. My dad was a central Illinois farmer just as generations before him were. A wealthy, libertine playboy like Uncle Chuck may as well have been an immigrant from an exotic Pacific island.

"So, you drink something every day?" my dad asked. He did not judge. He probed Uncle Chuck like Captain Cook examining a Maori's tattoos, with excited fascination.

"No, no, Rich." Uncle Chuck patted his thigh. "Well, maybe, but not to excess."

This seemed to be true. Uncle Chuck was always lucid and in control. On the other hand, there's more than one way to define excess. For example, having a season of the year dedicated to drinking $200 bottles of high-end liquor would likely qualify to most people.

"Which is your favorite?" my father examined the syrupy brown liquor in his glass. He brought the booze to his lips and tasted the tiniest amount. My father would make that glass last clear through dinner.

"Rich, I don't believe in having favorites. Everything has its time and place." Uncle Chuck sipped his cognac. "Like gin, in January, in Florida."

"Are you heading down to Florida again this year?" my father asked.

"Absolutely, we leave Christmas day. Best day of the year to travel," Uncle Chuck said. "Do you want some cigars? I got a guy in Naples that gets them straight from Cuba."

"I'm all set, Chuck, but thank you," my father leaned closer to Uncle Chuck. "What do you do with yourself while you're down there?"

"Lots of fishing, deep sea charter action, Cuban cigars and Black Marlin . . . Hemingway style." Uncle Chuck set his snifter down and rocked back and forth in his chair as though he was reeling in a big one. He caught me smiling, so he exaggerated the motion even more.

"Every day?" my father asked.

"Just about, weather permitting. And in the evening we hit the hounds. Dog races," Uncle Chuck said. I looked to see if he had a charade for that, but he didn't. "You know, Rich, if you ever wanted to come down, we could put a nice week of fun together for you."

"I'm not much of a sailor, I'm afraid. I once threw up on a charter boat in Lake Michigan." My dad frowned and shrugged.

"Well, that's OK. They put together some nice dog racing junkets out of Naples. We hit Fort Myers, St. Pete, and Orlando over four days. Let me tell you, they may call South Florida God's waiting room, but some of these silverbacks know how to get filthy wild. I hopped on a party charter last year with these guys and we ended up at the skin bar every night."

I looked straight ahead at the TV. There was a pause in the story. In the periphery I noticed Uncle Chuck casting an eye to see whether I noticed that he had broached an inappropriate topic. I pretended not to notice so the details would keep flowing.

Uncle Chuck returned his attention to my dad. "So, we're on our third straight night at the booby bar and I swear I hadn't seen this one guy sleep yet. He was filthy, filthy wild. He had this way with the girls that nobody else did. He wasn't even doling out much cash, but he kept taking them in the back. I saw him get a lap dance right out in the open, too. She sat on his face. This old man was giving them mustache rides right out in the open."

"Um, Chuck," I heard my dad say.

"Right. So anyway, we're heading back on the charter and this guy is sitting next to me. Do you know what this geriatric tells me?" Uncle Chuck asks.

"What's that?" My father leaned in even closer to my uncle.

"He says, 'Chuck, you got to chase the dragon. You got to ride the lightning.'!" Uncle Chuck yells.

"What does that mean?" My father was oblivious.

"Chase the dragon. Chase it," Uncle Chuck implored. "Find your catalyst. Go after whatever gets you geeked up in the morning."

"Geeked up?"

"Whatever makes you randy!" Uncle Chuck urged my father.

I looked away from the football game that I wasn't watching to see my father's puzzled face. He wasn't sure what Uncle Chuck meant by "randy." For a moment I was sure my father was going to say, *My name is Rich.*

Uncle Chuck continued, "Now it turns out that this clown wasn't all that old at all. He was a Florida beach bum with a satchel full of meth and meds. He was buttering up the girls with coke you see, so that's why he was getting all the extra-curriculars. He looked like hell, let me tell you, but his words still resonated with me. I always say that it's important to always listen because you never know where your next dose of good advice is going to come from."

"What happened to the guy?" I asked.

Uncle Chuck was startled to see that I was listening. "Don't know, Nicky. Don't know. He got up to use the bathroom on the bus and I never saw him again. But you missed the point. The story is not about him."

"What's it about?" I asked. My father looked to Uncle Chuck for an answer as well.

"Tomorrow is promised to no one, guys. You wake up in the morning and run toward whatever your heart desires." Uncle Chuck leaned forward with his elbows on his knees. "Of course, we all have our responsibilities. It's important that you fulfill your duties, but after that, go nuts, man. Go nuts." He drained the remaining balance of brandy into his mouth.

Even on Thanksgiving my father had risen from bed at 5 a.m. to tend to the livestock. He found a polite way of inquiring about whatever responsibilities Uncle Chuck ever had. He asked, "What would you say is your work versus life balance, Chuck? Fifty, fifty? Forty, sixty?"

"You smell that food?" Uncle Chuck nodded toward the kitchen with his nose in the air. "I shot every piece of meat that's going on the table today. I'm up almost every morning during the seasons. Duck, pheasant, turkey, deer; I plugged them all.

After my morning hunt, I usually head out and do my charity work."

Uncle Chuck's charity work consisted of canvassing bars, bowling alleys, and off-track betting outlets across central Illinois. He was a monitor for Heartland Helpers and it was his duty to make sure their clients were not playing reckless with the charity's money. Uncle Chuck's spending habits, on the other hand, were not subjected to the same scrutiny.

"If I see another three-and-out in this game, I'm going to just shut it off." Uncle Chuck was frustrated with the football game for some reason.

"Are you rooting for Detroit, Uncle Chuck?"

"I'm rooting for points, Nicky, forty-eight-and-a-half or more, to be specific. I don't care who gets them," he replied.

"How does a team score half a point?" my dad beat me to the question.

Uncle Chuck chuckled. "The half point is to make sure there are no ties between me and the house."

"Whose house?" I asked.

The chuckle turned into a belly laugh. "Belongs to some guy named Ron in Decatur. Let me tell you, it's a nice place."

Aunt Jan walked into the room. "Charles, Florence just called. They'll be here in ten minutes and we're going to sit down right away because they have to head straight from here to Danville. Would you please put that away before supper?" Aunt Jan cocked her head toward the assault rifle mounted above the fireplace and below the stuffed deer head.

"Yes, ma'am." Uncle Chuck popped the recliner upright and stood in one fluid motion.

Aunt Florence was the youngest of my mother's two sisters. She was coming to dinner with her husband and my twin, five-year-old cousins in tow. They were clever as monkeys. They would have that AR-15 off the shelf the second they saw it.

I followed Uncle Chuck back to the rear addition of the house. Aunt Janice may have insisted on never moving from her first house, but she never stopped Uncle Chuck from making improvements as he saw fit. The addition contained a treasure trove of marvels that made my young mind reel.

There was a billiards table, an electronic dartboard, and six leather recliners staggered in two rows of theatre seating in front of a retractable screen. The walls were adorned with the many busts of Uncle Chuck's conquests. The wild boar he had bagged in Florida was my favorite because it was festooned with a derby cap and had a cigar hanging out of its mouth. The advanced weaponry hanging along the back wall was the clear reason why the holiday festivities were forbidden from the rear addition, but I never really understood why my older cousin Michael stayed holed up in the dank basement while Uncle Chuck's treasure room sat empty.

"What's Michael up to, Uncle Chuck?"

"Probably downstairs making cheese."

"What?"

"Never mind, Nick, never mind." He chuckled and rubbed my head.

Uncle Chuck closed the two, oak sliding doors to the rear addition and turned the latch to lock them together. He slid the bottom bolt of the door closed and did the same to the top bolt. He added a medium weight padlock around the metal loop in the top bolt and then locked the door latch with a key.

"Tell you what, let's go down and see Mikey right now. I should tell him to come up for supper anyway." He slid his keys into his pocket.

I had an ulterior motive for asking about Michael. I was looking for a glimpse of my yearly haul of gifts from Aunt Jan. Since she always headed down to Florida for Christmas, she would hand out our gifts at Thanksgiving. I hadn't seen any stacks of gifts in the rear addition, so I figured they had to be in the basement.

The silver-blue glow of a large-screen monitor cast the only light in the basement. My cousin, Michael, sat in the center of a loveseat between two luscious cushions. He wore headphones and a pair of glasses with an attached wire that led to a gaming console. He was playing a combat flight simulator game. He either ignored us or did not notice us enter his domain.

"Mikey," Uncle Chuck called out but received no response. The monitor showed the cockpit view of a fighter pilot in pursuit of an enemy fighter. "Mikey," Uncle Chuck called out again and clapped his hands twice.

My cousin flinched at the sound of the clap and lost some range on his target. He sat forward on the edge of the couch to refocus his hunt.

Satisfied by Michael's passive acknowledgment, Uncle Chuck focused on the dogfight as well. The opponent was no match for the aggressor. Armed with only a novice understanding of what I was watching, I could still see that Michael's fighter was equipped with its full complement of weaponry. He drew closer to his prey and engaged the trigger button on his joystick. He shot three rounds from his gun as tracers. Satisfied with his range and trajectory, he opened both barrels on his opponent. The other fighter absorbed the fiery projectiles and burst into flames.

Michael removed his glasses and headphones. "What's up, Charlie?"

"Supper," he answered and pointed upstairs.

Michael turned and saw me but did not say hello. I looked away and scanned the basement for any sign of gifts.

"I'll be up in a minute. I got to get dressed." Michael stood and walked from his side of the loveseat. He flipped a switch on the wall and lit the room. He wore boxer shorts and white gym socks with colored stripes around the calves. The socks did not match.

My reconnaissance continued as I ascended the staircase behind my uncle. I stopped at the last point where I would have a view into the basement. There, behind the bar was a flash of red. I locked my focus; there were red and green wrapped boxes with gold bows. The pile ran the full length of the rail and was almost as high as the bar top.

My cousin walked by and saw me staring down into his room. "Jesus Christ, kid, give me a break."

***

The following Thanksgiving at Aunt Jan's table was quiet. Uncle Chuck had left early for Florida and she was to follow him down the next week. Michael was gone, too, not that he would have been a conspicuous presence in any event.

"He chose the Air Force," Aunt Jan sighed. "U of I was here for the taking but I knew he'd fly away. By the grace of God, I hope he ends up in Rantoul when his specialist training is over but I know it will never happen."

There's an Air Force base in Rantoul, just north of Champaign. Whether it was there or the University of Illinois, the Altgelds likely had the pull to see Michael land safely. However, Aunt Jan was on the outs with her inlaws.

"Chuck wanted to be here, he really did, if only for deer season. He just couldn't handle his mother anymore. I told him to just get out of here." Aunt Jan waved her hand. "He's no help to me when he's all stressed out like that."

"What was her problem?" my dad asked. He was perhaps the most disappointed by Uncle Chuck's absence.

"She was upset that I took him off his rounds as a monitor," Aunt Jan said. "But he was unhappy. People were starting to avoid him, even folks not in the program. They treated him like a snitch because he was out checking up on folks. I know because that's how they treat me now that I pick up the slack." Aunt Jan let a tear slip.

My mother, the eldest of the three sisters, embraced her. "You're only looking out for their well-being."

Uncle Leo spoke up while reaching for the gravy boat. "They're damned ingrates if you ask me."

In contrast to her husband, Aunt Florence closed her mouth tightly. She even sucked in her lips and clamped down. She dug the handle end of her spoon into her napkin and wiggled it like she was writing something. She spoke without looking up, "Jan, didn't you tell me that Chuck was being a little reckless, too? Did you tell Olivia about that?"

Aunt Jan released a long breath and sat up in her chair. "Flo, he wasn't reckless. He has no obligation to be a choir boy all the time. Just like you or me."

I never once saw Aunt Jan drink, swear, or lose her temper.

"But you said he showed up drunk to someone's intervention," Aunt Flo said. She still hadn't looked up.

"He'd been drinking. He wasn't drunk," Aunt Jan corrected.

"Come on, Jan, you can see how that shows some poor judgement, right?" My mother stepped in to arbitrate.

Aunt Jan's head fell forward. Her folded hands were in her lap. I saw two tears drop to her blouse. "Listen, he's gone. What's the point of dragging him through the mud while he's gone?"

"I agree, Jan," my dad said.

"Thank you, Rich." Aunt Jan raised her head, sniffed, and cleared a slick of mascara from below her eye with a wipe of each index finger. "How about we open some gifts?"

I sprang to attention. My sister followed and my twin cousins squealed with joy.

***

When we arrived for Thanksgiving the next year, the house was cold and odorless. We arrived to collect our gifts before heading down to spend the holiday with Aunt Flo, Uncle Leo, and the twins. Aunt Jan's luggage was lined up in the landing.

"I'm sorry we can't give you a ride to the train station, Jan, but with all the food and gifts there won't be any room at all in the car," my dad said. We had to haul all the gifts she had for me and my sister plus all of those for my twin cousins.

"Oh, Rich, don't you worry for a minute. I have a car coming to pick me up." Aunt Jan rushed us into the rear addition with a smile and a wave of her arm. The animal heads remained, but the weapons were gone.

The gifts weren't even wrapped, but I didn't care. It was the greatest bonanza of gifts yet. She got me the newest video game console and a handful of cartridges. There was a Lionel model train; the real heavy gauge one, not the cheap toy version. There were model planes and a remote-control car, too. She got me new baseball cleats and basketball shoes, and there was a large duffel bag to put everything in.

"What do you say, Nick?" my mother urged me as I marveled at the extravagant display of generosity.

"Thank you so much, Aunt Jan," I said. "This is amazing."

Aunt Jan smiled but her grin could not mask her mood. Her hair was mussed, and her baggy eyes told a story of a tired, stressed woman. My mother hugged her without saying a word. I sat on the floor and tore off my boots so I could try on my new sneakers.

***

That was the last time I ever saw Aunt Jan on Thanksgiving. She moved down to Florida the next year. We went to visit her for spring break some years later. She was living in a seafront condo complex with neighbors that were many years older than she. She was wearing a wedding ring but there was no sign of Uncle Chuck. His name did not come up all week. My father was at home tending the farm.

We woke early on Easter morning to catch the first mass. We would need to hit the road after lunch. Dad was already upset that we would miss school on Monday and Mom was anxious to avoid any potential delays.

"Thank you for bringing the kids down, Sissie. I really needed this," Aunt Jan said. She readied the bow atop Louisa's head. It matched the dress she had bought for her for the occasion. My little sister was Aunt Jan's goddaughter and the beneficiary of all her daughter-directed affection.

"Why don't you come back with us?" my mom asked as she watched her little sister dote on her niece. "You know there's plenty of room. Rich won't care."

"You are so blessed to have him. He's such a good man."

"He's no angel," my mother assured her.

"Angels fly away," Aunt Jan replied. There was a moment of silence and the sisters hugged.

My mother pulled away and gripped her sister by the shoulders. "So, what do you say?"

Aunt Jan shook her head. "Thank you, but I don't want to leave Charlie."

My mother's face was incredulous.

"And Michael said he might be on leave soon. I don't want to miss his visit if he decides to come," Aunt Jan added.

By then Michael was flying remote-controlled drones for the Air Force. The machines did surveillance and dropped munitions over targets in the Middle East. His actual location was undisclosed—undisclosed to Aunt Jan at least.

"Please come with us, Jan." My mother's concern for her little sister was as tangible as the smell of the lamb and thyme in the oven.

"I'm fine, I promise. I'll fly up once it gets warm up there." She patted my mother on her shoulder. "And as much as I'd love to come stay on the farm and get up at the crack of dawn, I still have the house in Monticello, remember?"

"OK then." My mother sighed.

"OK then." Aunt Jan smiled and then turned to my sister and me. "Now, let's see what the Easter Bunny brought for you guys."

Interlude 3: The Beacon

"I was only a boy. How could I have known?" I say to Andres, ashamed.

Andres is smiling and looking at the horizon. He does not respond.

I kick the ground and a plume of dust erupts and dissipates. I notice the heat on my shoulders again. "That must have been pointless for you. Sorry."

Andres turns his smile toward me. His grin widens.

"What are you so happy about?" I ask. "It was a boring story. All it did was make me look like a selfish ass."

"That story wasn't about you and it wasn't for you." Andres is delighted to the point of giddiness.

"Then why do I feel so horrible?"

"That's your compassion. Your aunt saw everyone she ever loved leave her, despite her generosity," Andres told me. "Now you see it and it breaks your heart. You are glowing with compassion for her."

"All I could ever think about was the gifts," I say. "I wish I could be with her now. I'd take her out for coffee and just listen to whatever she wanted to say. I swear I would listen for days if I could."

Andres nods. "You'd be amazed if you knew how many times I heard someone say something like that."

"She never changed, you know. She moved back to that house in Monticello once it was clear that Uncle Chuck was gone for good. She stayed sweet and generous. She gave Lori and me the largest gift of all the guests at our wedding. She begged us to visit."

"You never did," Andres says. He looks again at the horizon. We stop and turn in a circle. He is looking for something.

"We were up in Chicago. We were busy with our work and our travel." I am ashamed again. "I promised myself we'd come down to visit once we had a baby girl or boy to share with her."

"So she could shower the child with gifts? So they could experience the same excitement that you did?" Andres asks as he searches the distance.

I am more ashamed than ever now. I can't look at him. "Is it normal to feel so warm?" I ask.

"You're so fresh and pure that the truth is beaming from you," he says. "You're glowing with promise."

"Come on with this," I say. I'm in a foul mood and sick of enduring Andres' drawn-out explanations.

"Turn around," he says. "Do you see any sun?"

I turn. There is no sun behind me. I turn again. Still no sun. Our shadows are cast around us just the same.

"You're a beacon, a whisper of truth amongst a din of bullshit." Andres continues to look out at the distance. "There!" He points ahead.

There is a rider on the horizon. His horse is at full gallop and a cloud of earthy dust follows him.

"Who's leaving? Me or you?" I ask.

"Listen to me, Nick. You're going to be very popular," he says. The steward pulls the reins at an angle and the horse heads in our direction. "The things you have to say hold the promise of progress."

"Progress toward what?"

"In limbo, progress toward anything is a treasure."

The heavy footfalls of the horse distract us. The rider is close enough that I feel the pounding of the hooves pulsate in my legs.

"What did I even say?" I ask.

"You showed me a person of valor, a person who lost all the love she cherished and who tried to win it all back by giving her material wealth away. I think that's my lesson. I'm not sure, but I think that's going to get me closer. I need to give up some of those things that I love."

The steward has a collared shirt with snap buttons capped in mother-of-pearl. The collar is drawn closed with a bolo tie with a silver cinch in the shape of a steer skull. He sports blue jeans and a cowboy hat. His brown leather belt is fastened with a shiny silver belt buckle that's as large as a saucer. It reads RO-DEO CHAMPION along the top and CALGARY STAMPEDE '79 across the bottom. There was an engraving of a bucking bronco in the center.

The rider wears a mustache on his wind-chapped, leathery face. He extends a gloved hand to Andres, who accepts and is pulled upon the horse behind the steward.

"Farewell," Andres says. He salutes and the rider turns his horse in the opposite direction, but Andres turns his head back to me. "Thank you, Nick." He rides away.

"For what?" I mutter to myself. Then I turn to see a stampede of folks heading toward me. A young black man beats the crowd.

"Name's Cole," he says with a twang as he reaches out to grab my hand.

Story 4: Your Best Move

Cole wasn't nervous about screwing Fiore or passing bad information through the monks, but the next part of the plan made him nervous. Rossi told him to reach out to John Urso and tell him he had some information regarding his son. He also wanted Cole to tell him that he knew that Winters was a cop. Cole was not enthusiastic about Rossi's plan.

Cole pled with Rossi, "Come on, man. You want me to just hit up Papa Bear like that? It's not like Pauly ever had me over for Sunday dinner with the family."

"He wants to hear new information about his son. That's why he sent Big and Little over. He'll respect you for coming straight to him and then he'll want to keep you close. It's your best move," Rossi explained.

"You all still sending me downstate, right?" Cole asked.

"Yes. Once you handle all this, we'll send you," Rossi assured him.

Cole played the conversation back through his head and asked himself, *What good does it do to get on Urso's good side if they're going to ship me out? What does it matter that he'll want to keep me close?* He puzzled over all of it. *They gotta know I got picked up last night.*

Cole lit a smoke. He was sitting alone in his basement in the dark. The cherry of his cigarette glowed intensely as he took a deep drag. He turned on the TV. It cast a silver-blue patina across the room. The evening news was on. The sports anchor reported, "They're up three to nil in the fourth out in LA. They have runners . . ."

He changed the channel and then scrolled through the stations, never stopping on a program for more than a moment. Finally, he turned off the TV. The cherry glowed again.

***

Lunardi met Urso after dinner at Belrose Park, a harness racing track that was a dying holdover from their parents' generation. An evening at the races was now nothing more than a pleasant neighborhood ritual for the nostalgic. There was no money to be made in it anymore. Regulators and modern science made it too hard to fix races, not that anyone would bother anymore. The purses and pools weren't large enough to merit the risk. There used to be all kinds of cheats. Folks would drug horses, sneak higher-class ponies into races, pay off jockeys and forge tickets. Now that it was clean, the only folks who consistently made money were those who had a genuine talent for picking winners.

Lunardi met Urso in the club box on the first tier. He ducked under the canopy covering the box and sat next to Urso. Attendance was sparse. Few others chose to pay the premium for a club box; the enormous tier was filled with maybe another twenty folks spread across the area. Most of them were ushers.

Urso asked, "How was dinner, Lu?" He looked down at his racing form and crossed off a horse's name with a small pencil. His box was in the front row, in line with the finish line.

"We went to Mama G's. The boys like it there. Fiore was late." Lunardi pulled a leather cigar case out of his inside jacket pocket. He offered one to Urso, who declined.

"What did you find out in Rosehill?" There were nine minutes until post. Track conditions were fast.

"Our boy in the basement got picked up by the cops early this morning. Big and Little managed to get in their first. They're giving him a little time to think about what he wants to do." Lunardi carefully trimmed the end of his cigar.

"Who's giving him time, us or the cops?" Urso crossed off another horse.

"No, the cops put him right to work. They've got him talking to the monks, spreading some bad info. That's why Fiore was late." He pulled out a butane lighter and lit his cigar. The blue flame looked like the afterburner on a fighter jet. His cheeks sucked inward as he stoked the cherry. Lunardi could see that Urso was annoyed by the interruption, so he stopped smoking and continued, "He came running in looking for money for the DiScipio lot."

"Did he now?" Urso asked loudly. He dropped both arms to his sides and turned square with Lunardi.

"Yeah. We about laughed him out of the room. He said he got a call from one of the monks, who said he could have the corner that Pauly was giving up interest and they were going to give it to him."

There were seven minutes to post.

"So what does that have to do with the boy in the basement?" His attention was directly on Lunardi now. He was looking for straight information and Lunardi was giving him the run around.

"Cole. George Cole is his name. He must have been working with Pauly on whatever he is doing with the Jesuits. That had to have been what he gave the cops, so they're using it to mess with us to stir the pot. The cops had Cole call the monks to tell them to give Pauly's interest in the lot to Fiore."

Urso pointed the racing form at Lunardi. "Pauly doesn't have no interest in that lot! He knows that!"

"John," Lunardi said as he dropped his gaze in deference. "Pauly must have told them it was his or that he could talk you into giving it to him or something. He must be working some deals with them." He held the cigar off to the side between his thumb and index finger. "Even though you told him not to."

"So, Pauly says so and they think they can give it away to whomever? To Frankie Fiore? Get that clown over to the Capri tonight. I'll see him after the races." Urso turned from Lunardi and reviewed his sheet. There were six minutes to post in the eighth race. The number three horse, Butter Whip, was the favorite paying three-to-two.

"What's the play, John?" Lunardi asked. He stood to leave and carry out his orders.

"Two, eight exacta box." Urso folded his racing form in two and tucked it in his inside coat pocket. They made their way to the concourse to make the bet. He had two guys with him in his box. One of them could have made the bet for him but he liked the ritual. He had his bet chosen since he picked up the form at lunchtime.

As they were walking through the tunnel past the usher, George Cole was heading up the escalator at the far end of the first tier. He came up to the tier and walked down to the club boxes.

The usher met him as he arrived. "Can I help you, son?"

Cole told the man his business and he whistled for another usher to walk over. That usher fielded the message and took it to one of the guys in Urso's box. The man emerged from beneath the canopy shielding his box and looked down toward Cole. The man was tall and thick. He kept his head bald. There were creases and wrinkles running every which way and there were nicks and scars from shaving wounds. Cole was frightened by his ogre-like appearance. The man made a small wave. The usher let him pass.

"You have a message for Mr. Urso? The ogre shook his hand with his right and patted around Cole's body with his left.

"That's right," Cole said.

"I want you to think about what you came here to say." It was Urso. He arrived through the tunnel. Cole and the ogre turned their heads around toward him.

Urso stared at Cole. "I bet you thought a lot about what you were going to say on the way over here. You probably played it through in your head a hundred times. Let me tell you something right now. It don't matter if you got it down cold; if you lie to me I will know."

The bell rang on the starting gate. "Aaaand there off!" the track announcer shouted over the PA.

"Come on, let's watch the race." He waved Cole over to his seats. The ogre and goon sat a row behind Urso and Cole. The three horse headed to the front and set the pace for the eight for the entire front stretch. The six horse moved forward but then broke stride and immediately faded to the back of the pack. The horses were three, two and eight as they came out of the turn and into the back stretch. The eight jockeys were whipping almost in unison as they hit the stretch, except for the jockey on the six horse in the back. He was whipping faster and without quarter.

"He's whipping that animal something fierce," Cole muttered, frowning. The three horse was ahead by two lengths at the top of the stretch. He was on the rail, with the two, Kay Katso Fay, to his right and the eight, Dani's Favorite, to the outside.

The PA man's breathless calling of the action screamed over the speakers. "KAY KATSO FAY splits to the front. Dani's Favorite tags along. Butter Whip is fading. It's Kay KATSO Fay and Dani's Favorite at the front with four furlongs to go. DANI'S FAVORITE has it by a neck. Kay KATSO fights back. It's a DING DONG BATTLE for the lead! Here they are at the wire and it's TOO CLOSE TO CALL." The crescendo of cheers from the crowd soon subsided to a murmur. After a pause, the announcer came back on, this time with a sober tone, "Photo finish between Kay

Katso Fay and Dani's Favorite, the seven, Rear Admiral, coming in third. Please hold all tickets until official."

"Who do you need to win?" Cole asked.

"I win either way." Urso gestured for Cole to sit down as he did so himself. "What is it you have to tell me?"

"I used to work for your son. Well, I do work for your son, but I haven't seen him in a while." Urso stared through him as he spoke. Urso's silent face urged Cole to tell him something of value.

Cole stumbled in his speech. "Your son is very good to me. He shares a lot with me."

The ogre walked around from his row of the box and sidled next to Cole. The goon moved down as well.

"I don't give the first fuck about what you think of my son," Urso said. "If me not giving a shit about you made a sound, we'd all be deaf right now."

Cole froze.

The ogre spoke. "Now is the part where you explain what the hell you're doing here."

"Rory Winters is a cop," Cole blurted. "He's tight with your son, he's like his foreman. And he's a cop."

Urso breathed in deeply through his nose. He cocked his head back slowly as he inhaled the puff of information that Cole released into the air.

Cole continued, "I didn't know about it when Big and Little came to see me last night, but I always had my suspicions. Player never stayed in town, but he always showed up right on time for the big job. The cops picked me up last night and confirmed everything."

There were ten minutes to post.

"And they just came right out and told you this?" Urso asked.

"No, but they told me they had a guy on the inside and they wanted to put me in, too. That other guy has to be Snowball . . . Winters. He has a lot of stuff in motion with your son. He had the most to gain and he just leaves town? No way."

The PA man announced, "Official results are in. Number eight to win, two to place, seven to show." A subset of the crowd cheered in appreciation.

"Anyway, I won't play ball, so they want to ship me out. I'm supposed to leave tomorrow," Cole said.

Urso signaled for the usher to come over and he told him to send the waiter down. Urso pulled out a smoke and offered one to Cole. He refused and showed him that he had his own.

The waiter arrived. "Yes, sir. What may I bring you?"

"Bombay Sapphire and Tonic. No fruit," Urso replied.

The waiter turned to Cole and asked, "And for you, sir?"

Cole looked up at the uniformed white man in Belrose calling him sir. He smiled. "I'll have the same. Thanks."

There were eight minutes to post.

Cole lit a smoke of his own.

"Tell me about the work you do with my son." Urso took a drag on his cigarette.

Cole told him about their deals up and down Roosevelt. He told him about booking inside and outside of the Roses. He told him about the monks. He made sure to tell him about Winters' role in everything. He was leaning forward with his elbows on his knees. He told him about his role as the money man. The cigarette dangling from his right hand hung between his knees as he spoke. He gestured with his left.

"So, you were his porta borsa for all this?" Urso looked Cole up and down.

"His what now?" Cole asked.

"His porta borsa. His purse man . . . Accountant."

"Yeah, yeah. I was his Petey Borsa," Cole agreed. Urso and his men laughed. The drinks arrived and they tapped glasses. There were two minutes to post.

"So, when are we going to see this Rory Winters again?" Urso asked. The two other men in the box turned to pay attention.

"I dunno. I'd guess they're going to put him back on the street as soon as I'm gone. He'll probably head to the monks or Fiore first." Cole took a drag and shook his head back and forth as he answered. He didn't make eye contact. He'd hit the hole in the plan: *Why would they ever let him go?* He knew it was a gamble, but there was nothing set up for him downstate. He was done hiding in a basement.

"Why do you mention those names together? The monks and Fiore?" Urso leaned in low, cocking his head to catch Cole's gaze from below. Cole did not look up or respond. "Come on, Petey. You were doing so good." There was one minute until post.

Cole sipped his cocktail then said, "I brought you something else. This is what Big and Little were asking for last night. I wanted to hand it to you myself." Cole handed him a bank statement that showed a series of transfers from Pauly's accounts to several accounts at the Bank of Belrose.

"You had this all along. Why didn't you cash out and run? Why did you let the pigs set you up?" Urso flashed a smile and looked to his lackeys. They smiled back.

"There's not much left to take. They said you'd respect me for bringing it straight to you. Maybe you could figure out who owns the other accounts."

The bell rang at the starting gate. "Aaaand they're OFF!" the announcer shouted.

"Why didn't you bring it to me a long time ago?" Urso ignored the race. He had not made his bet.

Cole took a large drink and answered quietly. "I thought it might help keep me alive one day." The horses were rounding the turn. "I want to show my respect for you here, today. I want to help you, Mr. Urso, any way I can."

Urso curled his mouth into a fake frown and nodded his head. "Is this all you got for me? One bank statement?" He flipped the sheet of paper over pretending to search for more information.

"That's all I got for now, but I can keep on with the cops. I can be a double-agent, ya know?" Cole sat back with a plaintive face. He put his arms on the armrests of the chair.

"But you said they were sending you away," Urso pointed out.

"Here they come spinning out of the turn . . ." the announcer shouted. Urso nodded to his men.

The ogre and his partner lifted Cole from under his armpits from behind. With their free hands they grabbed at the waist of his jeans, getting two handfuls of belt in the process. They swung back cradle like and then forward to launch Cole off the tier.

Instinct forced Cole to flail his arms and legs. He shifted his body weight to turn to face the rapidly approaching pavement of the empty concourse. He didn't scream. His panicked breath raced until just a moment before impact, when he inhaled fiercely. He contorted his body to land on the left shoulder and he shielded his head with both arms.

"And it's Pillow Bandit AT the wire!" the announcer screamed. A small group within the crowd was still screaming after the rest of the place went quiet.

There was a piercing ring in Cole's head like feedback from a concert speaker. Even with his arms wrapped around his head, the force of the impact instantly broke Cole's jaw and most of his teeth skipped across the concourse. They sounded like a bracelet of enamel beads breaking loose across the pavement. His neck was broken. His ribs had served to protect his still beating heart, but they pierced his other organs and abdominal flesh. His racing heart pumped measure after copious measure of blood from his body. The feedback faded. He bled out and died.

"Please hold all tickets until official," the announcer said.

Interlude 4: Deputy Cole

Cole is dressed as a deputy. A tin star shimmers on his leather vest. He stands with arms akimbo and faces Nick. "So?"

I feel pressured. I imagine sweat on my brow and so it drips down my nose. "So what?"

"What's the point of all that?" Cole demands. "You think I like reliving getting launched off a thirty-foot tier?"

I am stunned silent. I felt the story pulse through him, and I sensed the trauma. It was not as traumatic as a first-person re-telling, but it was harsh.

"I'm shocked," I say.

"You're shocked?" Cole gapes. He turns to the crowd. "He's shocked." No one laughs. No one smiles. They listen intently.

"Just give me a moment, OK?" I pant as though I just raced up a flight of stairs and need to catch my breath. I don't know what to do. I don't know what is expected of me.

"Take your time," Coles says sarcastically.

"Maybe . . . maybe you should just sit tight in your basement with your mother." I feel a pang of regret in my stomach. The shame of my poor first effort with Andres echoes through my mind.

"So Big and Little can come back and kill me and my mom?" Cole's face pinches to a scowl.

"Maybe you need to pick one side or the other and just stick with it?" I ask more than suggest. I shake my head and look away.

The features of my setting fade. Cole faces me with his arms folded. Behind him stand rows of good citizens waiting their turn to speak with me, the oracle of the celestial plain. I let the pressure channel my concentration, like I used to do before sitting for an exam. I tell myself that I am prepared for this, even if I'm not.

"George, you need to retrace your steps," I assert. "Trace your steps back to the crossroads that led to that racetrack, to that predicament."

"Do you have any idea what it's like where I'm from, man?"

"I imagine it's pretty rough." I stand resolute. "But everyone has options. I work at a school in a rough part of Chicago. Only a small number of the kids end up graduating from high school, but there are plenty of kids who make it out."

"What about the bad kids, Nick? What do you do for them?"

"I talk them into doing their best."

"What about the really bad kids, the kids who don't want your help?"

"I put them in the back of the class." I shrug. "I tell them to stay quiet. And if they keep out of the way and don't distract the others, I give them a C and push them out the door at the end of the year."

"Do you ever feel insecure, Nick?" Cole asks me.

"Sometimes, yeah, but we have security guards in the halls at school. They even escort us to our cars if we ask."

"Not at your school, Nick. I mean every day. Do you feel insecure?"

I make an attempt at humor, "Only about my appearance."

"You think you're doing those good kids a favor, but you're just teaching the bad ones to bide their time," Cole says. "They'll see you again on the streets and they won't give a shit about the pass you gave them."

"They don't listen when I scold them. If I send them to the principal, she sends them right back. I can't beat them."

"People respond to incentives, even kids."

"That's right. I incentivize them to behave by promising them a passing grade."

"You are rewarding their viciousness. They are learning that if they show their teeth, you will placate them," Cole says.

I want to change the subject. "How does someone get away with throwing people off balconies at a crowded racetrack?"

"It's his racetrack. I'm sure he told them I jumped." Cole shrugs.

"And people believed that?" I ask.

"Who would care either way?" He laughs. "Just another troublemaker getting out of the way for the good kids, right?"

"Fuck you."

"Fuck me? You were supposed to hold the truth," he growls, "but it looks like I'm the one preaching to you, don't it?"

"You can let go at any time."

Cole looks at the crowd of semi-damned awaiting their turns to grip my hand.

"All right, fine. I'll roll the dice," he says.

Story 5: Jay Hustler's Lucky Day

Jay Huntsfeld was a good friend from Effingham. He was a few years older than me and my buddies, but he fit in perfectly. We met when he was in high school and we were still in junior high. I think our first encounter was outside the drug store when Phil Maloney was trying to find someone to buy him chew tobacco.

Everyone called him Jay Hustler. He always had some scheme going on; often more than one at a time. He was the guy who got the keg for the party after the football game and then he found the barn to have it in, charging $5 for every cup he sold. He sold designer sunglasses and car audio equipment; his inventory was of unclear provenance. Jay Hustler was the man to call when you needed tickets to the Cardinals game. He even got me and my friends a car service for prom. Mind you, this was in southern Illinois, where most people had only seen a limousine on reruns of Dallas. He knew where to find things. He also knew where to lose things.

Jay got a lot of guys out of trouble. He earned everyone's admiration this way. The fact that it was probably his goods or services that got the guys in trouble in the first place always went ignored. He always knew whose name to drop if we were partying a county over and got into trouble. He knew where to find the doctor who wouldn't tell your girlfriend's parents about her unscheduled visit. If you crashed your mom's car, maybe Jay could make it look like it had been stolen.

Mitch Pollard was the first of our close group of friends to get engaged following college. I wasn't the best man but when it came time to plan the bachelor party, the guys asked me to reach out to Jay to set things up for us in Vegas. Of course, I obliged and so did Jay. He had rooms, meals, car service and club reservations set up in a day. It was like he was expecting my call.

"Ninth of June. Caesar's. You're all set," Jay told me over the phone. "You can bunk with me in the suite."

"You're coming too?" I asked with surprise.

"Come on, Kraus, don't be a penis," Jay said. "You think I'd miss Pollard's last hurrah."

"Well, I . . ." I stammered, "I figured you might have better things to do." I wasn't intimidated by Jay but I was impressed by him, so much so that I would sometimes forget that we were true friends. The others guys were tight with him too, but we shared a lot more with each other than with the others.

Jay had found a great career as a sales agent for a private aircraft company that chartered planes and helicopters for corporations, celebrities, and the ultra-wealthy. While my buddies and I were finishing up our studies, he was flying around the country to attend galas and golf tournaments. I was sure he had seen things beyond what we could ever hope to experience during our three-day trip to Las Vegas.

"I can't wait to be there with you guys," Jay said. "It's going to be epic."

***

Showing up with a massive white bird turd dripping down the shoulder of my polo shirt was not the impression I wanted to make when I met Jay in our hotel lobby.

"What's up, amigo!" he exclaimed as the automatic sliding doors closed behind me. He spread his arms wide to hug me, but I flinched and pointed at the stain on my shoulder. "Oh yeah! That" good luck, Kraus. That's good luck, on your first day in Vegas!"

Mitch and the rest of the guys trailed in after me and received Jay's embrace. While they laughed and slapped backs, I looked around anxiously for a bathroom. I packed light and was hoping this shirt would last me through the first night out here.

Without breaking his hug with Keith, the soon-to-be brother-in-law, Jay, caught the concierge's attention and nodded him over to take care of me. This nice gentleman took me aside, took my shirt, put me in a robe and pushed me back toward my friends. Later, I was barely into my second beer in the bachelor's suite when my shirt, laundered and pressed, arrived at the room.

***

The bar in the suite was resplendent with every kind of potable concoction devised. The bottles were arranged in a chromatic sequence from the top left of the top shelf to the bottom right of the bottom shelf. There were clear bottles of clear liquor at the top left followed by yellow liquor, then orange, then brown and finally ending with green bottles in the bottom-right corner.

Jay and I shot pool on the billiards table set in the middle of the suite. A crystal chandelier swung six feet above the table in place of the traditional pool table light with a beer logo on it.

The west wall was completely covered with four massive TVs. Mitch and Keith played a video game on the TV at the bottom left. To their right was Brad, Mitch's younger brother, who was watching porn. The dimensions of the unit made the scene nearly life sized. The top two TVs were showing baseball games, which we all ignored.

The best man, Gary, had a beer in one hand and a mouse in the other. He was watching instructional videos on a computer about how to win at craps. The last two guys in our group were the Maloney twins, Phil and Mike. They were camped behind the bar devising new cocktails. We would be lucky if we made it through the weekend without them getting in a fight. The best we could hope for is that they would just fight each other.

There was loud rock music pulsing through the suite. Mike shouted to Mitch above the din. "What's the first stop tonight?"

The suite was filled with a sonic soup of classic rock, clapping pool balls, cursing, video game soundtracks and the ecstatic exclamations of the copulating couple on Brad's TV.

"I don't know. Ask the best man," Mitch shouted over his left shoulder toward the bar.

"Gary," Mike shouted. "Gary!"

Gary had his headphones on, and his concentration was devoted to the gambling strategist on his monitor. I tapped him on the shoulder to get his attention and then pointed to the bar.

"Jesus Christ, Hendricks, get your face out of the computer," Mike pled and spread his arms wide like a game show hostess highlighting to the contestants what they could win. "What do you have planned for tonight?"

"Nothing. I mean, we're in Vegas. I thought we'd go gambling." Gary shot looks around the room searching for an agreeing face.

I looked at Jay and smiled. He saw me and smiled back.

"Two, four combo off the rail, corner pocket," he said. He nailed the shot, stood, grabbed the chalk, and applied it to the tip of his stick. "We have reservations at 8:30 for dinner at Tao. We'll hit the Lotus lounge at the Cosmo after that and then head upstairs to the club around one."

"Nice," Phil muttered. "All comped?"

Jay lined up his next shot and called it. "You know it." He nailed that shot too.

"Fucking A, nice!" Mike added. "Full hookup."

"One a.m.?" Gary asked.

All the guys laughed. No one was really counting on Gary to plan anything. Gary was Mitch's neighbor from across the street and his lifelong best friend. As sure as we were that he would be the best man, we were even more sure he would be a dud when it came to partying.

Jay finally missed a shot and then I missed mine.

I looked over to Gary. "Listen, Hendricks, it's 7:00. You've got about one hour of gambling time if you want to get a shower in before we have to leave for dinner."

Gary looked at the clock on his computer, logged off, and headed toward the door. "I'll be back in an hour. Don't leave without me, Mitch."

"Good call on best man, Mitch," Keith said as the door shut behind Gary.

"Give him a break, Millman. He's known him since he was five," I said.

"Yeah, almost as long as Pollard's been banging your sister," Jay joked.

All the guys laughed, especially Brad. Keith shot him a nasty look. He was a youngster and not entitled to get a laugh at his elder's expense.

***

The pace of the evening accelerated when we left the hotel and hit the strip. We rode down the boulevard in our limo and gawked at the lights and signs adorning both sides of the street. The sidewalks were as large as the concourse on my old college campus and they were filled from edge to edge with people. If there was a large group heading in one direction, folks coming the opposite way would have to yield passage to the herd.

I had never been to Vegas and it all felt surreal to me, like an animated film. Every hotel was like a theme park; there were rides, theater productions, light shows, and fountains. Street performers and vendors claimed toeholds on the edges of street corners. It was frenetic. It was exhilarating.

The Maloney brothers opened the sunroof and went topside to review the landscape.

"No, trust me, horrible, horrible choice," he replied to whatever she said in response.

"Caesar's, tonight! Suite 2020!" Mike shouted to a group of girls. "It's a *suite*. Ask for Mike."

They carried on while we blasted music and slammed beers. The talk was juvenile. We mostly made fun of each other and our respective ex-girlfriends. Jay picked on Keith because he always thought he was a bully. Jay didn't like bullies, probably on account of the fact that he had a younger sister with Down syndrome.

"You still got that fancy car, Keith?" Jay asked, knowing full well that he didnt'.

"Nah, man. Got rid of that one."

"Got rid of or lost it to the bank?"

Keith was the same age as Jay. He was our friend but not so close that he would have been invited if Mitch weren't marrying his sister. He had bought a nice German sedan just after high school. He briefly had a sweet gig at a tech company that his uncle got for him down by St. Louis. He rolled back into town one weekend, jangling the keys in everybody's face. He had a good run for a few years but lost that job. He got greedy and started making unreasonable demands for more pay and more liberties. I guess he felt he was essential to the enterprise and entitled to more. They let him go without severance.

Jay smiled and stared at Keith, confirming his place above him in the order. It was awkward for a moment, so I pulled Phil down into the limo and took my turn topside. Looking down the strip from up there was like looking down a runway at night, but brighter. The lights of the town eclipsed anything the desert night sky could muster in terms of celestial brilliance. Meanwhile, Mike continued to harass passersby.

Mike had his right hand shaped as an M and his left shaped as a W. He slapped his hands against his chest and shouted, "Midwest *side!*" at a group of guys crossing the street in front of the limo. I laughed at his idiocy and retreated to the safety of the carriage below.

Brad had somehow managed to get a porno film to play on the limo's AV system. A bottle of hard liquor that someone had swiped from the bar was passed around. It was all laughs now. No heavy subject matter. No talk of cars or work or family or the forthcoming harsh realities of adult life. We were children, children with money and freedom and a fully comped trip to Vegas.

***

"Krug. Most expensive on the menu," Gary bragged. The sommelier brought the bottles to the table and the busboys set the ice buckets atop their pedestals.

"Yo, Hendricks! Not everything is comped." Jay put his hands to his forehead. "I mean, there's limits."

"No, no, don't sweat it, Hustler." Gary waved him off. "I got this. I won big at the craps table."

I smiled wide, feeling so satisfied for him. Gary could put his nose down and learn anything. I wasn't surprised he mastered craps from some course he bought on his computer.

"How much?" Keith asked.

"About $2,000." Gary's proud smile matched mine.

Jay shouted "Hey, hey!"

The rest of the table lit up with hollers and we raised our glasses. "To Mitch," we said in unison.

"To Gary," Mitch answered.

"To Gary," we echoed.

Tao looked like a large ballroom with a terrace balcony extending around three walls of the main floor. At the end of the room was a fifteen-foot-tall statue of Buddha seated on an ornate six-foot pedestal. It was painted gold, but special lighting flickered deceptively on the surface to make it shimmer. Lanterns hung from the ceiling on chains. Red curtains hung in panels along the walls, interrupted by columns festooned with tapestries that looked to be Southeast Asian in origin.

Our crockery was made of black stoneware. The tablecloth and napkins were crimson red linen, the utensils were silver with gold accents and our glasses were crystal with gold plating on the rims. A saxophone player complemented the DJ's trance groove.

"How long is dinner?" Mike asked. His brother nodded in agreement that this was a worthwhile question.

"I don't know, Mike," Jay said. He raised his glass toward the brothers. "Try to enjoy it. This whole weekend's going to fly by."

The captain of the waitstaff arrived to greet the table. "Good evening, Mr. Huntsfeld. Thank you for joining us this evening." The man wore a black suit over a black, collarless dress shirt. The shirt was buttoned to the top so that the band of fabric encircling his neck seemed like a choker. "And good evening to our special guests. Congratulations to you, Mr. Pollard. I hope your weekend is as special and lucky as your bride-to-be."

We each said thank you to the kind man. Jay smiled and winked. The captain clasped one hand over the other and bowed slightly. When he walked away, a squad of waiters set to delivering our first course of noodle soup along with a special spoon that looked like a little boat with a handle on it.

Jay grabbed the spoon and brought it to his mouth with a loud slurp. We all followed suit in pantomime.

"You're amazing, Hustler," Mitch said between slurps. "Thank you."

"Cut it out, Pollard," Jay answered.

"Yeah, Mitch, the lap dances are tomorrow night," Keith told him. "You don't have to rub him off here at the table." Keith was jealous of Jay.

"Seriously, how many kids from central Illinois are walking around Vegas right now on a first name basis everywhere we go?" Mitch insisted.

The staff came and removed our soup bowls. They placed woven bamboo baskets in front of each of us, paused and lifted off the tops with a flourish. Plumes of steam wafted straight into the air and for a moment there were eight little mushroom clouds ascending above the table. When the smoke cleared, we saw that each basket held a small pile of dim sum dumplings.

"I want to be Jay when I grow up," Brad said, half joking. He was only twenty-one and content in his kid-brother role. He took his lumps from us, but he enjoyed the fruits of having an older brother who didn't mind him tagging around everywhere.

"You want to know the secret, Bradley?" Jay asked.

The table went silent. Brad had pierced a dumpling with two chopsticks. He held it aloft at the end of the sticks and it dripped condensation onto the tablecloth. "Yes, very much so, Mr. Hustler, sir."

The only sound from the table was chewing.

"There are jobs you like. There are jobs you're good at. There are jobs that pay well," Jay said. He looked around the table to make sure we were paying attention. "If you don't want to be miserable, you have to have at least one of those things. If you want to be happy, you have to have two of the three."

"What about three for three? What's the payout on that?" Gary asked in gambler's speak.

"That's the jackpot, Hendricks. That's the jackpot, " Jay told him.

Everyone nodded except for Keith. "Bullshit," he muttered.

"What's that, Millman?" Jay asked.

"Bullshit," Keith said resolutely.

"What part?" Jay smiled and looked around the table.

Keith took a long gulp of his beer and set down the glass. He shook his head and sneered, "You didn't get some sweet gig flying from pro-am to pro-am because of some bumper sticker philosophy."

"What do you want, a seminar?" Phil asked. "We're having a good time here, Keith."

"You're right. You're right." Keith raised both hands and pushed them forward.

Jay raised an eyebrow at Keith. "No, no, please continue, Keith. Do you think I'm a fraud?"

The squad of waiters circled the table, ready to snatch any empty baskets or fill an empty water glass.

"How does a guy from Effingham end up living the high life out west without, you know, getting his nose dirty?" Keith asked.

"Oh, I see. I'm dishonest." Jay laughed.

"I don't know about dishonest," Keith said. "I'm just saying I bet there's a little undeclared cargo in those international flights you're taking."

Mike Malone's ears perked up. "Hey, Jay, you got any undeclared cargo on you tonight?"

Everyone laughed. We were happy that Mike broke the awkwardness.

Jay wiped his face with his napkin. "You got me, Keith. You got me. I've got half a kilo of blonde molly keistered right now."

The laughter grew. Even Keith cracked a smile, unsure whether he had scored a hit or not.

"In fact, I didn't even bring a change of clothes for the weekend. That bag I wheeled in was packed with Amys, Special K, Blue Dots, Horse Hair, Donnas, Benzos, and Kitchen Tile."

I wasn't sure how many of those names he made up but there was no doubt that Jay knew a thing or two about designer drugs. The Malone brothers hung on Jay's every word.

"So, Jay, about the Special K . . ." Phil smirked and furrowed his brow.

"As the guest of honor this weekend, I propose a change of subject," Mitch said above all of us.

"All right, put a pin on that." Phil pointed at Jay.

The waiters cleared the table for the next course. In two laps of the table, all the remnants of the dim sum were gone and there were four Peking ducks placed on the table. Each had its head intact; the one placed between me and Jay was looking at me. His bill was open as if he had a wide-mouthed grin when he was tucked in the oven. His eyes were gone, replaced by blackened marks that looked like the backsides of sewn-on buttons.

***

The lounge at the Cosmo was arranged as a series of terraced, concentric circles. The central circle was a bar, which folks stood around and mingled. The next circle was raised above that one with booths along the back partition of the wall of the next circle. There were three more circles of larger and larger circumference continuing upward to the top concourse. It was like the Roman coliseum but instead of lions and gladiators at the center, there were douche bags.

Poor Brad was cornered by one such douche bag who had wandered past our booth.

"I said listen, honey, you're gorgeous but that's just way too much ham for my eggs," he bellowed.

The guy was drunk but so were we. We could have saved Brad, but we figured we'd let him learn his lesson. It was amusing to watch him try to extract himself from the guy's grip.

"So, she gets all miffed and takes off. I realize that I'm surrounded by a bunch of consultants on discount junkets. So, I tell my buddy that we should split and he suggests we head over to one of those day-club pool parties," he said. "So, we come here to the Cosmo but I ain't got no trunks, so I head to one of those trendy shops in the gallery. Turns out the only thing they got are those skin-tight things that look like briefs and a bunch of banana hammocks. So, I said screw it. I tell Rafael to give me the tightest little marble bag he can scare up and we hit the party."

"Did you get the bottle service?" Phil nosed into the conversation. Mike punched him in the thigh, hard.

"No, no, not right away," he answered, perturbed by the interruption. "So, I'm standing at the edge of the pool in my robe. I wait for the music to stop then I open the robe and drop it off my shoulders to reveal all my girthy splendor. Raffy had given me the Old Glory model, a grape smuggler with the American flag across the front and the back. It was majestic. The DJ sees me, and he just starts chanting *U-S-A! U-S-A!* and then the whole crowd busts into it. I took three steps back to let the crowd feast their eyes and then I rocked the most epic cannonball that place has ever seen."

The guy laughed so hard he became breathless. He was oblivious to the fact that no one else was laughing. He was oblivious to the fact that he was there alone, talking to complete strangers on a Friday night.

"Where's your buddy now?" Jay asked the guy.

"Not sure." He looked around with what seemed like genuine concern.

I saw two dazzling waitresses approaching from the corner of my eye. One carried a large bottle of tequila that was wrapped in golden foil with sparklers attached to the top. The waitresses boxed out our nuisance and placed eight shot glasses on the table. The guy took the hint and moved on to latch onto another group.

"Oh man, we ain't going to make it to the club, Hustler!" Gary cried.

"You'll be fine. We'll get some energy drinks," Jay said. "Serene?"

"Yes, Jay?" the blonder of the waitresses answered.

"Would you please bring us some Flying Tigers, at your convenience?"

"Of course, Mr. Huntsfeld."

"Of course, darling," the lesser blonde added and stroked his shoulder.

"Darling?" Brad smiled at Jay with admiration.

"Man, it's too bad Jack couldn't make it," Mike lamented as he poured out the shots. Phil portioned out the salt and lime for each of us.

"The legend of Jack Decker!" I shouted. I was excited just to hear his name. "Oh man, I haven't heard from him in years."

We saluted each other with our shot glasses and then downed them in unison.

"Didn't you try to find him?" Mike asked Gary. It was almost an accusation.

Gary shrugged. "His cousin told me he was living on a boat in Puerto Rico, but that's all he had. His mother is long gone. He said she got married again."

"What is that, like five?" I asked.

"Who knows? You keeping track?" Keith returned.

Jack Decker was the wild man of our group when we were in high school. He was the guy who accepted every dare. He was the guy always hurting himself trying some stupid challenge. The mere mention of his name provoked a showdown of Jack Decker stories.

"Do you remember the time Jack tried to jump the homecoming bonfire on Brad's little BMX?"

"Do you remember the time Jack stole his stepfather's credit card and had a hundred and forty-four prairie dogs released on the school grounds?"

"Do you remember when he took a stripper to prom?"

Each story carried us through another round of drinks. My diaphragm ached from convulsing in laughter. The evening was spectacular. I felt higher than I'd ever felt in my life.

"Do you remember the time Jack was living in a cave out by Funkhouser?" Jay asked.

Silence. Smiles. And then an eruption of laughter.

"I'm serious." Jay pled. "He lived in a cave for a summer."

I shook my head. The guys were transfixed. This was new Jack Decker material. The legend would grow.

"He was in junior high or maybe fifth grade," Jay began. "It might have been before you guys met him. He was still kind of tame. The only reason I knew about him is because his mother married my best friend's dad and he would tell me the stories."

"What number was that?" I asked.

"How do I know, Kraus?" Jay dismissed me. "That woman was like a doorknob."

"Shut up, Nick." Mitch shoved me playfully. "Jay, continue."

"So, Jack pulled some shit with his BB gun. I think he shot the neighbor's cat in the ass or something." Jay sat back in the plush booth and looked around at his audience. "The neighbor made a fuss with the cops and his mother didn't want to deal with it, so she sent him down to Missouri to live with his father."

Gary nodded. "That's why we never really saw him around before high school."

"Well, not exactly," Jay continued. "You see, his dad passed away not long after he moved down there."

"How?" Phil asked.

"He accidentally drank antifreeze," Jay answered, paused, and look at the ceiling. "Or maybe it wasn't an accident. I'm not sure."

We absorbed the information for a moment and then erupted in another spasm of laughter.

Phil composed himself for a moment. "I heard it tastes great. I see how that could happen."

"I guess it was a dare," Jay said. "A drinking game taken way too far. Maybe that's where Jack got his habits from."

We were brimming with booze and copious doses of B-12 from the energy drinks. I was drunk, but ecstatic at the same time. I saw Brad's obnoxious friend from earlier patrolling the aisle of the tier below us looking for someone to talk to. Perhaps he was looking for Brad.

"So, he came back to Effingham?" Mitch asked.

"Not exactly, but this is where it gets good." Jay reviewed our faces and laughed. "His mom took him back in but then he got in trouble again, so she sent him straight back to Missouri to live with his father's family." Jay paused and took a sip of water. "Jack had other plans though. He didn't want to go back there. He didn't care for his kin down in Missouri. He said they were too trashy."

"We got some family down there." Phil looked at Mike. "We can confirm that."

"OK, you guys know about those the limestone caves along the Little Wabash, out toward Funkhouser?" Jay looked around to make sure we knew what he was talking about. "Jack knew that river like the back of his hand. He would spend his summer days fishing in the river. And sometimes he would escape the afternoon sun in one of the caves. Maybe even catch a nap, you know?"

"Like a siesta," Gary offered.

"So, his mom puts him on the bus for Mizzou, but he hops off in Funkhouser. He doesn't know what he's going to do but he figures he better lay low, so he made his way over to the riverside." Jay traced Jack's movements with his finger on the table. "Next thing he knows he spends an entire summer and a good part of the school year in those caves.

"What did he do for food?" Brad asked.

Jay sat back and explained with an open hand. "Well he caught fish and stole corn from the fields. And then think about all the orchards and berry fields around there. There's lots of healthy grub for the taking."

Gary scratched his cheek. "I suppose you could boil the river water and drink it."

"Didn't the family in Missouri make a fuss when he didn't show up?" I asked.

"I dunno. Maybe he called them to tell them he wouldn't be coming," Jay said. "I don't know."

"So, did he get caught or did he just head home when the weather got cold?" Brad persisted.

"He got caught before the winter. That's actually a pretty funny story, too." Jay sat up in his chair. He was giddy.

"Jack kept going to school, bless his heart," Jay said. "One day he was in line with another hundred boys for a mandatory physical from that local doctor, Dr. Tennison."

The boys groaned at the mention of the doctor's name. "I remember him," Mitch said. We nodded.

"Yeah, real sweaty hands, remember?" Jay continued. "The school called for physicals for the boys because there was an outbreak of crabs."

"I remember that," Mike said. He squirmed and subconsciously scratched at the crotch of his jeans.

"Was Jack patient zero?" Phil asked.

"No, no. Jack was clean . . . or maybe he wasn't. That's not important." Jay waved off the question. "The thing was that when Jack got his turn after a hundred or so other boys, he refused to submit to the examination."

"Why?" I asked.

"Dr. Tennison only used one glove." Jay smiled.

"You mean he used one bare hand and a gloved hand?" Gary asked.

"No, I mean he only had one glove. He gave a hundred robust examinations of each boy's junk without changing gloves," Jay said.

"Not once?" Gary asked.

"The boys ahead of him tipped him off. Jack asked Dr. Tennison to change gloves and he refused, so Jack refused to let him touch him," Jay said. "Can't say I wouldn't have done the same."

"The principal had to call his mother. She refused to believe that her son was in the school. She thought they were making a mistake." Jay smiled. "That's when they found out he had been living in a cave."

The blonde waitresses came and cleared the table, spilling the one shot glass that was still full. The lesser blonde wiped it up and apologized, though no one except Keith and I noticed.

***

The club was called Pandemonium and it was aptly named. We lost track of the Maloney twins almost immediately. They were off towards the dance floor even before Jay found his connection to have us seated. He had scored us a table in the VIP section with bottle service.

"Everything is comped, but you still need to tip," Jay instructed us. "Start big and then dial it back as the night goes on. I already gave our girl $200, so you guys need to scare up $100 for the next pass."

Gary pulled out a fresh $100 bill and flashed it at us. He was lucky and generous, and I was most grateful.

I was expecting more luxury from the VIP section. The table was a black high-top that you would find at any corner bar in Chicago. The stools were upholstered in black vinyl, some of which was tearing at the edges on some of the seats. On top of the table were two large ice buckets. One contained a bottle of vodka, a bottle of rum, and a bottle of tequila. The other had small carafes filled with juice, soda, seltzer water and more energy drinks.

The VIP section garnered us a heightened level of attention from the other club goers, especially the ladies. Several ladies passed by the velvet rope more than once to scope out the chosen people of the evening. The interest of these ladies was not lost on Brad. He mixed two strong drinks at the table, and then walked toward the rope, ready to hand one off to the next curious woman who walked by.

"What's he doing?" asked Keith, pointing at Brad with an open hand.

"Trolling for tail," Mitch answered and we laughed.

Brad landed a striking tan woman with black hair and red fingernails. The bouncer released the clasp on the hook of the velvet rope and allowed her passage to our realm. She sat in one of the seats left vacant by the Maloney brothers' absence.

"What's your name?" Brad asked.

"Destiny." She smiled.

I nudged Mitch beneath the table. He looked at me, smiled, and gave a small wave of his hand to tell me to let this play out.

Destiny only had questions. She wanted to know where we were from, where we worked, where we were staying. Anything we asked her was met with a vague answer and another question for us.

"Where are you from, Destiny?" I asked.

"I've been out in Vegas for years," she answered. "What brings you boys out this weekend?"

"How old are you Destiny?" Brad asked.

"What are you a cop?" she joked. "Old enough to be in here, How about you?"

She talked to Brad like he was a child, just as we did.

"Do you live around here?" Keith asked.

"I'm out for the night, sweetie," she said quickly and smiled. She seemed to be growing impatient. I noticed that every time she flashed her wide toothy smile, her eyes stayed squinty and suspicious.

The waitress returned to refresh our mixers. She cast a leery eye at Destiny but evaded her stare. Gary gave our server the $100 bill as she left, which caught Destiny's attention. This time her smile was genuine, as told by her lifted brow and wide eyes. She sidled next to Gary. Both Gary and Brad grew anxious.

Jay pointed to the crowd of people dancing. "Brad, why don't you take Destiny to the dance floor? She didn't come here tonight to stand around a table with a bunch of guys."

Destiny was clearly keen to peel one of us away. She didn't seem to care whom. "Sound good, Brad?" she asked. She could not have sounded more indifferent.

"I don't dance much," Brad hesitated.

"Go show him what it means to take a girl dancing in Vegas, Destiny." Jay winked at her and she returned another sincere smile.

The bouncer removed the velvet rope to let them exit. They bounded into the crowd.

"How long?" I asked.

"Twenty minutes," Keith said.

Jay outbid him. "Thirty. Let's give Bradley some credit."

"Are they going to have sex?" Gary asked.

We looked at Gary in silence. Once it was clear he was serious, we laughed in unison at his naiveté.

"Was that a prostitute!?" Gary couldn't believe it. "Oh my God, that was a prostitute."

"Little brother is going to have some story to tell," Mitch laughed.

"If he's not back in twenty minutes, we should go up and make sure she's not ransacking the suite," Gary said. He was ever the thinker, and prudent at that. We ceased laughing and looked at each other with concern.

We debated whether to act but after a few minutes the point was moot.

"Forget something?" Jay asked Brad as he returned to the table.

"That was a hooker!" Brad pointed his thumb back over his shoulder.

"And an eager one at that!" Mitch said.

"Why didn't you guys tell me?" Brad said. We all laughed except for Gary.

"Hey Gary, she can't be far." Keith pointed to the dance floor. "Now's your chance."

I was proud of myself for maintaining my party composure. We had only spent ten hours in Vegas but it already felt like a whole weekend of partying. Half of the crew flamed out in the club. Mitch was the first to pass out, likely on account of us force feeding him booze without quarter. His little brother followed close behind. The Maloney twins were thrown out before they could get in a fight and we were all thankful for that.

We took the Pollard brothers up to the room and settled in for the night. We had a 10 a.m. tee time on the course.

"Damn, Jay, 10 a.m. is pretty early, ain't it?" I asked.

"Would you rather tee off in the noon, desert sun?" Gary answered for him.

"Oh, yeah."

The Maloney twins were restless. I didn't know what they got into at the club, but they were pacing like caged animals.

"Let's go out," Phil said.

"Yeah, let's find some whores," Mike agreed.

This was a dangerous prospect. These two were in no shape to distinguish a random civilian from a professional. That's what led to their ejection from the club. Making matters worse, we knew they would bring them back to the suite. That would mean no sleep for anyone.

"Let's walk down to Fremont street. Old Vegas," Jay suggested.

Keith shook his head. Gary groaned; I did, too. Phil and Mike clapped like they were about to hit the field for a big game.

Jay looked low and whispered, "It's a little bit of a hike and it's kind of chilly. They should be out of gas by the time we get there. We'll take a car back."

***

The Maloney's did not run out of gas. Jay, Keith, Gary and I walked three steps behind them as they rambled down the street. There were signs inviting us to try the "Fremont Street Experience" as we approached the bedeviled pedestrian mall that was the old main strip of Vegas. To many, it represented the original Vegas and had never ceased to be the main strip.

To the more puritan of locals, it was the deepest pit of hell. Plainly dressed families, with children in tow even at these little hours of the morning, stood like turnstiles handing out pamphlets to those entering the strip. A teenage girl in a frock and a bonnet handed me a folded pamphlet. The front read IS THERE A HELL? I opened it to find the answer. YES, AND YOU ARE GOING THERE. I folded it and put it in my pocket; Lori would get a kick out of this little memento.

There were other bands of folks trying to coax our money from us. Freaks, side-acts, and charitable-minded folks waited patiently for us to pass near before hitting you up. A young man wearing a smock that indicated he represented an animal rights group positioned himself square in front of Mike Maloney. "Do you love dolphins, sir?"

Without hesitation, he replied, "Yes, they're delicious."

The young man froze, speechless, as Mike and Phil walked past him on each side.

Gary was interested in the Fremont Street Experience, which entailed a tour of the historic spots in old Vegas and culminated in a zip line ride above the center of the street. "It looks neat," he said.

Keith took another chance to ride his ass. "Did you dip into Hustler's stash of dope? Why aren't you exhausted?"

"Why aren't *you* exhausted?" Gary returned.

"I tried to conk out when we got back to the suite, but all those damn energy drinks had me buzzing," Keith said.

"Well me, too, I guess," Gary said.

"What did you just say about me and my dope?" Jay asked Keith with a laugh. He didn't seem miffed, but he wasn't going to let it slide either.

"Come on, Hustler, you didn't have a drink all night besides a small sip of the fancy champagne before dinner. I was watching you." Keith seemed surer of himself now. "You got to be rolling on something."

It was true; I had noticed it, too. It was Jay's shot of tequila that was left on the table at the lounge. At the club, he filled his glass with ice and juice. I looked at Jay for the answer.

"I'm just trying to get the most out of this weekend," Jay assured us. "You never know which one of these will be your last."

"That's kind of dark," Gary said.

"Tomorrow's promised to no one, Hendricks," Jay said as he smiled and squeezed Gary's shoulder.

Keith kept on him. "Screw that, a jet setter like you is always partying. Spare me the BS."

"This again, Millman?" I shook my head and looked at Jay, who grinned. Gary squirmed from the awkwardness.

"Oh, sorry to pick on your butt buddy, Kraus," Keith mocked me.

"Why'd you even come out here?" I yelled at him. "Did you just tag along so you could blackmail Mitch one day?"

"Mitch is family now, Kraus. He won't be hanging out with you tards anymore. Not that he would be seeing anything of you, anyhow, now that you're living up in the ghetto."

Keith was bitter and mean. I thought that maybe he just had too much vodka, and this was some angst boiling over. We were all really drunk, and it was only the euphoria of the setting that kept us coherent. The lights and sounds of the marquees flashed around us, the crowds swelled and flowed; the whole scene could be overwhelming if you were in a foul mood. Or maybe he was just tired. Whatever the case, I wanted to give Keith a pass because I didn't want to ruin the weekend.

"I'm sorry you're not having a good time, Keith. Why don't you head back to the suite with Gary? Jay and I will look after the twins," I offered, even though the Maloney's were nowhere to be seen.

"Why don't you head back to the suite, you fucking queers?" Keith scoffed.

A group of flashy fun boys were strolling past and one took offense. "Heyyyyy," he said and frowned in our direction.

Jay stopped walking and looked at Keith. "What's your problem with me?"

"You think your shit don't stink, Huntsfeld. Instead of Hustler, your nickname should be God because that's who you think you are. I can't walk two feet in town without hearing about what Hustler is up to these days." Keith started talking in a girly, mocking voice, "Did you hear Jay went to the Oscars? Did you know that Jay met Jay-Z? Did you see Jay at the Super Bowl?"

"Jealous much?" Gary asked.

"I'm not jealous, Hendricks. I'm not jealous. You know why? Because ill-gotten, ill-gained." Keith shook his head and stabbed his finger toward Jay. "You're a crook. You're a scumbag, drug dealing, pimp."

Jay took a deep breath and exhaled heavily. His shoulders sank. "I'm sorry things never worked out for you, Keith. I know you had a lot of potential. I saw it in you, so did everybody else." Jay put his hand on his shoulder, but Keith slapped it away. Jay continued, "You're a young man. You're still so young. You have so much time left . . . so much time. "

"What the fuck is this? Are you my life coach now?" Keith put his hands on his hips. He twisted to look at Gary and me before returning to Jay. "You think you're going to sweet talk me? I ain't your little brother. I ain't no waitress."

There was a commotion up the strip. It was too far to see through the thick crowd, but we heard shouts and breaking glass. The disorder was enough to disrupt the prevailing current of the crowd. The turmoil grew louder as it headed in our direction. We began to hear the shouts more clearly, but only the exclamations.

". . . assholes . . ."

"Stop them."

". . . fucking assholes . . . "

". . . kill you . . ."

The crowd unzipped before us like a fly on a pair of jeans. Phil and Mike Maloney were at full sprint leading a pack of large men and angry women.

"Step aside." Jay ushered us aside as they approached. "Don't stop them. We'll work it out later."

Mike was in the lead. He held a lime green bikini top in his right hand. Phil was shirtless but had two tasseled pasties stuck to his nipples. They twirled like propellers as he sprinted. Both brothers wore massive grins as they ran past.

***

The golf course was hot and I was miserable. My head throbbed. My vision was blurry. There wasn't enough water in the state of Nevada to quench my thirst. My hands trembled; the energy drinks left a residue of anxiety and irritability. My concerns wavered between fear of fainting and fear of going berserk.

I held off on throwing up until the second tee. It would have been a bad look to evacuate my gut right in front of the course starter. Jay walked over with a bottle of water and a pill in hand.

"What's this?" I asked.

"Water."

"What's THAT, asshole?"

"It's Polase. Mostly magnesium and potassium," Jay explained. "You need to take it or you're going to shrivel up out here."

Jay handed me the round, white, chalky pill with no markings on it.

"Why do you have this?"

"Lots of clients get airsick. We give this to them, so they don't pass out. It's really dry inside the cabin, just like out here. Trust me."

Jay left me to tee off. I stared at the pill in my hand. I thought of Keith's accusations. I watched Jay, lean and athletic, swing in perfect form and strike the ball straight down the fairway. He was spry and happy. I lifted the pill to my mouth with my palm and pounded the bottle of water.

I was next on the tee. I dribbled my shot past the rough and out of bounds. I could see the ball amongst the stones and cacti. I waved to Jay to just keep driving to his ball, but he stopped and retrieved it for me.

"Just keep pounding those waters. You'll be fine by the fourth hole."

Only four of us had made it out to the course. Mitch and Brad were actually well rested and eager to go in the morning, but Jay had to put me on a guilt trip to drag me from bed. Keith was awake but he ignored us; he said something about going to shoot machine guns in the desert. Gary studied craps on his computer.

The Maloney twins were asleep in their room when we left. We didn't even ask them to join us. Somehow, they had outrun their pursuers and made it back to the hotel without consequence.

As bad as I felt for staying out all night, the Pollard boys felt worse about missing the excitement. They begged us for the details.

"One of the guys chasing them looked like Jimmy Superfly Snookah." Jay laughed. "He alone would have ripped them apart but there were like three more after him."

"They actually touched the girls at the strip club?" Brad asked. He seemed intrigued.

"So, they pay to get into this place and the sign outside says *fully nude*," Jay explained. "When they get in there though, all the girls have bikinis on. They get upset and one of the girls explains that to see them fully nude they have to take them in a back room and pay extra."

"Isn't that expensive?" Brad asked.

"It's Fremont street, Brad. Discount Vegas," Jay said. I propped my feet on the dash of the golf cart, tilted my head back and poured half a bottle of water over my face.

Jay went on. "So, they squirrel their funds together and take her to the private room. She starts dancing, she takes her top off and throws it to Mike, but then she bends over and does something. When she stands up, the top is off but she has tassels on her nipples."

"And that's when the Maloneys lost it?" Mitch guessed.

"Yep. Phil grabbed the tassels and ripped them right off. The girl screamed and the boys bolted without paying her." Jay laughed. "Then it was a naked rampage down Fremont."

"Why did Phil have his shirt off?" Brad asked.

"To show off the tassels," Jay replied.

"He put the tassels on? That's amazing!" Brad screamed and the brothers laughed.

I didn't hit another ball until the ninth hole. It was a par three to the clubhouse, so I got up and whacked one. It fell about twenty yards short of the green. My stomach felt better and the ball-peen hammer in my head had slowed, but I still felt anxious.

We hit the clubhouse grill for lunch, and I tucked into a greasy bacon cheeseburger and fries. The boys had Bloody Mary's with their lunch, but I stuck to water. I felt a little better but there was no way I was making it back to the course.

"How about we bail on the back nine and we hit the poolside cabana?" I suggest.

They took mercy on me. None of them were too keen about heading out in the afternoon sun anyway. The heat in the desert was so intense that it radiated up from the ground and off the rocks aligning the course. It was like golfing in a convection oven. The heat was worse when we dragged our bags out to the parking lot. The sun reflected off the shimmering skins of the cars and hit us in the face with focused intensity.

Our ride arrived and the air-conditioned cabin felt like heaven. I wouldn't have cared if it took eight hours to get back to the hotel. I nodded off. I woke to Jay prodding me to get out. He had my clubs slung over his shoulder.

We found the Maloney twins in matching trunks lying beneath the misting hose strung across the top of our cabana area.

"How'd you hit 'em boys?" Mike asked.

"You're back early," Phil observed.

"Kraus strained his vulva," Mitch answered.

"Let's see if you make it past 2 a.m. tonight," I defended myself.

I desperately wanted to return to my slumber. I found myself a comfy recliner inside the tent of the cabana, but the whir of the air conditioning unit bothered me. I dragged the chair outside, but the fans were too intense to relax.

"Where's Keith?" Brad asked.

"Sports book," Mike answered.

"Hendricks?" Mitch asked.

"Craps," Phil answered.

I didn't care where anyone was. I was frustrated and wanted to lie down. Jay sensed my distress.

"Come here. Take this." Jay held out his hand. Another pill. Smaller. Diamond shaped and pink.

I turned and looked him straight in the eye. I didn't say anything, but he knew exactly what I was thinking.

"It's not what you're thinking." He shook his head and smiled. "It's medication, an antianxiety pill. It helps me deal."

"With what?" I ask.

"We can talk about it later. Just take it." He plucked the tiny pill from his hand and placed it in mine.

I never broke eye contact. He reached into his satchel and pulled out an orange prescription bottle. It had his name and address on it as well as the name of the drug it contained: Haloperidol.

I committed the name to memory and swallowed the pill. What followed was a half hour of nervous anticipation followed by a pleasant descent into a state of pure mellow. I don't know when I fell asleep or for how long I slept, but when I awoke, everyone was gone but for Jay.

"Everyone's upstairs getting ready for tonight." Jay smiled.

"Ready for what?" I had forgotten where I was. I felt rested, but still in a haze.

"We're going to dinner and then a special show for Mitch afterwards." He winked.

I yawned. "I feel odd."

"Yeah, you might want to lay off the cocktails until after dinner," Jay suggested.

I blinked my eyes fully open and rubbed my head as I stood. I remembered I had a burning question on deck for him. "What's with the pills, Jay? What's going on?"

Jay looked around to verify that we were well enough alone. He shrugged and put on a childish frown. "I'm sorry, Kraus. Keith nailed me. I'm a drug dealer."

I didn't care. For as long as I had known him, Jay had danced over the line between legitimate and illegitimate enterprise. I was disappointed, sure, but I could digest this without straining the relationship. "I mean, it's just recreational . . ."

"Look at you!" Jay cut me off. "You're such a penis, Kraus. I'm not selling drugs."

"All right, fucker. Quit fucking around." I pushed him and tried to act pissed, but I was still in a state of mellow grace.

"I'm sick, Nick," he said and then quickly added, "It's not that big of a deal though. I'll fight through it, I'll be all right. Don't worry."

I hadn't even had a chance to worry yet.

"I've got some treatment and then some recovery to get through, but then I'll be fine." He added this, as if rehearsed.

I rubbed my eyes and sat back down in my chair. I had no words.

"I started last week. The chemo," he continued. "I'm lucky you guys picked this weekend, or I wouldn't have made it out."

I stared at him. There were tears in my eyes. "Cancer?"

"The big C." He smiled and slapped my shoulder. He kept his hand there and patted me. "I'm going to make it, Nick. I know it."

"Where? What kind?"

Jay sat down next to me. "Can I ask you a favor?"

"Anything."

"Please don't tell anyone, OK?"

"OK."

"And please don't worry." He patted me again. He smiled.

"OK," I said.

Jay looked over my head at something in the distance, but he continued talking. "I want this weekend to be about Mitch and the boys and us. I don't want to be looking at you all teary eyed when we're at the club later. That's a real mood killer with the ladies, you know?"

I giggled a little and wiped my eyes. "What are you going to do after this weekend?"

"I'm going back up to Seattle to continue my treatment," he said. "And then I'm going to put it in the hands of God."

"You believe in God, Jay?" There were church-going families back in Effingham and there were those who never went. And everyone knew who was who.

"More and more, as of late."

"Wow, did you have some type of epiphany up there at 50,000 feet?"

"What was that old saying on that plaque under the cross at the VFW hall?"

"The one where you bought the beer when we were six-teen?" I smiled and laughed. "I don't recall."

"There are no atheists in a fox hole." Jay smiled and popped to his feet. "Come on. We're late."

***

Dinner was early, fast, and greasy. Jay knew that if lingered around a table for too long we would crash before 10 p.m. The menu described the cuisine as "Upscale Americana Trash" and it entailed fanciful versions of otherwise recognizable dishes, like Pâté Hot Dog, Bon Mi Sliders, Korean BBQ Pork Belly, and Fried Chicken with Waffles. For cocktails, they specialized in sugary tropical drinks. There were Margaritas and Piña Cola-das, as well as more potent concoctions like the Singapore Sling and the Tahiti Titty Twister.

No one had much to say before the drinks kicked in. We were all content with each other's company. We had been through this so many times before; the early Saturday evening recovery before the late-inning rally. It was twilight when we left the res-taurant to walk the strip down to the club. Some of the guys grabbed beers or drinks for our stroll but Jay and I stayed sober. Well, we hadn't had any alcohol at least.

The fountains pulsed jets of water in synchrony with orches-tra music. Wagner, I believe. Actors played through their scenes on open-air stages of impossible design and imagination. Obvi-ous vagrants intermingled with the ostentatiously wealthy without any acknowledgement of the absurdity of the situation.

As the sun descended and the lights of the casinos were cast to full power, Vegas put on her evening face. Spirits lifted. The anticipation of the night's festivities, the last night of festivities, crept into our collective mood.

We passed a homeless person who had a pet cat on a leash. She had a pile of coins collected in an empty tin of cat food.

We passed her without comment until Phil turned to Mike and said, "Do you remember the time you took a shit in the litter box at Hendrick's house?"

"That was you?" Gary shouted.

Mike slapped Phil. Phil shoved him back. I was laughing so hard that no sound was coming out of my mouth and I struggled to breathe.

"We thought Mittens was dying!" Gary kept shouting. "That's a real thing. That's a serious thing. You guys are assholes."

"He dared me." Mike pointed to Mitch.

Mitch tried to curb his laughter to explain, but only laughed harder. Even Keith couldn't resist a smile and a chuckle.

"At least now you know that Mittens was OK," Jay said.

"My mom spent like $800 on meds," Gary whined.

"Jesus." Keith rolled his eyes and his sour attitude returned.

"You'll win that back in three rolls of craps tonight," Jay said.

Mitch tried to change the subject. "How much did you win today, Gary? "

"I won another grand or so rolling dice, but I put $500 of that on the Card's game tonight," Gary said. "I ran to the sports book while we were waiting for Nick."

I was a step or two behind everyone; slow but sanguine. I watched my dearest group of friends and Keith cavort down the street like I was watching a home recording of a past vacation together. I had no fears or worries. I felt secure.

***

On the continuum from pathetic to classy, The Velvet Curtain Gentleman's Club placed toward the top end of the gauge. The bouncers wore suits and ties. There were crystal light fixtures. The cover charge was exorbitant.

"Thirty bucks to walk in the door? Get the fuck out of here," Keith pouted as we entered the marble-ensconced vestibule.

"We're not paying that," Jay said as he shook a finger in the air. He strolled forward and shook a man's hand. "Rico, so good to see you."

"Mr. Hunstfeld," Rico smiled and then turned to us. "And friends, welcome."

"Gentlemen, this is Rico Renzi. His is a name to remember when in Vegas," Jay announced.

"And so is the name Jay Hunstfeld," Rico replied and winked at us.

"Hustler," Brad piped up. "We call him Hustler."

Rico loved it. "Hustler. Oh, that's good. That's apt. Very nice."

"So, are we all set for tonight?" Jay placed one hand on Rico's back and another in his palm.

"Yes, Mr. Hustler, of course. Everything according to your specifications."

Rico led us to two large, regal doors eight feet high. Both had three-foot-long brass handles manned by two very large, very thick-necked men in black suits. They opened the doors like royal guards allowing the king's courtiers to enter the throne room.

"I can't wait to see the specifications." Brad bounced with anticipation.

The main stage was an island in the middle of the room raised about three feet off the floor. The dancer on duty was an impossibly gorgeous woman of Asian provenance. She would entice men to the edge of the stage, tease away their money, and then retreat back to the safety of the interior stage.

The booming voice of the night's MC spoke like the voice of God. "Everyone give it up for Lotus. She's headed to the VIP balcony after this set. Annabelle, everybody's favorite Georgia peach, is up next. Chastity, you're on deck. Chastity, to the winner's circle please."

The VIP balcony was eight steps above the main floor. It was close enough to enjoy the girl on stage without having to mingle with the rabble. Aside from the showcase dancers, the choicest women at the club prowled the deck. Jay had reserved a large box for us at the center of the stretch of seating. No sooner than we sat down, a blonde girl with red garters came and took Mitch by the hand. She led him to a red velvet curtain leading to places unknown.

"What's this?" Mitch was startled. "I don't think I can." He wore a wide grin, yet his face begged for help. He looked to Gary and then to me. We shrugged in unison.

"These are the specifications, Mitch," Jay said. "A girl for you at all times. If you get winded, you can defer to one of the boys."

Two girls arrived and sat on each arm of the lounge chair where Jay was seated. The conversation was effortless, casual. There was no sign of expectation or entitlement on the part of the girls. It seemed like they would be fine sitting there with Jay all night.

Valentina was Hispanic; Puerto Rican as it would turn out. Monica was Italian. They both had the same caramel complexion and dark brown hair. Monica had grey eyes and Valentina had brown eyes. Their outfits were sporty; each wore white thigh-high stockings that looked like exaggerated versions of the crew socks I wore as a kid in gym class, complete with the three little stripes at the top. They wore sports jerseys as tops, Valentina in number six and Monica in number nine. The jerseys were made of nylon mesh. From my seat to the left of Jay, I could clearly see Monica's cinnamon-brown nipples through the material.

We were mesmerized. No one said anything except for Jay and the girls.

"And you're still out in the condo by Henderson?" Jay asked them.

"We sold that place and bought a house." Valentina shook her head. "We needed more room for when Mona's family came to visit."

They really were a team, as it turned out. We were all titillated and I'm certain we all had the same thought at once. Phil spoke up first.

"So, are you ladies, like . . . ?"

"Go ahead sweetie," Monica encouraged him.

Phil looked at his twin brother. Mike stared back. They were suddenly bashful. I had never seen it before.

Mike continued. "I mean, would you guys, like, kiss if we asked you to?"

The girls looked at each other and giggled. Valentina ran a finger slowly down Monica's cheek. "You could see us do a lot more than kiss."

Jay told us in a hushed tone, "Remember boys, these ladies are working tonight." He held his hand out and rubbed his thumb against his index and middle fingers.

Gary had a crisp $50 bill on the table before the Maloney brothers could put their drinks down.

"The Cards won," Gary said as a matter of fact. "I'd like to hear more about the sleeping arrangements at the new house."

The girls led Gary away behind the curtain. The twins sat back in a slump on their chairs.

"Boys, boys, patience. This place has more fantasies to fulfill than you have money in your pocket. I promise," Jay assured them.

The Maloney's were riled up now. They moved down to the edge of the main stage with Brad following. The only people remaining in the box were Keith, Jay, and me.

Keith drew closer to Jay and me. He cut straight to it. "Hustler, listen, let me get one of those pills that you gave Nick earlier."

I was dumbfounded. I looked at Jay and I read disappointment on his face. I shook my head and shrugged.

"Come on, don't play dumb. The Haloperidol." Keith nodded and pointed at Jay. "Brad saw you slip him something and then he was knocked out. So, I did a little snooping while you were getting ready."

"Dude, what the fuck?" I began.

"What do you want it for?" Jay asked him.

"Are you kidding me? That shit's currency for chicks like this." Keith's right hand gestured to Jay to come forward with the goods. "Come on, here comes the Oriental broad."

It was Lotus. She had changed into an all-white outfit of stockings, garters, and bustier. She had an orange hibiscus blossom tucked behind her left ear. She was trailed by a waitress with a bottle of champagne and a tray of glasses. Lotus sashayed into our box and sat next to Keith, at his urging.

"Too late," I said.

"Too late for what?" she asked.

"Nothing. Nothing at all," Keith assured her. He shooed me away with a flick of his hand.

Keith grabbed two glasses of champagne from the waitress and handed one to Lotus. He whispered something in her ear. She smiled and looked at Jay. She whispered something to Keith.

Keith looked around and then drew closer to Jay. His hand beckoned again as he spoke close to Jay's face.

Jay shook his head as soon as Keith started talking. "I told you, man," Jay said, "no."

Keith was clearly frustrated as well as embarrassed. He looked to Lotus. Her face signaled dashed expectations.

"Well, this is really some bullshit," Keith exclaimed. "You got the hookup for everyone but me."

"You're making a scene, Keith. Stop it," I told him. A boiling anger bubbled in my stomach. I swallowed hard.

"Fuck you, Kraus. What are you on right now? I'm just trying to party like everyone else."

Lotus sipped her glass of champagne and furrowed her brow.

"We're not partying, Keith." I tried to reason with him. "Not like you think."

"I'm sick of you two. You've been like two little lover boys all weekend. Whispering shit and holding out on whatever you're holding." He sneered contempt at us.

My anger burned, my mellowness long gone.

"I'm going to tell you something later and you're going to feel like a real fucking jerk," I growled.

"Tell me now, faggot," Keith yelled. He spread his arms to invite me to come at him.

Jay put his arm across my chest. "No."

"I knew it. I knew you two were gay. That's why your girl Lori is jocking all the guys when she comes to visit."

I flew into a blind rage. I stood and moved to strike Keith while Lotus simultaneously chose to stand and exit our company. I tripped on Jay's chair as I advanced toward Keith and fell forward. The crown of my skull landed square in the middle of

Lotus' dainty face. I felt the cartilage of her slight nose crackle and disintegrate.

Lotus screamed through her hands. Blood streamed down her arms and all over her white bustier. The petals of her flower adornment lay strewn across the floor. Rico and his bouncers were on us in a flash. They dragged all three of us through an emergency exit, choking and punching us the whole way. Not even Jay was spared.

***

"Mitch wants you to come back up to the room," Jay told me. His lip was split, and his left ear was swollen and red.

I held a bundled towel of ice to my eye. I was sitting at a nickel slot machine, passing time until the airport opened at 5 a.m.

"Is Keith still up?" I asked.

"They wrenched his neck pretty bad. He might need to go to the ER," Jay told me. "I offered him a pill, but he doesn't want it now."

I laughed a little bit at the irony. "I'm just going to run out the clock down here if that's all right? My flight's at 10."

"Of course, of course, I'll stay with you. I have to be at McCarran by 7 a.m. I'll just stay up, too." Jay patted me on the shoulder, and I winced in pain. The reels spun and came up all 7s. The machine flashed and rang like a calliope.

"Would you look at that?" I said, my shoulder still smarting. Five-hundred dollars' worth of nickels began cascading into the tray with a steady clang.

"Oh, wow. Nice. I'll go get you one of those buckets." Jay walked away.

I had no joy. I could really use this $500, but I was physically beaten and emotionally exhausted. My best friend had cancer. I had been beaten up by bouncers. I was probably no longer welcome at Mitch's wedding.

"Here you go, man." Jay began grabbing handfuls of nickels and dropping them into the bucket. "Listen, how about we pool our funds and go throw some craps? I think I saw Gary over at one of the tables. He'll tell us what to do."

I kept putting nickels in the bucket by the handful. "All right, let me go cash these in and I'll meet you over there."

The line at the window was pretty long for 2 a.m. It took me about twenty minutes to exchange my nickels for cash, but it didn't take me long to find Gary and Jay after that. I just followed the shouting.

"He's on fire!" Gary shrieked. "Twenty-two rolls in a row."

"I don't even know what I'm doing, Kraus!" Jay yelled.

"You're winning!" Gary yelled back.

He rolled again. He won again. People from other tables stopped playing and turned to watch. Folks at Jay's table clamored to place their bets. He rolled again and won his twenty-fourth in a row, then his twenty-fifth. I noticed two guys betting against him. He won again and again and again. Their bets got bigger each time he won. After he won his thirty-third in a row, they were both out of chips. Then Jay lost on his very next roll.

"Oh my God, what a run." Jay exhaled. "What a run."

"Nick, get over here and help us haul these chips." Gary waved me over.

"Are we really quitting?" Jay asked with total seriousness.

"Let's take a blow, chief," Gary told him. "That was nuts. You'll never see that again."

"How much is it?" I asked.

"I don't know," Jay answered. "How much is it Gary?"

"I don't know. It's six figures though."

We started counting. It looked like more than two hundred thousand dollars. A casino manager approached, "Congratulations, sir. We have a private room for counting if you would like to use it."

The squat man wore a poorly fitted suit. His pants were sand colored with pleats that bloomed out like they were filled with air. His blazer was maroon with gold flashing along the lapels. He led us past a guard and through an obscure door with a one-way mirror as a window. On the other side we found an entirely different room that we had not seen before.

"High-roller room," Gary murmured.

"The private counting room is right over here sir," the manager directed us.

We didn't make it to the counting room. Jay sat down at a Blackjack table and continued his run of luck. He started playing hands of $5,000 and won or pushed every hand until the dealer changed decks. He went to $10,000 and won. He went to $25,000 and won. He went to $50,000 and won.

"Oh my God, Kraus. I'm so sorry. Your $500." Jay put his hand to his forehead in despair. "We were supposed to pool."

I wasn't the least bit upset. I was happy to be along for the ride. I handed him my $500 dollars.

"I'm sorry, sir, you can't fund another player once he's seated," the dealer scolded me.

"Don't sweat it." Jay placed a bet for $50,500. He was dealt a pair of kings.

"Split 'em," he told the dealer and placed another $50,500 down.

Another king and a nine.

"Split the kings again. I'll stand on the nineteen." He placed another $50,500 down. The dealer dealt him a seven and a six. The dealer was showing a five.

Jay had three bets of $50,500 placed on hands of nineteen, seventeen, and sixteen. The dealer had no more than sixteen. He had to hit.

Jay looked at Gary. Gary bit his knuckle and bounced on the balls of his feet. He looked at Jay and shook his head no. Jay looked at the dealer. "I'll stand on both."

The dealer used the five card to flip his down card over. It was a ten. He dealt himself a card from the deck. Another king. He busted. Jay collected $151,500 in winnings.

"Half is yours," he told me.

***

I wanted the limo ride to the airport to last forever but it only took ten minutes at five in the morning. So, we sat in the car outside the private jet hangar and talked.

"One point two million dollars, Kraus. One point two *million*." Jay laughed.

I'd never seen him get excited. He always played it cool.

"I won't have to ask my parents for anything," he said. "They had already mortgaged a hundred and twenty-five acres."

I was puzzled. He saw it in my face.

"Chemo is expensive, Kraus," he said.

I was still puzzled.

"I'm an agent, buddy. I work for myself."

"Insurance?" I asked.

Jay shrugged. "Whoops. I thought I was going to live forever."

"But what about all the money you spent on us this week-end?" Even if most stuff was comped, he was still throwing $50s and $100s around like dimes.

"That was a drop in the ocean at this point. I planned on go-ing bankrupt anyway. May as well go out with a smile."

I put my hand on his shoulder. "I'm coming to see you. Soon. Lori and I will drive out."

"No. I don't want to see anybody. I want to put my nose down and get through this on my own," he said.

I was quiet. Tears welled.

"Nick, you're such a penis," he told me. "Cut it out. I'm going to be fine. God has my back."

"God?"

"Yeah."

"I thought you were joking about that," I said.

"I might have been then, but not anymore. I said a prayer, Nick. The first time in my life I ever said a prayer. No shit, the very first time."

"What did you pray for?"

"I said, 'God, give me what it takes to get through this.'" He laughed. "And then bam, one point two million dollars. It's almost exactly what the treatment will cost. I mean, come on, is that God answering your prayers or what?"

"How short are you?"

"Nothing much, 50, 60K. I can scare that up. No problem," he said.

I thought of the $75,000 I had strapped in bundles around my waist.

"I'm going to say another prayer. I'm going to say another one." He laughed and began. "Hey there, Lord, it's me Jay." He laughed again.

His eyes were shut tight. I slipped off my money belt and tucked it into his travel satchel.

Jay kept praying. "Thanks for the big win. Much appreciated." He smiled. "If it's no problem, I just want to ask one more thing. Can you help me get through this as quickly as possible? I mean, I still want the best possible outcome, but let's just get it done sooner rather than later. Thanks, buddy."

"Amen," I said.

"Amen," he repeated. He opened his eyes and gave me a high five.

***

I trudged down the terminal hallway like a zombie, sure that my left eye was blackened by now. I dragged my duffle bag on the ground behind me, hoping to get two hours of sleep in before boarding. I found a seat at my gate, placed my duffle on my lap and then plopped my arms and head atop it.

I awoke and looked at my watch. It read 10:10. I panicked and bolted to the gate agent. "Why didn't you wake me?"

"We're delayed, sir, and you looked like you could use the rest," the young lady pursed her lips and assessed me with a slow look.

"You're right. You're right," I said. "Thank you."

I trudged back to my seat. I noticed a crowd of people packed against the far windows at the end of the terminal. I looked at the woman seated next to me. She was older and she looked agitated.

"Do you know why we're delayed?" I asked.

"You must have really been out cold. Didn't you hear the sirens?" She wrung her hands.

"No," I said.

"Oh dear, it's horrible." She had a hard time speaking. "There was a plane that crashed on takeoff."

I turned and looked at the crowd of gapers at the end of the terminal.

"It was a private jet," she whispered. She shook her head and made the sign of the cross. She clasped her hands, bowed her head, and prayed.

Interlude 5: Jackass Redux

"Your boy Jay started that shit when he was dogging Keith that first night. You get that right?" Cole asks me.

"No, I don't see it that way," I answer.

"Dude, Jay made sure Keith and all y'all knew who the alpha was," Cole says. "He embarrassed Keith, and Keith fought back. Simple as that. I would have done it, too."

"Keith was a jerk for a long time. Jay just wanted to let him know that he hadn't forgotten," I reason.

"Man, you're letting your love for your friend cloud your judgement," Cole shakes his head at me. "You're a loyal friend, Nick, I'll give you that. But you have to be honest with yourself."

"I don't feel sorry for Keith."

"I'm not saying you need to feel sorry for him. But he was right," Cole says.

"Right about what?"

The crowd creeps closer to listen to our conversation. The characters of the plain are more detailed than before. There is a woman in formal prairie style dress, the skirt swells out like a bell. She is carrying a parasol with lace frill around the edges.

"He was dealing drugs. He was pimping the ladies." Cole smiles. "Jay Hustler was a mother fucking hustler."

"So what?"

Cole lifts his arms as if to take his hands off the judgement he just passed. "Nothing, man. That's his business. Didn't sound like he was hurting anybody to me. But he *was* a pimp."

"Fine, but so what? Is that my lesson? Is that what I'm supposed to learn from this?" I ask.

"You need to be more objective," Cole says.

The woman twirls her parasol. The horizon behind the crowd is more vivid now. I see a frontier town in the distance.

"I don't care if he was a pimp. I don't care if he was a dealer. I sure as hell don't care how much he embarrassed Keith Millman!" I yell. "I loved him. I admired him. I needed him to help me."

I begin to cry but I'm self-conscious of the crowd, so I choke it off and wipe my face with my sleeve.

"Nick, you're a naive, country-fried white boy."

"Maybe I was but I'm not anymore. I won't be anymore," I mumble.

The crowd surrounds us now. Some of their faces are dirty and their clothes are torn and disheveled from their time on the plains. Others are tidy and well-tailored. They must be from the upper crust of frontier society.

"All right, what am I supposed to learn here?" Cole asks. "Don't take my private jet to Vegas to hang with a gang of stiffs from the sticks?"

"I can't believe that was all you heard. Maybe we should part now," I suggest.

"Not until you tell me the point of that story."

"If I have to tell you, then you clearly didn't understand in the first place."

"Tell me the Goddamned point, Nick," Cole demands.

"I don't know the point!" I scream in return. "I don't know why I'm here. I don't know what I did wrong and sure don't know what I did right. I don't know why anyone should give a flying fig about how I lived my life when I ended up here, just like you."

There are murmurs in the crowd.

Cole nods to himself. He turns towards the crowd and nods again. He accepts that he's had his turn. He looks over the crowd to the horizon, hoping to see a steward on approach. There is none.

"Thanks, Nick," he says but he doesn't mean it.

"Best of luck, Cole."

I watch the crowd absorb Cole in their midst. I scan the faces of the people in the throng. They are silently begging me to take their hands. There is one man with an older face that does not look as plaintive. He doesn't look as needy. I am drawn to him.

"You need to stop looking right at it," he says without prompting.

"I can't help it. It flashes on every surface."

"Not at your glow, at your story."

We are face to face.

"They are just tiles in a mosaic, Nick." He is distinguished by his apparent older age. His skin isn't as tight, there's a flash of grey at his temples. All the other people appear to be in their thirties. "Some tiles are light, some are dark. They only reveal an image when we stand back and rest our vision."

"I would like to talk to you," I say.

"And I with you."

I clutch his hand and pull him from the crowd.

Story 6: The Opportunists

I f you ask ten Germans if they speak English, nine will answer "yes" and the tenth will say "of course." They are intrepid tourists and they tell you exactly what they want. The Germans were the first to start going up to Harlem on Sunday mornings to hear the Gospel choruses. They explored Chelsea way before it was chic to be gay friendly. I'd prowl Times Square with an ear tuned for their accents and then steer my people toward them.

The mayor had dedicated his first term to cleaning out Midtown. It had ceased to be the whore-filled skid row it once was but people still showed up to be titillated. Once the hookers went underground and the peep shows were pushed into Hell's Kitchen, the vacuum was filled by opportunists like me. We filled the streets with performers, character models, portrait sketchers, and the occasional perverted thong bearer. It was this latter type that always intrigued the Germans and it was their penchant for the salacious that put me in some tough predicaments.

***

I was restless growing up in Mamaroneck. It was a pleasant but sleepy commuter suburb of New York City. The town had a main street that ran from the train stop down to a harbor on Long Island Sound. There was a barber shop, a diner, a deli, and a toy store along the way. It was literally a Norman Rockwell painting. The painter had spent some of his formative years there and the town was the model for several of his iconic suburban scenes.

Mamaroneck was just twenty miles north of Manhattan on the Metro line but my dad rarely took us down to the city. He would tell us how fortunate we were to be growing up in Westchester County. He would say it was verdant, bucolic, idyllic, and a bunch of other words I equated with boring. I was a boy when the corporation he did accounting for moved their headquarters from Manhattan to a patch of forest along the Taconic Parkway. He was content to leave Gotham to the rats and gypsies. It was the '60s and he called anyone without a suit or a uniform a gypsy.

I did well in high school, and I wrestled my way into Columbia. I had opportunities at other schools and my mother was surprised I didn't go farther away. My ennui and my contempt for the cradle of suburbia was no secret. What she didn't understand was that it didn't matter that I remained close if I never had any intention of going back. I would go back, however. It was the only place I could go to get clean when I needed to.

I devoured Manhattan and all it had to offer. It wasn't cheap, even then, so I learned every gimmick. I befriended the theater folks right away and I learned to take advantage of the food-service trailers around Broadway. The artsy types were my ticket to the disco scene, and that was my ticket to a teenage coke addiction. I'd go to Spanish Harlem for some Latin jazz and to feed my habit. That's where I found the best deal on product. Four years of high school Spanish paid off, I guess. I spent my Sundays smoking free weed in Washington Square with the NYU kids when I needed to wind down. I was much more in rhythm with the bohemians than the Ivy League crowd at Columbia, not that I got to know any of them very well. I stopped going to classes and practice entirely by my sophomore year. I was asked to leave the school, but I kept my dorm room for the full year.

I got by as a drug courier to the businessmen downtown. I wasn't really a drug dealer as much as a conduit for Luis to get his product from East Harlem to the Battery. Luis' look made him stand out on Wall Street and the cops would shake him down for his stash and his cash as soon as he stepped off the 6 Train. I always looked older than my age and my slacks and loafers raised little suspicion.

I'd go to the bars off Broad Street at happy hour to make my exchanges. When my duties were completed, I got right back on the 6 and head back north. I got off at 116th and walked up Lexington to a place called el Barrio. They had live music every night and a set of timbales was on stage at all times. Some nights the crowd was so thick and the music so loud that an impromptu dance floor would manifest on the sidewalk in front of the bodega next door. The small shop had cold cervezas in the cooler and it became an extension of the club on warm nights.

"You got to cool it with the loafers, man," Luis said. He always watched for me as I walked up the street to the club. Sometimes he'd be waiting for me on the subway platform.

"Eh, amigo, what do you want from me? I can't change on the train," I protested.

"You stand out," he said. He pulled me over to a small wrought iron table in front of the bodega.

"What about them?" I pointed to a white couple dancing awkwardly on the sidewalk. I set my satchel on the table. I had already removed my share of product and payment while on the train.

"Germans," he said and dismissed them with a wave. He pulled the bag onto his lap.

***

I was what the pop economists at Columbia called a "social hub." I was the nexus of a system of friends, acquaintances and purveyors of contraband. It helped that I had a knack for meeting people and I always liked to hear people's stories. People love to talk about themselves and I guess this endeared me to them. I was everyone's first call on a Friday night, so I was hip to every scene around the city even if I never planned on showing up to all of them. Some nights I did though, supposing I kept a full nose of powder.

I snorted the spoon of chemicals into my face and my nasal cavity sparkled to life. The sensation spread through my sinuses and then my psyche. So instant was the sensation of confidence and euphoria that I resented my sober self and the trepidations I carried just a moment ago. I had achieved a better me, the best me.

I was on the Midtown shuttle from Times Square to Grand Central. I had met some theater friends in Hell's Kitchen, and they were tagging along as I made a delivery on the Upper East Side.

"You been in the city long?" I yelled over the sound of the train to the ambiguously gendered person next to me. We'd never met before, but he was with my crowd.

"I was down in Philly until I made it in the cast for this show as a dancer," he said. I was now sure he was a guy based on the sound of his voice. "The first run just started. I hope we survive the first review. It's a solid gig, my first time working on Broadway."

He carried on and on. I nodded and smiled, never breaking eye contact. I logged all the details. He was twenty-two, from Florida originally, and he now lived in the Village with a friend who didn't like it when he brought friends home to spend the night. He would kill for a speaking part, but his dancing is what kept his bread buttered.

"This is the stop," I interrupted him. We exited at 86th. My merry troop and I skipped down Lexington to 80th and then walked a block toward the park until I found the address. It was a four-story, brownstone townhouse with two gas lamps affixed to each side of the front stoop. The flames licked the glass casing of the lamps and their light flashed on the walls. I bounded up the stairs and rang the bell as my company waited on the other side of the gate.

Peter answered the door. He was in his thirties and was wearing a white silk shirt with black buttons that were open to mid-chest. "Are you Luis's friend?" He asked.

"Yep." I fluttered and twitched. "It's $325."

"That's a lot."

"You asked for a lot."

"All right; let's go upstairs and I'll get it," he said and pointed over his shoulder. "Come on."

I stood still and cased my setting. I turned and looked at the fay gang of thespians waiting by the gate. Peter noticed my hesitance.

"All right, them too." He waved us all in.

Peter escorted us to the parlor on the second floor. There was funk music on the stereo and the sound of cocktail glasses clinking on glass-topped tables. Peter was hosting ten or so guests from the upper crust. In the middle of the room was a trolley of brown liquors in crystal decanters that I thought only existed in midday TV shows.

There were two women dancing though not with great vigor. The early hour and the neighborhood dictated a minimum level of rectitude. One of them noticed us as we entered ,and she took a recess from her swaying. She approached one my theater friends, Gabe, and traced the outline of his pectoral muscles with a red fingernail. "Peter, who are our new friends?" she shouted without breaking eye contact with Gabe. Peter had left to fetch my payment.

Without saying a word, Gabe began to dance to the syncopated funky rhythm. He added a thrust on the one beat and the two women cooed.

Peter returned with my payment to see a cast of Broadway dancers gyrating in the middle of his parlor. Someone had dialed up the stereo. Peter and I completed our transaction and he lined up a few rails on the glass table. A joint appeared and migrated around the room. I drank champagne.

We spent an hour in the parlor with our new friends and I signaled to Gabe that I had to bolt. I had another delivery in SoHo. Gabe looked to his new lady friends and cocked his head toward the door.

"Peter, fetch our coats dear," the girl with the crimson nails shouted.

Peter and the remaining guests looked dejected. I dropped the volume on the stereo and waved at Peter. "Come on, you guys, too."

We marched to the subway and dominated one of the cars. We were a crowd of young souls captivated by the mystery of each other's company. We had danced and frolicked for the past hour but barely spoke to one another. The car was a buzzing hive of young people exploring whether reality aligned with the fantastic images in their minds.

We got off at Pearl Street and deployed toward a loft apartment in a warehouse. The industrial lift accommodated our whole group. The gate opened and we walked onto a floor brimming with the largest concentration of beautiful people I had ever seen.

If there were living quarters on the floor, they were concealed or removed for the purpose of the party. The only indication that the open space was a residence was the couches. There were many couches and loveseats surrounding an open space. A white sheet hung from the ceiling and a home-recorded movie was projected upon it from a lofted space above the main floor. The movie consisted of recorded frames of tulips in graduating states of blossom interspersed with recorded frames of women in graduating states of nakedness. Some of the beautiful people at the party were recognizable in the movie.

"Are all these people models?" the new fella from Philly asked me in a hushed tone.

"Maybe . . . Probably." I searched the crowd looking for my client. "Do you see any redheads?"

"What about her?" he asked, pointing to a girl in a green paisley dress with an aggressive V-neck that plunged to her belly button.

"No, that's a strawberry blonde," I replied and continued to look.

"Her," he said, pointing confidently.

"That's a black girl with a dyed afro." I flashed a smirk his way.

He put his hands up in surrender. "Does this redhead have a name, or should I just start shouting out for Ginger?"

"Veronica!" I shouted. "Her name is Veronica."

She was standing right behind me.

"I'm Veronica!" she shrieked. "Are you Luis's guy?"

Veronica was gorgeous. She was striking in different ways from different angles. Her left eye was blue and her right eye was brown. They were as round as jumbo marbles and the blue one had flashes of gold brilliance. Her stare was hypnotic. She had a perfectly straight nose that descended to plump, elastic lips. Her smile extended across her face and reached upward so that the outward creases of her eyes crept upward too, as though they wanted in on the show.

"*Mi despues, habla Espanol usted?*" she asked.

"Huh. *Si.* What?" I stammered.

"*Me llama Veronica. Conosce Luis?*" Veronica said. A red renegade curl fell across her face.

"Yes, yes. I'm your guy. Do you have a place we can go?" I responded with a blush.

"Sure, sure. We need to find Karl first though."

I deflated when she said this. An extra breath that had been trapped inside me escaped and my chest shrank. The idea that she was acquainted with any other man in the twenty years it took us to meet was heartbreaking. It was heartbreak at first sight.

"Stay here, OK? *Aqui,* OK?" she giggled and turned.

I may as well have been standing on a landmine as I watched her walk away. Veronica had perfect poise and posture. She wore a simple white blouse over blue jeans and moccasins. There were high-heeled fashion models sporting expensive cocktail dresses teeming about and Veronica outdid them all. Her legs were long, sturdy stems and she walked on the balls of her feet like a ballerina. She weaved through the crowd like a ghost.

The Philly dancer clapped his cupped palms twice. "Yo, man, still here?"

"Yes, still here. Sorry," I said. "Man, I've seen a lot of women in this city, but I've never seen anything like that."

"Not without makeup," he said.

"What do you mean?"

"Theater folks can work magic with the makeup, but she's a natural beauty." He nodded as he commended her. "She's a soap-and-water beauty."

"Soap and water. I like that."

Veronica waved from the other side of the floor. The tall, Teutonic man at her side waved, too, but with less conviction.

"They're waving us over," I said.

"Us?"

"It will only take a minute."

The Philly dancer stared down the tall blonde from afar.

"Come on. Let's go," he said and led the way across the floor.

Veronica introduced Karl. We did not give our names.

"It's $100," I told him.

Veronica told him the price in German. He nodded in agreement.

We retreated to a stairwell. It was painted institution green and was lit with fluorescent white bulbs. The lights were linear tubes that ran in pairs about eight feet off the floor and traced the walls of the landing on which we stood.

We made the exchange. Veronica said something in German and Karl nodded.

"Do you guys want a bump?" she asked as she pulled a tiny spoon from the coin pocket of her jeans.

The four of us took our turns with the spoon and returned to the floor.

"Suddenly this seems underwhelming," Veronica said as she stood just outside the event horizon of the social circle on the floor.

Karl and the Philly dancer stared at each other. They traded smiles.

"How many languages do you speak?" I asked.

"Just the big three: Spanish, French, German. A little bit of Russian, too, but I'm out of practice. All I really remember is what I learned from my *bubbeh*," she said. "I work for the tourism office and it's not like we got a lot of visitors from Moscow, you know?"

"You're not a model?" I asked.

"I do some modeling, but my Heterochromia keeps me from getting the big gigs." She pointed back and forth at each eye. "I do mostly black-and-white stuff."

"I think your eyes are amazing."

"Thank you." She was dismissive, as though she pitied me for finding beauty in her imperfection. "Do you want to get out of here?"

"What about Karl?" I stabbed my thumb toward the big German.

"He's just a client."

"I'm sorry?" I was taken aback.

"Not like that, silly." She laughed and slapped my chest with the back of her hand. "I told you, I work for the tourism office. I make extra scratch as a fixer for our, um, more adventuresome customers."

"So, you like score coke and stuff for them?"

"Sure and take them to parties like this and then maybe hit some underground clubs," she said. "Looks like you already did me the favor of finding him a companion for tonight."

I looked at the transatlantic love connection. Karl was dispensing a long whisper in the Philly dancer's ear.

"Let's take the *fräuleins* dancing," she said.

I found Gabe and told him the plan. He still had the attention of the two ladies from the Upper East Side. He had one on each arm as we broke camp. Veronica and I walked down Broadway toward Canal, followed by a swarm of dandy actors intermixed with elitist yuppies, models, fashion moguls, and two darling gay men who could barely communicate.

Veronica turned to appreciate our crowd. She walked backward as she asked, "Do you always roll this deep?"

I turned to admire the group as well. "Some nights."

"You never told me your name," she said.

"It's Jeff."

"You're not a Jeff," she declared.

"Tell my father."

"I'm going to call you Piper," she said.

"Piper?"

"Like the Pied Piper." She laughed and cocked her head toward my crowd of followers.

***

Dad was pissed. "All you hang with down there are those Goddamn gypsies!" he yelled.

I had to take it. I was back under his roof, the dorm being closed for the summer. I hadn't told him yet that I had dropped out before Christmas.

"How dare you show your face around here in such a state," he said.

He had picked me up at 7 a.m. from the Stamford station. That was thirty minutes past Mamaroneck at the very end of the train line. I had partied straight through the whole weekend and passed out on an early train that left Grand Central Terminal with Monday morning's reverse commuters.

"They thought you had OD'd on junk!"

His screams were all that kept me awake. I sat stock still at the kitchen table and absorbed his abuse while sipping a cup of black coffee that my mother had slid in front of me. She would withhold any words she had for me for days. That hurt more than my father's scolding.

"I have to go to work now and face the secretary who kept your ass out of jail this morning. How does that make me look? Do you even care?"

I kept my father's business card in my wallet. The conductor called his office and told whoever answered that they had twenty minutes to pick me up or I was heading to the railroad's jail cell.

"Tell her I said thanks for getting to work so early," I said and I meant it.

"Is that supposed to be funny?" He was in my face now. He put his finger to my nose. "Keep this shit up. Keep it up and there won't be anyone there to pick you up next time. You're damn lucky you're in school or I would take you down to the recruiting office myself."

This statement caught my attention. Nixon was at war in Vietnam and he would gladly invite me to the party if I was not otherwise occupied with college. He passed on my friends. The foreigners, the queers, and the rich kids he could do without. I guess that's why I neglected to appreciate that he would still take me.

"I wasn't trying to be funny. I realize how lucky I got. Thank you for helping me. I'm sorry I've put you in bad light," I said.

He backed off. "Is that all you're sorry for?"

"I'm sorry for my behavior," I lied.

"What are you going to do about it?"

"I'm going to straighten up," I lied.

"Starting now?"

"Right now," I lied. He marched out of the room to head to work. I was asleep in my bed before his car left the driveway.

***

I moved in with Veronica at the start of what should have been my junior year. The arrangement was not as intimate as I desired. I slept on the couch of her two-bedroom walkup in Hoboken. Her friend, Jane, was the occupant of the second bedroom. She had the same résumé as Veronica. She was a semi-employed model who worked at the tourism office and moonlighted as a liaison for libertine Eurotrash tourists.

"Are you wearing the jeans tonight?" Jane shouted to Veronica from behind a crack in the bathroom door.

"All yours, I'm in tonight," Veronica shouted from her spot behind a crossword puzzle on the couch. She returned to her task and mumbled, "Deadly lady savior? What's that supposed to mean?"

Both girls were cast from the same mold of 1970's fashion model and were the same size for all their garments. They saved money by sharing a wardrobe. They typically only had a single specimen of their choicest wares, so these were always referred to using the definitive article, as in *the* jeans, *the* heels, *the* dress, and so on.

Jane prepared herself and trotted into the living room. She always walked like she was on a runway and her arrival was foretold by her rhythmic cadence. Her hair was a natural blonde with curls that framed her oval face. She had blue eyes and ivory skin. Her natural breasts tumbled unconstrained beneath her silk blouse.

"One who is constantly pursuing happiness?" Veronica looked to the ceiling as she thought. "Hedonist!" She wiggled the tip of her pencil and jotted down the answer.

The closest that most men ever got to women of this caliber was a lucky seat for a few stops on the same subway car. I shared a tight apartment in Jersey with two of them.

"You need anything for tonight?" I asked Jane. I wasn't a complete freeloader. I had my income from my job as a runner for Luis, so I pitched in on the rent. It was an arrangement of convenience for all of us. I had neither the means nor the need for my own place, and it was helpful to have no known address for the recruiter to find me. Meanwhile, the girls appreciated a male companion to escort them from time to time. I had ample treats to offer as well.

"Can I get a bump before I run?" Jane responded.

I portioned out a line on the mirror of her compact. She snorted it and wiped her nose with the back of her finger.

"Do you have any spots for tonight?" Jane asked.

"East Village or Lower East Side?" she asked.

"Lower East Side, a new speakeasy called Lansky's. The only real sign is an L spray painted on the steel door of the bodega out front. You have to walk down a gangway and go in through the back. Kinda groovy."

"Lower East."

"Pass," she said. "What else you got?"

"New place called Milkdud, in Meat Packing. Satin T is spinning tonight," I said. "That's a late scene though."

"Nice. You got anything for the pre-party?"

"How many are you?"

"Just me and a Spanish girl."

"Spanish from Spain or Spanish from Harlem?"

"Spain," she answered.

"There's a private showing at the Frick. There will be a lot of avant-garde, Warhol-wannabes there." I watched her prepare herself in the mirror. She was her own muse. "Play it cool and you'll get in."

"Gotta name I can drop?"

"Gabe will be there," I said. "He's on the list at least."

Veronica spoke to the ceiling again, "The blank in the room. Eight letters."

"You know, you'd be really good at this," Jane told me. "Better than me, clearly."

"The next time you get a gorgeous exotic girl who needs entertaining, you be sure to let me know," I urged her.

"She's right, Piper. You'd be perfect," Veronica added without looking up from her puzzle. "Elephant, duh." She filled in the squares.

"I'm looking into it tomorrow," Jane decided.

"You mean the tourism thing, too?" I sat up a little.

"Casanova style is *romantic*," Veronica said to no one.

"Yeah, that's how you score the evening clients," Jane answered me.

"Oh, no thanks, J. I got a day job." I waved her off.

"Hold on. You could be a guide. You could make your drops as you zip around the city with the O'Learys from Ohio," she urged me. "The fuzz never fusses with the tour groups you know."

"She's right, Piper," Veronica repeated. "Pen sounds are *oinks*." She penciled in another answer.

She got me a job offer and I took it. I eventually took her job and her room in the apartment after she overdosed and died.

"Ah ha, *heroin*," Veronica said. "Heroin is the deadly lady savior."

***

The first time Veronica let me make love to her it was Christmas night. We were drunk and alone in the apartment with nothing to do. Dinner in Chinatown with some Jewish friends was the most social interaction we had had for the holiday and we had nothing left to do to stem our melancholy.

"Was that worth all those years of effort?" she asked.

"I would rather have waited longer if it meant you would have enjoyed it," I answered.

Veronica was passive for the entire event. I felt like one of those little fish that darts around the tentacles of a sea anemone, like a benign parasite frolicking safely while the host ignores its presence.

"Do you still want to be my friend?" she asked. She pulled the sheets up to her chin.

"Of course. What a stupid question," I said. I turned to my side to face her.

"I needed to know."

"Know what?" I slid my arm beneath her shoulders in an attempt to cuddle.

She turned to her side to face me—and escape my embrace. "I wanted to know if all this time you were just trying to fuck me."

"I've known you for like, eight years." I pretended to take offense.

"I love you, Piper, but not like this."

"What an odd time to tell me."

"In a week it will be 1980. I couldn't let you go the entire decade in vain; that would be cruel," she smiled.

"I love you, too, you know?"

"We'll see for real now," she said.

Our relationship was indeed parasitic, and we traded the role of host and parasite back and forth throughout the eighties. We were codependent companions with a stronger bond than most married couples. Sex was infrequent and essentially constrained to our Christmas ritual.

My value proposition to Veronica, aside from rent and drugs, came from playing the role of guidance counselor. Veronica was blessed with talent and looks and cursed with the impulse control of a young Labrador. She sprinted in the direction of any attractant with her tail on full wag. Frequent were the conversations to convince her to reconsider some new foolish venture. In no particular order and with varying degrees of effort I had talked her out of getting a boob job to land a movie role, adopting an orphaned African teenager, and buying a scooter.

Veronica moderated my consumption habits. She would ignore me just like my mother would whenever I went beyond my limits, and this was my signal to tone things down. There were a couple times when she was in serious relationships and she couldn't look out for me. Those were the times that I would oscillate between black-out drunk and staying up for days on a coke bender. I ended up at home with my parents in Mamaroneck on one such occasion.

"Oh, my drug-addled, gypsy son is home. What a treat," my dad said as I walked in the door on a cold Sunday in January.

I had bought a bouquet of flowers from the bodega at the entrance to the station at 125th Street. "Where's mom?"

New York was getting destroyed by Chicago in a playoff game. Still, he could not be bothered to look away from the TV. He extended his arm and pointed to the kitchen.

She knew I was there. She waited for me with her back to the sink; she leaned back on the counter with her arms extended across the edge for support.

"Happy birthday, Mom," I said and extended the clump of yellow daisies toward her.

She smiled but did not move to accept them. Her lip began to quiver, and her eyes turned red and shiny. Her only child stood before her with a pallid face in clothes that draped over his emaciated body. I made no effort to act like I was there to celebrate anything, but at least I didn't forget.

She turned and reached into the cabinet above the stove. She took out a vase, grabbed the flowers and slammed the stems into the hole. She filled the vase with water from the sink and set it on the sill.

"There is going to be discipline this time," she said. She stared out the window. Stray drops of water fell from the foliage of the flowers onto the sill.

"OK."

"I will drive you to work and pick you up." She turned and faced me now.

"Mom, I have to work really late sometimes."

"I don't care, I'll be there." She was crying again. "And if I show up and you're messed up, I am going to leave you where you stand. So help me God, I will turn my back on you forever."

She was yelling and crying hard enough to attract my father to the kitchen.

"Thanks for coming home, son. We always enjoy your visits so much," he said.

***

The sad prospect of failing on my mother's ultimatum kept me in line. I made arrangements with my friends in Harlem to meet me along the guide route. Veronica was right; the tourism gig was the perfect gimmick for porting drugs around the city. As for the moonlighting gig, I couldn't do that without a cocktail or two. It would be extremely awkward for the client if I did not partake, as they ingested all manner of intoxicants in their whirlwind romps around the city.

After a couple months of passing my mother's tests, I convinced her to let me stay at my place in Hoboken for those late nights. It was exhausting for her to keep those hours and I felt guilty for putting her in that position. I was also hoping to run into Veronica. As long as she was in that relationship, I would only see her when we ran across each other at the office. She would spend every night at his place, and I was anguished that she would never move back in. Sometimes I would ditch work for a day and just stay at the apartment, hoping she would come home to change.

It was a June night when I hit the jackpot. I had lied to my mother and told her I would be working late so I could spend the evening at my place. I heard Veronica fumble her keys at the front door lock. She cursed and pounded the door in a fit of frustration. I rose and opened the door for her. At first, I didn't recognize her. Her face was a scowl and she was wearing mascara, which had run and dried on her cheeks. She must have been crying at some point.

"Thank God you're here," she said.

My mind pumped endorphins when she said this. She reached to embrace me. I clutched her bosom close to mine and kissed the top of her head.

"He dumped me," she said.

"I'm sorry," I lied and caressed her back. We had still only moved as far into the apartment as her first embrace had pushed us.

"Is there anything to drink?" she asked in a meek voice.

"Not a drop. Do you want to go out?" I said.

"Yeah, come on." She locked the door behind us.

We walked down 10th Street to the Elysian and sat at the zinc-topped bar. She ordered a Cosmopolitan and I asked for a seltzer water with a lime.

"Seltzer?" she asked.

"Things got a little hairy during the winter. I've actually been spending most nights in Westchester, you know?"

"You're with me tonight, Piper. I'll take care of you." She was seductive. She used the stem of her cherry garnish to stir the surface of her pink drink. The bartender placed a coaster on the bar and set a high ball of bubbly water on top of it.

"Let me get a gin and tonic, too, please," I told him.

I drank while she talked. It turned out that her erstwhile boyfriend was a jealous man. He had started following her while she was out fulfilling her duties as a social liaison.

"So, I have this guy named Heinrich from Stuttgart, and he just falls in love with the table showers down in Chinatown. You know what I'm talking about, right?" She put her hand high on my thigh as though I needed assurance to keep up with the story. There were massage parlors in Chinatown where pairs of women would steam, oil, rub, and then wash your body for a very reasonable fee. The Germans loved it.

"Of course." I put my lips to my straw. The sound of air being sucked around the ice at the bottom of my empty glass signaled the bartender to begin another drink. He didn't even ask.

"Well, it didn't seem like Hank was really all that pervy. He just seemed to love the experience of getting hosed down. We went every night this week and tonight he asked to skip right to the table shower. Of course, I say fine and by now I'm used to seeing this guy get rubbed every which way from Tuesday, so I just stick around while he hops up on the table."

"Hold on, you were getting the treatments too?" I ask.

"Yeah, but I hadn't done the shower thing up to that point. He was springing for everything and he paid me a nice premium for the whole week, too," she said. "So, he's up on the table with this little Asian woman lathering up his lower quarters while another stands on a stool and works his shoulders and chest. He's moaning with delight. Then he starts extolling the virtues of the experience, trying to get me up there."

"So, you did?"

"Yeah, what the hell, I thought. It's not like they put me up on the same table. There was another stall next to his."

I dropped my face into both palms. "Then what?" I peeked through my fingers.

"It was glorious. These little hands flitting about every crevice. It wasn't nasty. Just little, teasing strokes randomly dispersed between a routine of lathering and rinsing."

I looked up. "Were they naked?" I asked, like an asshole.

"No, they wear bikinis," she said. "I thought you said you were there?"

"I said I knew about it. Not important . . . tell me more." The gin aside, I was processing her story with crystal clarity.

"For the final rinse, they fill these wooden buckets with warm water and pour them over your head before hosing you down with a fine, warm mist," she said.

I chewed my straw until I had rendered it useless. The image of the water pouring down her shining, wet body flushed the chemical blur from my mind.

"I still had my eyes closed when they started with the final rinse. The warm water sprayed over me from head to toe," she continued. "It was bliss."

"Sounds wonderful."

"It was until Jacque started screaming and yelling," she said.

"Jacque? You said his name was Heinrich."

"Jacque, my boyfriend Jacque," she said. "My ex-boyfriend Jacque."

She hammered the top of the bar with the bottom of her fist. The bartender looked in our direction. I waved him off.

"What was Jacque doing there?" I asked.

"He had been following us all week. He stalked us at the clubs, he knew the peep shows we went into—everything."

"So what? He knew the score, right?"

"Yeah, but he was never really cool with it. He was convinced that there was more on the program than I ever let on."

"But there never was . . ." I said but there was question in my voice.

"No," she sneered at me.

"So, what happened with Hank here that got him all bent out of shape?"

She hesitated. She took a sip of her drink, paused, and said. "When I opened my eyes, Heinrich had the hose between his legs. He was rocking back and forth on the tube as he stroked the nozzle and sprayed me down."

I laughed. "And that's when Jacque sprung his trap!"

"You got it," she said, still angry. "I swear to God, I thought it was the little Asian woman rinsing me down. I had my eyes closed."

"Jacque wasn't hearing any of that, though."

"Nope." She stared into the bottom of her drink. She closed her left eye and peered down the barrel of her straw with her blue eye. She looked at me and smiled. I laughed again and she did too.

***

We awoke in the same bed the next morning. We did not make love, but it was the first time we actually slept together all night in one bed. We fell back into our silent morning routine. We prepared for work and walked to the PATH train together. I spent the ride thinking about how I would persuade my mother to release me from our agreement.

It was a Friday and I was busy, too busy to partake of any accelerants or straighteners. I convinced myself that I didn't need any of that stuff anymore. I would be much more convincing to my mother if I believed it myself. Being truly sober wouldn't hurt either.

Our bus drove from midtown to downtown, straight down Broadway. We parked near city hall. I led the group east down Wall Street and stopped at the Broad Street. I released the group to take photos of JP Morgan's bank, the New York Stock Exchange, and the statue of Washington. I made my drops at each spot as well. I took a bunch of photos of each family in front of the Wall Street sign and then we made our way to the Brooklyn Bridge.

"All right folks, we are going to walk to the middle, stay five minutes, and then meet back in that park." I pointed to the park surrounding city hall.

"Are you coming with us?" a man with a fanny pack asked me.

"Of course. I'll be right behind you."

Fanny Pack never wandered more than five feet from me during our trek.

"What's that bridge?" he asked.

"That's the Manhattan Bridge, sir."

"Are we going to walk across that one, too?"

"No, sir, it doesn't have the nice boardwalk running across the top like we have here," I answered.

"Are you going to tell us the names of all those buildings?" He turned and walked backward while pointing to the downtown skyline.

"Sure thing, as soon as we get to the middle."

My contact was walking his bicycle behind us. The continuous *click click click* of the hub turning on the idle sprocket reminded me of his patience.

"Tell me, sir, what's your name?" I asked Fanny Pack.

"I'm Stan, from Ohio." He was older than me. He wore a grey, push broom mustache on his upper lip. His shorts were khaki and pleated.

"Damn glad to meet you, Stan." I extended my hand. "I'm Piper, from New York City. How do you make your living, Stan?"

"I'm a cop in Dayton."

"No shit," I blurted. My client with the bike hopped on his saddle and rode off.

Stan the cop watched him ride off. "He sure left in a hurry."

Stan eyed the messenger bag slung across my chest. I self-consciously held my forearm over the top flap.

"Do you have any questions about the tour that I can answer for you, sir?" I asked.

"You answer a lot of folks' questions, don't you, son?" Stan asked.

"That's my job, Stan, to satisfy people's curiosities."

"Do you have a lot of friends in New York?"

"It's a big city, I make a lot of friends."

"I can tell. I see you keep bumping into them wherever we go." Stan smiled.

"Let's catch up to the group. They may have some questions, too." I smiled back.

This wasn't the first time a tourist spotted my gimmick but it was the first time the tourist was a cop. A loose twenty and a powdering wasn't going to distract Stan.

"On the first day this bridge was open to the public there was a stampede," I told my group. "A rumor had spread that the bridge was falling, and people started trampling each other to get back to the banks."

Stan looked up and down the boardwalk in search of something.

"Don't worry folks, this structure is fantastically over-engineered. There is no danger of it falling down—perhaps ever. You see, the engineers were so concerned about safety that they took their first calculations for the required structural support and multiplied them by six," I said while watching Stan.

Stan seemed to have found what he was looking for on the Brooklyn side.

"When the bridge first opened, Brooklyn was not yet a borough of New York. In fact, it was the third-largest city in America by population and would still be today," I said.

Stan had spotted a pair of beat cops walking the bridge. I watched him greet them.

"At this time, we're going to start heading back toward Manhattan," I announced. "Let's all walk this way." I waved my arm over my head.

"Come on, Dad," a girl yelled to Stan. He held up an index finger to urge her to wait. He spoke with the cops and pointed to me. The cops looked dead at me and my satchel.

"The group is leaving," the girl yelled again.

Stan cocked his head in my direction and the troika of cops began walking behind the group.

We walked from the wide center deck of the bridge. We were at the choke point where the boardwalk narrows as it descends toward Manhattan. "Oh, pictures!" I exclaimed. "I forgot about pictures."

I scurried to collect cameras from my customers. I had them line up across the width of the boardwalk and commenced to memorializing their experience on the bridge. There were already dozens of people backed up behind our photo shoot by the time I was done taking the pictures of just the second family. I slowly walked over and returned the camera.

"Come on, Stan, get your ladies lined up here in front," I shouted. Stan's wife grabbed him by the hand and pulled him forward. I returned to my prior spot and noticed a throng of folks waiting behind me, too. Most of the locals were pushing through but a mass of polite tourists had clogged the way almost completely.

I prowled and pounced with the camera like a jackass photog on a fashion shoot. Stan's daughter ate it up. "What's your name, sweetheart?" I asked.

"Alicia," she squealed.

"You're looking good, Alicia. Do you think one day you might want to come back to the Big Apple as a model?"

"Maybe," she squealed again.

"Let's go, numb nuts!" somebody shouted from behind Stan. His two new friends in blue turned and glared. One of them raised his hand and gestured for the crowd to be patient.

"And what about Alicia's mom?" I asked. Stan's wife blushed.

"I think that's about enough," Stan said. "We're almost out of film."

An angry New Yorker pushed through using the front wheel and handlebars of his bike like a cow catcher.

"Just one more, honey," Alicia's mom said.

"Do you know how much film costs in this city?" Stan had lost his patience.

"Just one more, Stan," I said.

"Make it fast, asshole," someone said from behind me.

I gestured for Alicia's mom to move over, so the support wires framed her perfectly and the concrete towers loomed over her. I lay down on the boardwalk for perspective. I pressed the button, released the shutter, and registered a perfect up-skirt exposure of Alicia's mom's red striped panties.

"OK, who's next?" I asked as I walked over and returned the camera to Alicia's mom.

"Get the fuck off the bridge!" someone yelled from behind me.

"Just push forward!" someone yelled from behind the cops.

People squeezed around the margins on the side. A few nimble folks climbed onto the lateral I-beams and walked above and around the whole mess. I took note.

"You get down from there now," one of the cops yelled.

The crowds converged around us. My tourists were in the middle of the confluence of the opposing flows and the whole group spun counterclockwise like an eddy in a river. Stan pulled his daughter close and looked to his cop friends for salvation. Both cops gripped the handles of their clubs.

"Don't worry too much about sticking together. Remember to meet at the park next to city hall." I said calmly as I surfed the Manhattan bound flow. As a singleton I was easily able to out-pace the group back down the bridge.

I nodded to the guard in front of city hall and he opened the door for me. I had three drops to make and my bag would be empty except for the one I owed to the biker I left hanging on the bridge. I made my drops, hit the men's room and crotched the last baggie and the cash. Then I made my way to the park.

"That was exciting, huh?" I waved as I engaged the group.

"You almost caused a riot!" Stan shouted.

"Aw shucks, Stan. That's what we call a New York square dance." I sounded as oblivious as possible to the peril I had created.

One cop pulled me aside as the other took my satchel. "Cut the shit or you're gonna get a wood shampoo," he whispered. He gripped my wrist in one of his paws and stroked his club with the other. The name on his tag was Capetta.

"You're a clever little faggot, aren't you?" the other cop growled. His tag read BIANCO.

Bianco turned my bag upside down and dumped the contents on the bench. My clipboard rattled loudly against the wood. Receipts fluttered away in the breeze and my maps unfolded on the ground.

"If you guys are looking for directions back to Bensonhurst, all you have to do is ask," I grinned. Capetta squeezed and twisted my wrist in response.

"Did you find anything?" Stan stretched his neck over the cop's shoulders to review the mess.

"Just what are you expecting to find, Stan?" I asked.

"What's this all about? Can we get moving soon?" Stan's wife asked.

"They're just making sure all my papers are in order," I said.

"Seems kind of rude," she observed.

"Hear that boys? You're being rude," I said.

The cops found nothing. They left without an apology. I shoveled my papers back in the satchel using the clipboard and then we headed to the bus. We went to Battery Park and stood in line for the ferry to see the Statue of Liberty.

***

I met my mother near our rendezvous point by the West Side highway. I hopped in and gave her a big kiss on the cheek. I bounced on the seat and stashed my duffel between my legs.

"You're mighty chipper," she said.

"Exciting day, Mom, exciting day."

She wheeled the car around to get to the ramp that would put us northbound on Route 9. "Tell me about it," she said as she craned her neck to negotiate traffic.

"Veronica moved back home," I said.

"OK," she said.

"I want to start staying in Jersey again, Mom," I declared. "I'm clean. It's time."

"Unrequited love will exhaust you over time, Jeffery."

"I'm in my thirties, Mom. It's time I learned such lessons on my own."

"That woman corrupts you," she said. The steady wind from the harbor made white caps on the Hudson as it flowed south.

"Why would you say that?" I turned to view her profile to see if she was serious. Traffic crept.

"Because I'm the one who has to wring you out every time she flutters away on a whim, Jeffery," she said.

"That's why I have to stay with her. She's the one who keeps me straight."

The car was stopped in traffic. When the blue Datsun in front of us began to move, we stayed put.

"That's hurtful." She got misty. She took her foot off the brake and we moved.

"Mom, that's not what I meant. I'm sorry." I reached for her shoulder.

"Say what you mean then," she said, jerking her shoulder away.

"I mean, when I'm with her I don't need anything else," I said. "I stay out of trouble when I'm with her."

The buildings of the Upper West Side abutted the highway on our right side as we headed north on Route 9 toward Yonkers. The white lights of the George Washington Bridge sparkled to life in the distance.

"Every day I pick you up I can tell that you've been into something. Every day." She jabbed her index finger into the dashboard as she said so. "I'm your mother. I see everything."

I shrank in my seat.

"I let it go. You know why?" she asked.

"Why?"

"Because at least you have enough respect to not be a total mess when I show up," she said. "When it comes to my boy, I've learned to settle for adequate—not perfect. So, I ask you, who is it, exactly, who keeps you straight? Some flaky whore in Hoboken or your dear mother who will love you unconditionally, forever."

She wasn't asking. In the least, the correct answer was not open to consideration and she wasn't expecting a response.

"Am I sober right now, according to you?" I asked her.

"You are."

"I want to stay this way," I said. "And she makes me want to feel this way."

A highway sign foretold the approaching opportunity to the exit for Fort Lee, New Jersey.

"What if I refuse?"

"I will get out and go on my own," I said.

"I know you would." She jerked the car into the right lane, preparing for the approaching exit to the bridge. "I bet you'd swim to get there."

"I would, as long as I knew she was waiting on the other side," I said.

"You will surely drown," she said as we ascended the ramp to the bridge.

***

Lots of folks hit their flash point in New York City in their 30s. It's by this age that they see constant reminders of their inadequacies. The professional class of doctors, lawyers, and Indian chiefs starts to pull away from their cohort. Their promotions, their weddings, their new apartment with a doorman, the offspring they are somehow able to support—all a reminder that while you were out partying, they were studying, working, sleeping, and sowing the seeds of a wholesome future.

Those that are left behind have few options. Some frauds try to live above their means for a while, but that's not sustainable. Some lay in wait for a desperate yet wealthy mate to appear.

Success stories are few and far between. A 35-year-old single woman in New York is either married to her career, a closet lesbian, or a content old maid. Single males of the same age are inclined to stay that way.

Veronica and I survived by clinging to the edges of high society. These folks were insulated against the economic realities of Manhattan by their bountiful trust funds. While we were established among the initiated, we did not pay full fare when joining in their social exercises. Like the art that hung on the wall, the party hosts had only superficial understanding of our provenance, but they knew we provided legitimacy to their affair. No member of the liberal elite in New York is complete without a coterie of actors, models, and artists to add another dimension to the party. Exotic drugs were helpful as well.

"Piper, this is my wife, Bumple," Chilton said. He was a lawyer at the one of the "White Shoe" law firms downtown. She was some derivative of the Biltmore family.

"It's so exciting to meet you. Your friends are amazing," she spoke through her teeth as though her molars were fused together.

"Thank you for coming, Piper." Chilton shook my hand again.

He needed me there. Chilton and Bumple had money and pedigree, but when it came to Manhattan sophistication, they were as deep as a spilled drink.

"Your portfolio is impressive, Bumple." I referred to her menagerie of handmade lampshades on display. Her work was to be included in a charity auction to take place the following Saturday. The point of tonight's soirée was to showcase her work ahead of the event. The point of the event was to provide the ultra-rich the opportunity to show off their wealth by giving it away to fund causes about which they had only the vaguest familiarity.

Bumple stood just over five feet tall in heels. She was fit and she worked a tight black dress. She had a pearl white smile, hay-colored hair and an ugly face. Her brown eyes were sunken and set too close behind her thin, bony nose. Most regrettably, she sported a monobrow that was stubbornly untenable despite constant efforts.

"Thank you for saying so," Bumple said. "Now, please tell me how you are acquainted with such a large and fascinating group of people?"

Veronica and I called this the "resume recital" part of the evening. It was a routine and necessary exercise among the elite. It helped them to establish whether they needed to bestow deference or pity upon you. Some folks were pricks about it, too. They would call for your recital even though they knew exactly what you were all about. They would do it to remind you and the others around you of your place in the hierarchy.

"Piper is among the top 'Taste Makers of Manhattan,' according to the latest Core magazine," Chilton boasted.

This was true. It was also true that I had been delivering every manner of powder, pill, and smoke to Chilton and his peers for the better part of the eighties.

"So, these people just follow you around?" Bumple asked.

"That's why they call me Piper," I said.

Veronica had two models with her this evening: Nori was from Japan and the other, Akina, was from Rwanda. Nori's black leather tunic contrasted against her milky skin. Meanwhile, Akina was as black as Nori was fair. She wore a thin white garment through which her rich, dark skin was noticeable. They were admiring one of Bumple's lamps that stood on a pedestal in the center of the main foyer. The panels of the shade were made of magazine covers that had been cut and pasted over translucent nylon fabric. The three women were likewise admired by two Yuppie men. They wore blue, brass-button blazers over slacks. They wore loafers with no socks.

"Will you be at the auction?" one of the men asked Akina.

It was an innocent gaffe that would have passed without notice if not for the subtle chuckle from the second man.

"I mean, will you be at the event this weekend?" he corrected himself.

Veronica turned and spoke to Akina in French. Akina shrugged and smiled at the man.

"And you mama-san, will I see you there?" the joker asked. He looked to Veronica to translate.

"It's looking less and less likely," she responded without help.

The blazered boys were not among the established elite. They thought they were by virtue of their Ivy League degrees and solid careers, but they were not permanent. They had youth, money, and prestige but their blood was not blue, so they would be cycled out as routinely as the drapes. They would soon be spending their Thursday nights with their trophy wives in their high-rise nests on the Upper East Side—a consolation prize that the poseurs at the party would have killed to have.

Gabe and the Broadway crew were spread around, but never far from one of the bartenders.

"What your cousin needs to understand is that this is New York City," Gabe said to a female guest. "Even if she really is one in a million, there's still a dozen of her here and only one lead role for that show."

She was pretty, but not gorgeous. She was likely the prom queen in the town she came from, but she barely moved the needle compared to the talent in this single, albeit spacious, apartment.

"Do you know the casting director?" she asked.

"I do, she casted me," Gabe said.

"So, could you get her an audition?"

"It doesn't work like that." Gabe extracted his eyes from her plaintive glare. He swiveled his head around looking for salvation. He excused himself and joined two dancers at the bar on the opposite side of the room.

Gabe strolled past Ulderico and Alberto as they talked shop and surveyed the passing hors d'oeuvres. They both worked as restaurant managers for Carlo Capriani. Capriani owned many restaurants across the city and he had a material interest in several clubs as well.

"Those bacon-wrapped dates are tricky," Ulderico observed.

"Way harder than the scallops," Alberto agreed. "I have my guys leave the scallops a little gummy and then pour the hot bacon grease over them a few times to finish them off."

"Can't do that with the dates," Ulderico said.

"Nope, they'll shrink to raisins."

The collection of guests that Veronica and I brought to the party created a positive synergy. Capriani and his men courted the elite as the patrons of his empire of restaurants and clubs. Capriani's influential clientele would indulge him with the first notice when new spaces became available. Gabe and his troop created fanfare for their productions and made sure to put some hard-to-get tickets in the hands of the right guests. Veronica's clients received the attention they needed as badly as a plant needs sunlight. And most importantly, the host's shortcomings were mitigated by having such beautiful people in attendance. After all, they must be beautiful in some other way to keep such attractive people as peers.

Veronica and I received some compensation from our own clientele but the real value to us came by way of the complementary goods and services we would receive. We called this "payment in kind."

We dined out every night and never paid as long as we had the right guests with us. We used the service entrance at the clubs, and we might even get a take of the bar if we filled the floor for a special event. Miami Beach every spring was a given as was July 4th in the Hamptons. Our flights and accommodations were always private. How anything ever got paid for I still don't know. We entered art galas and show openings via the red carpet. The gift baskets we received were treasure chests of fine wine, caviar, and the latest advancements in gadgetry.

And yet, we had to move to Manhattan to maintain legitimacy and Manhattan rents were high. Cash is king and our landlord wasn't taking Pouily-Fuisse and fish eggs as payment. Even when we pooled my drug money with our clean cash flow, we still had barely enough to maintain life's basic necessities. Happily, the metamorphosis of Manhattan into a family playground in the early '90s provided a new opportunity for us to earn some decent money.

***

Tatiana took the corner seat at the bar of the Four Seasons lounge. The bartender nodded in her direction. "Good evening, Luke," she said with a slight Russian accent.

Luke started mixing a cocktail without saying a word. Tatiana cracked open a bound copy of *The Catcher in the Rye*. She wore a tight, gold, sleeveless cocktail dress with a hem cut high above the knee. Her hair was pulled tight in a bun above her head. Her makeup was limited to a fine patina with light accents around her eyes. She looked elegant and expensive.

Veronica and I sat in a booth on the street side of the lounge. The cushions were upholstered with rich leather and were generously padded. The undrawn drapes were made from tiny woven links of brass, like a knight's chainmail but much more delicate.

Veronica and I approached as Luke slid a martini glass filled with pink liquid and a cherry in front of Tatiana.

"The finder's fee is $1000," she said.

"A thousand dollars for just three?" Veronica asked.

"No, $1000 each; times three."

The two of them started speaking in Russian. Veronica was angry but she maintained composure. Tatiana was resolute.

"Fine, find a better deal," Veronica said in English. "We'll see how long the four of you last together in that hovel in Brighton Beach."

"In Russia, we endure more hardship then you could ever imagine," Tatiana dismissed her.

"In America, we pay rent," Veronica returned.

"Seven hundred fifty dollars for all three," I said. "Five hundred now and two hundred fifty at the end of the summer."

"Nine hundred. Now." Tatiana pressed her pointer finger on the top of the bar. "It's called a *finder's fee* not a *keeper's fee*."

We made the deal and added three Russian acrobats to our stable of entertainers. We put them near the fountain off the terrace in Central Park. They flipped and contorted themselves all summer, making a clean two grand on peak weekends. Veronica and I raked half of their gross. They kept this up for a season or two until they decided they could run the same show without our help. When they showed up to perform, the park authorities were no longer as permissive as they once were.

"We performed here all summer," Mikhail said.

"Well, perform your asses of this plaza," the park ranger told him. "You need a permit to perform here."

The two female acrobats began yelling at Mikhail in Russian as they rolled up their mats. The girls would eventually contact us for work, but Mikhail was too stubborn and proud. We set them up with a team of tumblers from Brooklyn and put them on the West Side promenade. We put a juggler near the fountain by the terrace.

We also had failed actors in production-quality costumes teeming Times Square to take pictures with tourists for five bucks. The costumes were discarded versions from the actual shows. They were beyond repair after many seasons on stage, as were many of the actors. Gabe and our other friends in the industry were a treasure trove of resources.

Our stable of freak show musicians lined the subway platforms. Give a concert cellist an hour to play Bach on the N Line and he'll make four bucks in nickels. Remove an arm and stick the bow between his toes and he'll make fifty.

We put the sketchers on the bridges and the caricature artists in the pastures in the park. The dance troops went wherever there was room for a square yard of cardboard and a crowd. The Chinese mafia dominated the masseuse trade, but we got some Indian yogis to stretch and rub the tourists in Union Square.

The perverts in swimwear were easy to find. There are an alarmingly high number of men in New York eager to sport tight briefs and commiserate with the masses. The biggest challenge with them was finding a place to attach the busker's license. We'd dress them for the nearest holiday: red thong and wings for Valentine's Day, green thong and top hat for St. Patrick's Day, pink thong and bunny ears for Easter, American flag thong and cowboy hat for the Fourth of July. They usually had their own thongs. We placed them on the fringes of Times Square in Hell's Kitchen but we'd have them lurk into Times Square after midnight. That's where I met David Hoff.

David wasn't taking any pictures. He just wanted to talk to our guys, who were cool with that as long as the gimmick wasn't a big come on. Nonetheless, at some point there was work to be done and money to be made so I would step in and run some interference so our creepy little pilgrim or elf could scurry away in peace.

"I love Halloween," I say to the man admiring Sergio's vampire costume. Sergio was wearing a black thong and bow tie, slicked-black hair and fangs. He posed with a tourist as though he were biting her neck.

"We don't have this festival in Germany. It's fascinating," the man with the idle camera agreed.

"Oh, you're from Germany?" I pretended to be surprised.

"Yes, but I have been here for many years now. I am an artist," he said.

"What is your medium?" I asked. Sergio wandered north up Broadway.

David extended his hand to reveal a Dictaphone. "My name is David Hoff and I am an audiovisual artist. My current project is focused on street performers."

"Nice to meet you, David." I extended my hand and he shook it. "This is interesting, tell me more."

"So, you don't mind?" he asked.

"Mind what?"

"Mind that I'm interviewing your employees."

"These folks are independent contractors, buddy," I said, a little startled.

"Half the performers I've met in the city tell me that Piper is their boss. And you're Piper, yes?" he asked.

I turned my head and stared down Broadway looking for Sergio.

"I'm not trying to get you in trouble; I've been eager to meet you. I am hoping to collaborate with you," David said.

"Collaborate how? You haven't even told me what you're doing?"

"Meet me at my apartment tomorrow night: 220 East 29th, apartment 1A, 7 p.m.," he said.

"What will I see there?"

"My progress so far. And you will see why I need your help."

***

Veronica wasn't keen on the idea but Herr David Hoff seemed to know enough about me and the performers that I was intrigued to see just how far down the rabbit hole he had gone. David welcomed me in and offered me a beer. I accepted.

The apartment was medium-sized by Manhattan standards, with a spacious sitting room off the kitchen. The room was windowless, and all three walls were painted white. There were three, small, digital projectors sitting atop an end table that was pushed to the middle of the room. There was no other furniture in the room.

David placed two chairs just within the wide archway dividing the kitchen from the sitting room. He handed me a glass of beer and pointed for me to sit. He killed the lights, sat, and extended a remote control toward the projectors.

The three projectors cast images on the three walls in unison but only the image to the left was in perfect focus. The sound of children laughing was dubbed over images of me unloading costumes from the back of a panel van.

"Obviously, I will need a release to use your image for any completed work that I intend to produce," David leaned over to say to me before I could vocalize my objections. His assurances about legal particulars did little to assuage my feelings that I had suffered a personal invasion.

The film continued with the soundtrack of children laughing set over sequences of costumed characters playing with kids and posing with families around Times Square. Then the film on the left wall began to lose focus and the film on the center wall came into focus. The soundtrack changed from laughter to the sound of a solo fiddler playing on an empty subway platform. His notes echoed along the vaulted ceiling of the 116th Street stop at Columbia University. He was a little person and his instrument was half the size of a viola intended for a child's hands. He was dressed as a gypsy and he danced in a circle as he played. A student passed into frame and dropped change into his hat. The focus changed from the center wall to the right wall just as the new coins splashed with the coins already in the bottom of the cap.

The sound of a crowd clapping in rhythm took over the speakers. The right wall came into focus on a team of dancers that popped, locked, and spun to a cadence of hip-hop beats. The setting could have been any crowded public square in Manhattan on a summer night. Two dancers feigned offense at one another and a dance off commenced to the delight of the public.

The film showed the whole duel and ended with the exalted victor receiving a final ovation from the crowd. Their applause faded to silence and all three walls faded to black for a moment.

The left wall brightened. The film showed various characters transitioning from spot to spot across their territories in Time Square. The sound of David's voice came over the speakers. The edited content of his interviews was broadcast over the images of his subjects hard at work.

"Better than any opportunity I could find at home," a young man with a southern accent said.

"I'm just not ready to get off the stage," said an older voice.

"This is what it takes to get by in this city, man. I'll spend another four hours cleaning offices after I'm done here tonight," said another.

The camera panned up the skyscrapers. It panned back down and suddenly we were on the center screen, on the subway platform. David asked the little person questions and he responded with only head shakes and nods.

"Your name is Miguel?" David asked.

Miguel nodded.

"This is how you support yourself?"

Miguel nodded again.

The film told me what I already knew about Miguel. I knew he was a runaway from the circus who we found outside of Penn Station. I knew he was from Belize and that his mother taught him the viola while his brothers and sisters attended the school he couldn't go to because the other students would abuse him so viciously. I knew that he spoke with a lisp that he was very self-conscious about.

David leaned to me and said, "He didn't want to speak for the film . . ."

". . . because of his lisp," I interjected.

David nodded. The center screen faded and the screen to the right came up. The sequence continued. The dancers were interviewed. Then the performers were shown packing up and heading home. There was a scene of me loading up the van with costumes. The screens to the left and right faded as the center screen brightened. Miguel's tender face filled the screen.

"Do you work for Piper?" David asked.

Miguel nodded.

"Is he good to you?"

"Yes," he said, and a wide smile spread across his face.

***

David and I began regular sessions of interviews following that night. He fell in line behind me with the rest of the entourage. He recorded my life's events and acquaintances for posterity. He became my personal scribe.

"Don't you think you're being a little self-indulgent?" Veronica cautioned.

"It's art. You should see the work. It's an amazing production given his means," I answered.

"And all it's missing is you, right?"

"Number one, he wants me to make intros to all our characters. Number two, every featured subject is interviewed for their backstory," I said. "Well, I'm a featured subject."

Veronica shook her head. I poured a cup of coffee.

"He's coming here tonight. Is that OK?" I asked.

"Is that your way of telling me to leave?"

"Not at all. I think it's a shame you haven't really gotten to know him yet. He really is impressive."

David arrived with a lot of gear. Our place in Murray Hill was near his so I was surprised by his insistence on doing the taping at our place. He said he wanted to capture me in my home setting.

"Tell me what you mean by addictive personality?" he asked. We were a half hour into the session.

"I bet if you looked in my brain and found all the pleasure receptors, they would lead to one master circuit that pumped all its energy toward whatever thing put the biggest smile on my face at any moment. There's no such thing as too much of a good thing in my mind."

"So, what keeps you sober?"

"Oh, don't get me wrong. I still party," I said and took a sip of my coffee. "But these days I'm able to pull back the throttle before things get out of hand."

"Tell me about this throttle. How do you know when to pull it back?"

Veronica was leaning against the counter in the kitchen with her own cup of coffee. She had no expression.

"She's my throttle," I said. "Hers is the voice of reason in my head."

David smiled and shut down the gear. He approached Veronica, who remained expressionless.

"You do not approve of this project," David said, true to his direct, German nature.

"It's invasive," she replied and took a sip of coffee.

"Clearly if you thought it was harmful, he would have pulled out by now." David grinned.

"I'm not as influential as he would have you believe," she replied.

***

David followed me for the rest of the season. He finished the film and when it debuted at the Tribeca Film Festival the next spring, I was delighted to see that he had awarded me credit as a co-producer. The film received commendations and accolades but none of the grand prizes. David still counted it as the top achievement of his career to that point.

"I want to go deeper for the next film, Piper. I want to peel the onion, as you say in America," David told me during the post party.

"You want to do a film about me?" I asked, holding the stem of a champagne flute in my hand. "What did you have in my mind?"

"I want Gabe and the dancers, Chilton and Capriani . . . and I want Veronica," he said. "I want the whole club to tell me about how they met you and the places you've taken them."

"They've taken me to more, I assure you of that," I tell him.

"You see? That's exactly the type of insight I want." He sipped his champagne. "I want Luis, too."

"Luis is going to be tricky," I said. Well-wishers brushed past and congratulated us.

David was by now familiar with my courier gig. Even though the Luis of my youth was long gone in a cell or a grave, I still called my connections by his name. Luis was followed by a succession of Armando, Raul, Esteban and even a woman named Agrapina. There were other names along the way that I forgot. At the time of his request, a guy named Keith was my man in the barrio.

"Are you familiar with the California Gold Rush, David?" I asked.

"The '49ers?"

"Yes. It ruined many men. They left home and risked everything to find an easy fortune," I said. "The majority found a pan of dirt and two lungs full of opium."

"What does this have to do with Luis?"

"Luis is one of those fortune seekers."

"And who are you?" he asked.

"The folks who got rich off the gold rush never really took the risks," I said. "They were the guys who sold the shovels, the guys who rented out the mules. The opportunists."

"The Opportunists," David said as he smiled and looked up at a billboard he was imagining.

"I take no risks, David. I'm just a courier," I said. "Not very exciting."

"I disagree. And it's part of who you are."

"No, it's not. It's just a gig," I said. "And I'm not too keen on letting the world know about my side job, you know?"

"I'll shoot it point of view, with no narrative," David replied.

"You want to send me to a business meeting with a camera on my head?"

"I have small cameras, small as buttons."

"Not a chance, David. Sorry, buddy." I clinked my glass to his and we both sipped. He stood, pensive.

"I'll do it. I'll make the run," he said with conviction. "You said the guy playing the role of Luis changes all the time. Well, the guy playing Piper can change just this once, right?"

I laughed and shook my head.

"I don't need you to be in the scene. There will be no discussion. Just a pickup, right?" he reasoned.

"David, forget it."

"But why not?" he whined.

"Because I know how to get out of a jam and you don't," I said.

I saw Veronica alone at the bar. I broke from the discussion and moved next to her. Her dress was white with a floral pattern tracing up from the bottom hem, around the waist and across her bosom.

"No client?" I asked.

"He's smitten with the starlets. No time for an old hag like me," she whipped her luscious red curls from across her neck so she could sip her cocktail. Her plump, nude lips left an impression of moisture on the rim.

It wasn't late by party standards, but I was satisfied with myself for the evening. I was emboldened by my taste of fame. "Let's go home and finish the celebration," I said with a wink.

She extended her hand and caressed my left cheek with a sweep of her thumb. "Go ahead of me. I'll be right behind you."

I was giddy. It had been some time since she had allowed me. "I'll get the place ready."

"Find some candles," she whispered.

The cabbie made his way to the Bowery and then shot up 3rd Avenue. I rushed up the stairs and into the apartment, and then immediately hit the shower. I made myself clean and then started on getting the apartment in order. I made the bed and set out the candles. I gambled that I had enough time to make it to the liquor store for a nice bottle of wine.

I hustled back up to the apartment with a bottle of Barolo in hand. I had expected her to be there, but the place was as I'd left it. I exhaled and told myself to calm down. I opened the wine and poured a glass and then lit the candles. The sterile odor of the unscented candles made me think of church. As I lit the scented versions, their bouquets mixed with the church smell into an indiscernible medley. The tongues of fire flickered in the silence. I turned the stereo on, and I set the volume low.

I returned to the kitchen and poured myself another glass of wine. There were only three inches of liquid left in the bottle. I finished the glass and checked the clock. It was nearly 1 a.m. I blew out the candles and went downstairs to hail a cab. The lights turned green in sequence and I made it back to the party faster than I had returned home. There was line of hopeful guests outside of the building and I had left my credentials at home. I surely knew the rope crew, but I didn't want to cut the line and I didn't need to. I walked between buildings to the rear exit, where I had escaped for a smoke a few hours earlier. There would be a doorman there too and I would know him as well.

I walked down the dark gangway and as I approached the corner of the building, I heard a man and a woman arguing. The voices were familiar, but they were arguing in a language I couldn't understand. It was German.

"*Nein, nein, nein!*" the woman yelled.

I turned the corner and the woman was pounding on the man's shoulders with the bottom of her fists. He absorbed the punishment. She became exhausted and finally relented. She put the crown of her forehead to his chest reluctantly and he pulled her into an embrace.

***

They came clean the next morning. It was a Friday and I needed to head to Harlem to pick up my packages for delivery. The time pressure added to my anxiety and I wasn't keen to listen to their explanations.

"You betrayed me. Both of you," I said.

"My work stands on its own," David stated. "I sought her out to get to you. The project was always supposed to be about you."

"Why couldn't you just tell me?" I asked. I looked at the clock on the wall. I needed to make it to 116th and back downtown in an hour.

"She wouldn't let me," David shifted the blame.

"That's not true. I wanted to introduce you on my own, on my own terms. But you said that would corrupt your precious project." Veronica had her back against the wall. She held her left arm across her chest and her right hand against her face.

"Just how long ago did you guys meet?" I began to move about the apartment collecting my gear for the day.

"About a year before he met you."

"A year!"

"It was casual. I had met your acrobats on the promenade, and they told me when they would be meeting their boss," he explained.

"If it were anyone else, he would have met you first," she said. Only Veronica dealt with the Russians. I typically handled all the other business meetings.

I went to the fridge and grabbed a bottle of water. I placed it in the bottom of my satchel. "I'm really late. You guys can fill me in on the details later."

"Piper, I need to get this out there now. I've been keeping it in for too long." She was still leaning against the wall in the same pose, guarding herself.

"I don't feel like catering to your needs right now," I said.

"David and I are in love," she said. "There're going to be some changes."

I made my way to the door.

"Piper, please." She walked after me.

I turned and faced her. "David and I are doing the next project. The changes will add another dimension to the story."

Veronica glared at David. He took a deep breath and began to speak, "Piper, listen . . ."

"Fuck you," I said to David and pointed at him before turning to Veronica. "And fuck you, too," I said, this time pointing at her. "You two kept me in the dark for two years while you exploited me. Now you plan to take everything I hold dear. The least you can do is finish the job. It'll be a masterpiece."

They had no response. I grabbed the handle of the door. The phone rang. It rang again and Veronica stayed fixed in her guarded pose. I returned and answered the phone.

"Hello."

"Piper?" a man asked.

"Speaking."

"Don't go uptown today. Keith's in a pinch with his supplier and he set you up," the voice said.

"How?"

"He got busted the other night. Everyone thinks he's working with the cops. He is, but he told them you were instead. He goated you out."

The man hung up, but I kept the phone to my ear.

"Thanks for letting me know. See you soon," I said.

I turned to Veronica and David. She was in the same pose. David was stoic.

"Do you still want to meet Luis?" I asked him.

"Don't you dare," Veronica said.

Perhaps David did love Veronica, but I was betting he loved his art more.

"This is your only chance," I said. "Are we doing this or not?"

David checked the stash of gear he kept in his satchel. He found a tiny, wireless camera.

"If you walk out that door with him, don't come back," she said. "Either of you."

"We owe it to him, Veronica," David crooned, making a weak attempt to stem her objections.

"Don't forget this." I tossed him the wireless mic from the table.

Veronica was starting to cry as we walked out the door. I was sure I could convince her later that he was a mistake.

"What should I do when they answer?" David asked as we walked from my building.

"Tell them your name is Piper and then follow their instructions."

David was excited, but nervous too. He fumbled with his gear then patted his pockets to make sure he had everything he needed. "What if something happens? Like you said, I don't know how to get out of a jam."

"Don't worry, David. I do."

Interlude 6: I Love New York

The transition from 1990's Manhattan to the back of the steward's horse was as abrupt as waking from a dream. "I didn't even get to share my story with him," I say.

"Piper is only interested in sharing his story," the steward replies. His name is KO.

"I thought the point was to share our stories to learn how to get out of here?" I speak over the hoof beats of KO's gray horse. The saddle is sized for two. The leather is worn smooth from an eternity of use.

"Piper likes it here," KO says.

"What about David? What happened to David?" I ask even though I already have a good guess.

KO shrugs. "Piper gets his way in the end."

"He gets the girl?"

"Not exactly," KO says and looks to the horizon. "He makes sure that David doesn't either, though."

I smile, but then I'm ashamed by my reaction, so I wipe the grin from my face. These stories aren't fiction. I realize that Piper surely set David up for a grim and violent demise at the hands of his suppliers.

My purgatorial plain is abloom with detail. We are riding across a high desert plateau. There had been a rain shower and the landscape is a chromatic delight of new flowers. They are determined to flash their brilliant blossoms before their existence is extinguished by the blistering sun.

"I bet this all looks like a bustling city to him," I say.

"No doubt."

"And you're what, a taxi driver in his world?"

"Bus driver."

"And he's content with that existence?" I am intrigued by the potential option.

"Not exactly, but he loves that story. He loved his life," KO says. "He tells that same story over and over again. It's the only one anyone can pull out of him. It never changes. And every time we take him back, he does the same exact things and makes the same exact decisions."

I linger on the notion. What chapters of my life would I enjoy repeating forever?

"Where will you take me now?" I ask KO.

"You will return to a critical juncture in your life. You will have no recollection of having been here, but you will be equipped with the lessons you learned here," he tells me the same things Andres did, more or less, but I still don't understand completely.

"I mean, how will I know if I get it right this time?"

"I don't know, Nick. But if you end up back here, I'd say you left some meat on the bone," he says. "Rely on your instincts. That's where your lessons here will manifest."

"Tell me something about Piper," I say. "How is it possible for him to enjoy a life that is so utterly miserable?"

KO shrugs and answers, "Some people really like New York, I guess."

Story 7: Déjà vu

"Nick, I don't want to see the country with you. I'm sorry. I don't want to." She begins to compose herself. "I want to go back. Before I hurt you again."

"You could never hurt me so bad I would stop loving you." I squeeze her. From the river below, we hear the distant hoots and cheers of rafters as they shoot a set of rapids.

"I know. That's why I have to do this." She begins to weep again. "It's not right."

"What's not right?" I try again to pull her away and, again, she resists. She is strong.

"I'm going to keep hurting you until you resent me. I know it." She cries harder. She's burst the levee holding back her emotions.

The episode weakens her clutch. I remove the sunglasses from her bloodshot eyes. They are blue with streaks of gold and I love her even at her worst. I can fix this. I will fix this.

Lori catches her breath. "Let's go home. We'll talk to someone. We'll try. OK?"

"No, I can fix this," I declare. "I know what you need."

"No, you don't." She pounds my body with her hands.

"We need to move forward. We don't go back, we never go back." I pull her close to my chest. I am looking upriver. Her chin is on my shoulder. She has stopped crying. I've reached her.

"Nick, listen to me. Whatever damage that's been done is small potatoes right now," she says. "Let's be smart. Let's work through this so we still like each other in the end."

"What end?" I say.

"There are no kids. We rent our place."

I know where she is headed and I don't want to accept it. I saw this coming, somehow. Instinctively, I know my best move is to acquiesce. I release her from my arms and begin walking the trail back the way we came.

***

"What would you do if you won the lottery?" Lori asks me.

I haven't spoken any more than necessary since we left Glenwood Springs to head back east. We are back in the middle of Kansas. I need some stimulation, or I am going to fade right into the steering wheel. I submit to her small talk, but not without some bitterness.

"What would I do if I won the lottery? Give you half and watch you walk away, I guess," I say.

"Nick, come on. We are going to talk to someone when we get back, OK?" she says.

"Why bother, Lor?"

"I'm not giving up on us, Nick. I'm not," she says.

"Do you promise?"

"Yes."

We ride in silence for a bit. The weight of the stress dissipates in stages. The sting numbs quickly but the pressure weighing behind my eyes disappears more slowly. I replay her words in my mind. She's not giving up. She promised. Still, the prospect of a life without her is real. The subject has been broached. It is a possibility now, whereas before it was not.

"What would a life apart look like to you?" I ask. "I heard what you just said but still, it's out there now."

"Let's talk about something else, Nick. Please."

"I'm sorry, I just never imagined I'd ever have this conversation," I say.

"So, let's not have it then," she smiles and slaps my thigh. "What about the lottery question?"

"I don't know. What about it?"

"What would you do? How would you spend it?" she desperately wants to change the tone of the day. It's late and I'm exhausted so I indulge her.

"I'd get us a boat, a sailboat. We'd put it in at Belmont and host a happy hour every Friday for our poor friends who still had to work," I dream aloud. "We'd sleep on the boat and maybe Shanghai whatever stowaways we had with us in the morning. We would head across the lake to Saugatuck. We'd have them back in time for work on Monday, of course."

"Of course." She laughs. "What else?"

"I don't know. It's hard to imagine. I would definitely need to find something to fill my day." I ruminate on the idea. "I suppose I would start writing more. I'd like to volunteer, too."

"There you go," she encourages.

"We'd build a house and have a room for each hobby. I'd dedicate a room to music. We'd line the walls from top to bottom with albums and then start a collection of antique record players."

"I think that's the only kind you can find now." She laughs again.

This is fun.

"There'd be a fitness room too," I say, grabbing a handful of gut and shake it. "This would have to go."

"You know, it occurs to me that you can do a lot of those things even if you don't win the lottery," she points out.

"The boat would be tricky," I reply.

"They say that the two happiest days of your life are the day you buy your boat and the day you sell your boat," she says.

"Yeah, I heard that. And that you don't want to own a boat, you want a friend who owns a boat," I return.

"The guy down the hall, he has a boat."

"Craig, the finance guy?"

"Yeah, I think that's his name," she says.

"We don't like him very much, though," I point out.

"Maybe we should give him a chance," she says. "We shouldn't disqualify people just because they work a certain trade."

I change the subject. "In any case, the house wouldn't be possible."

"Houses come in all sizes, and all at prices," she says. "Have you ever seen what you can get down south of Kankakee?"

"That would be a hell of a commute," I turn and cast a suspicious glance. "Have you already looked into this?"

She shrugs, "If we can live on two teachers' salary in Lakeview, imagine what we could do in Kankakee."

"Skip stones? Count cows? Die of boredom?"

"Do you know how happy it would make my mother to have us closer to home?" she says. "And the train line runs right through there; we could hit the city whenever we pleased."

"Oh my God. Is that what this is all about?" I put my hand to my forehead and run my fingers through my hair. "You miss your mother?"

"Why do you have to say it like that? I think it's normal," she turns and looks at me with narrowed eyes.

"No, I'm just saying, we can go see her anytime." I begin to feel relief. Maybe we are going to be fine. She just needs to see her mother.

"Nick, we spend all our vacations driving all over the country," she declares, "and we spend every weekend at a bar or at a ball game, and then at brunch."

"Let's go there now." I feel ashamed that I have only been thinking about myself, but I also feel relief that I might have found a way to work this out. I just have to stop being so self-centered. I congratulate myself for my epiphany.

"It's 11 p.m. and a day's drive from here."

"We'll hit the hay now. No camping tonight." I spy a blue highway sign displaying local motels. "We'll get right back on the road in the morning and be there by suppertime."

***

We park in the back of the white farmhouse. Lori's mother, Carol, is waiting for us on the back porch. Lori nearly tumbles over backward as she meets her arms. Carol's enthusiasm spills over and I enjoy a dose of affection as well.

"How was your trip? I thought you were going to stay out west this summer?" Carol looks puzzled.

"The car wasn't cooperating, so we turned back. Couldn't handle the mountains," I nod my head toward the Subaru. "Would it be OK if we spent a couple weeks here?"

"Of course!" Carol shouts. We walk into the kitchen.

"Hello, Father!" Lori yells from the kitchen.

"Hello, honey, welcome home," he says from his reclining chair in front of the TV. "Did I hear something about a broken-down car?" Lori's father, Emil, collapses the chair and walks slowly to the kitchen.

"She was running really hot up in the mountains, but she cooled off now that we're closer to home." I smile at Lori.

"Could be the thermostat," he says.

"Yeah, perhaps the altitude was making things screwy." I smile again at my wife. "But we're looking good now."

"Let me know if you want to take a look," he does not insist.

"How is your summer, Father?" Lori asks.

Emil thinks it over and answers, "Feed corn got a little expensive on account of the dry spring. It hasn't been too hot, and we need to catch up on some rain."

The chit chat continues as Lori and her mother set the table. A breeze blows through the window above the kitchen sink and the lace window dressings undulate. The surface of the kitchen table takes shape as slowly as the conversation. Like dance steps executed from rote memory, the exercise of preparing the table, serving the food, and clearing the dishes occurs effortlessly. We repeat the ritual for several nights and soon find ourselves retiring to bed shortly after sundown. We begin to take on her parents' rhythm of life. I wake with Emil and help with the morning duties. It may not be the farm I grew up on, but I know which chores I can cover without Emil's direction. The turmoil of the prior week seems absurd now.

There is a one-gallon glass jug sitting on the top step of the back porch. The afternoon sun is heating the liquid inside. The essence of the tea leaves and the lemons leach into the water. Carol concocts this elixir every other day so a constant supply is chilling in the fridge. It's 4 p.m. on a Friday and the four of us are relaxing on the back porch with our iced teas in hand. Each glass is garnished with a sprig of wild mint picked from the creek side.

"Are you going to Jeanine's wedding shower tomorrow?" Carol asks Lori.

"I was going to play it by ear," Lori answers. "Are you going?"

"I bought a gift. I figure that entitles me to at least a piece of cake," Carol jokes.

"Sounds reasonable," I say. Emil nods his agreement and smiles.

"What time does the shindig start?" Lori asks.

"Noon, in the basement of the church," Carol says.

"I suppose we could drive out to the mall to fetch a gift after supper," Lori figures. "You don't mind that I go, Nick?"

"I'm sure your father and I can find a project to dive into," I say.

Emil sets his tea down after a sip. "We got part of an old oak that split and fell across the fence on the back thirty. We could clear that up and mend the fence."

"That should fill the afternoon," I say.

Emil takes another sip and sets the glass down. "We could start right now if you're up for it."

The weather is sunny but mild for an early summer evening in central Illinois. I tip the remainder of my glass back and get set to work.

***

The fence is a big project for two men to handle by hand but it's satisfying work. We had cleared the oak last evening and spent this morning hauling the wood to the log splitter behind the barn. It wasn't until after lunch that we began mending the fence. It takes hours to saw off the broken railings and dig out the old posts.

The main road is at least a mile from where we stand at the far east end of the Muell family property. We see Carol's white Ford turn left onto the drive. It hasn't rained for the entire week so far and the road up to the house is dusty and dry. The sedan leaves a powdery contrail as it approaches the house.

"Suppertime?" Emil asks as he leans on a post hole digger.

"Got to be close," I say.

We cross two fence posts in an X to cover the segment of fence that has been compromised. We use some of the old rails to support the new beams where they meet the ground and then use wire to fasten them to the fence posts at the top.

"That should hold for the night," Emil says.

A horse or an ambitious cow could jump over the barricade, but it serves as an adequate deterrent for the time being. Satisfied with our day's work we load a few leftover railings onto our vehicle and head back toward the house.

Carol has changed out of her church dress and into a house dress. She is wearing a white apron over the flower-patterned garment. She has begun the evening ritual of preparing supper.

"Where's Lori?" I ask. I do not hear anyone else stirring in the house.

"She wanted to spend a little more time with Joanne and Wendy," Carol says. She washes carrots in the sink. "I needed to get home to make supper."

"Oh, OK," I say. "I'm going to get cleaned up."

As I shower and change, I think about our apartment and our evening rituals. I miss our home. I miss our routines.

"When do you think Lori will want to come home?" I ask over supper.

"We agreed that I'd fetch her after supper," she replies.

"Oh, OK," I say.

A front passes over the house from the west. A sudden gust flushes the pleasant odor of pork and vegetables from the kitchen. The screen door on the back porch claps against its frame.

"We sure can use this," Emil says. A distant thunderclap rolls across the prairie and slowly dissipates like the growl of a sleepy dog.

Carol begins to clear the table. I rise to fulfill Lori's duties.

"Don't bother, sweetie. I can handle this," Carol says.

"Maybe I could do you the favor of picking up Lori in that case," I say.

"That would be fine, dear."

"Are they still at the church?" I ask.

"That's where I left them," she says.

I certainly know the way; it's where we were married. The sky is grey and heavy above the highway. I'm headed north toward Clinton. There are storm clouds on the horizon. They appear black but they turn inky blue with each flash of lightning.

I arrive at the church. The parking lot is empty, and the doors are locked. I walk over to the pastor's house and knock on the door.

"Hello, Nicholas," Pastor Schneider says. "Such a treat to see you and your lovely bride in the same day." The air is sticky.

Pastor Schneider presided over our wedding. He seems as keen to talk as I am to find Lori.

"Good evening, Father," I say. "I hate to be abrupt, but I am hoping to find Lori before this storm rolls through."

Summer storm fronts in the central plains are tornado machines. Pastor Schneider, seemingly oblivious to the approaching tempest, peeks towards the storm. "There's going to be some real heat following that water. It's going to be steamy tomorrow."

"Indeed, indeed," I say. "Father, do you know what time the party ended?"

"The last of the ladies left about twenty minutes ago," he says. "What a wonderful couple the Kershaws will make. Will you be attending the nuptials?"

"Afraid we didn't receive an invitation," I say.

"Nonsense. You'll be a guest of the church," Pastor Schneider says. Lightning flashes and gusts whip the tops of the trees around the pastor's house. He looks to and fro, still not showing much concern.

"If we are still in town, I promise we will be there," I say. "Do you know where the ladies headed following the shower, Father?"

There is a flash and a crack of thunder that makes both of us duck and flinch. "You better come in until this passes, Nick," he says, finally showing some concern.

"Thank you, Father, but I'm really eager to find Lori and get home."

"Mother Nature seems to be objecting to your plans, son," Pastor Schneider says. "Why not let this pass?"

The sky is purple with storm clouds. The winds are steady now and any small object that's not affixed is carried laterally across the yard. Loud thunderclaps immediately follow the lightning strikes. They are just about simultaneous now.

"I have to make sure she's safe," I say. I step off his porch. "Do you know where they headed, Father?"

He smirks and shakes his head. "No but probably to Clinton," he points west, down the highway, "for a cordial before supper."

"Thank you, Father," I say and head to my car.

"Be careful, Nick!" he shouts after me. "Your best intentions are no match for the designs of the higher power."

I know where they headed; it should have been obvious. Pins and Gins, a bar and bowling alley, was a favorite of Lori and her girlfriends. I had figured they would stay at the church, but it makes perfect sense they would head out for some cocktails after the mothers went home.

My wipers slap sheets of rain from the windshield. Torrents are buffeting the car and I cannot see for brief spells even with the wipers on full power. I arrive at Pins and Gins, park, and race into the vestibule. A WELCOME TO P&G neon sign salutes me once inside the first set of doors.

Every lane is occupied on this rainy Saturday night. Every stool at the bar is taken and there are lines for the pool hall and the pizza place next to it. The cacophony of bowling pins, billiard balls, clinking bottles, music, and laughter drowns out the calamity occurring outside.

I make a lap around the horseshoe bar but only vaguely recognize a few patrons. I check the pizza place and the pool hall to no avail. There is zero chance that they are bowling but I scan the lanes anyway.

"Excuse me, I'm looking for a group of girls," I say to the guy spraying shoes behind the counter.

"Ain't we all," he replies. He's wearing a black and red bowling shirt and it fits him tightly. The stitching on the left side of his chest suggests that his name is Rod.

"HA! Yes, well played," I say. "Did you see a large group of girls pass through here? Like, in the past hour?"

"Saw a gaggle of honeys strut through here, yeah," Rod says. "But, I mean, are you here for the party or are you the, um, entertainment?" His expression says he's doubtful that I could be very entertaining to anyone.

"I'm just looking for my wife," I say. "Is there a private party room here?"

He points over my shoulder past the first lane. "Do you see the west exit down there? Walk through the first set of glass doors and turn right. There'll be a set of fire doors; they're open. Go through those and walk to the end of the hall. There's another set of fire doors down there. The party room is through those.

"Thanks."

"Good luck," Rod sprays his can inside a size 12.

I reach the first set of glass doors. The heavy exterior doors guard the patrons from the chaos outside. It's as dark as night at 6 p.m. I turn right, open the fire doors, and walk down the hallway. The sound of shrieking and laughing women pierces through a pulse of hip-hop music.

I crack the next set of doors to see if anyone notices. The women are facing the center of the room, dancing and cheering for some spectacle I can't see. I slip into the room and stand on my toes to see what's going on. I am unnoticed amongst the music and excitement.

I see Lori's cousins and her high school friends. Lori is sitting on a metal folding chair in the middle of the floor. A tan, oily man is rubbing his torso all over her as she palms his buttocks. She has whipped cream on her face and in her hair. Lori's cousin, Joanne, turns to see me and gasps.

The crowd notices me. For some I'm just a benign intruder but the ladies who know me whisper to those who do not. The revelry drops a notch.

I'm locked in a stare with Lori. She begins to laugh. It's a drunken cackle, inappropriate for the circumstances. It makes the scene more awkward.

"I suppose you want me to leave," she says. A speck of whipped cream drops from her face and to her blouse.

Several giggles escape from the group.

I turn and exit through the fire doors. Lori follows. An eruption of laughter swells from behind the doors just after they close. The music is turned backed on.

"My mother was supposed to pick me up," she laughs again. She is drunk.

"Is it better or worse that she didn't?" I scoff. "You said it was a wedding shower."

"Guess what, Nick? There was a bachelorette party, too!" she cackles.

We negotiate the puddles in the gravel parking lot. The initial deluge of the front has passed but there is still a steady, heavy rain. We make it inside the car, but I do not start the engine. I savor our shelter for a moment and try to stay calm.

"Do you want to clean yourself up?" I hand her some napkins that I nicked from the last fast-food place we had visited.

Lori snatches the napkins from my hand and slaps the sun visor down to see the vanity. She dabs at the whipped cream on her face. Most was washed away by the rain but there is some residue around her nose. She tries to do the same for the stains on her blouse. She doesn't notice the cream that is caked in her hair.

"Way to ruin a great party, ding dong," she says.

"How was I supposed to know there was a bachelorette party?" I say. I start the engine, put the car in gear and pull the car onto the road.

"You're so stupid. You think you're so smart but you're so stupid," she stammers. "And fat, too. You're fat." She pokes me.

"I won't let you provoke me. You're just drunk," I say. The sky has turned from purple to green.

"You'll still be fat when I get sober," she cackles again. "Did you see Danny Boy back there? He'll still be firm. You could bounce quarters off that ass."

"Please, stop," I plead. The rain eases and a pitter-patter noise begins. There are tiny pebbles of hail skipping off the road and the car in an excited dance.

"All the other girls got to stay and have a good time, but I have to go home with my chubby hubby, Nick. I'm married to Nick," she explains to no one. "He's the chubby English teacher from Effingham. The effing hick from Effingham."

"Who are you calling a hick?" I lose my cool for a moment. "Did you see that crowd back there? Your aunt looks like she has a mouth full of dominos. Growing up north of Decatur doesn't make you urbane, honey."

The hail is larger now. Dime- and quarter-sized balls pelt the skin of the car. I'm sure it's damaged.

"You're a hick, and you're fat, and you're a buzzkill," she says, counting the insults off on her fingers.

"I need to concentrate right now."

Thump. Thump. Thump. Larger balls of hail assault the car.

"And you've got a tiny wiener," she counts off a fourth and cackles.

"Shut the fuck up!" I scream.

"HA! You're provoked," she cackles.

A large hail ball smashes against the windshield. It leaves a spiderweb crack in the glass.

Lori laughs again. "Did you see how provoked I had Danny Boy back there?"

I put my palm on the left side of her head and push. Thump. The right side of her head smashes into the passenger window. There is a smear of whipped cream on the window.

Lori haunches forward and rests her head in her hands. She is silent for a moment and then I hear her breath deep sobs as her back heaves. I pull the car over and put it in park. The hail stops.

I want to say that I am sorry, but I know it will sound empty. It was no accident.

Lori lifts her face from her palms. She is not sobbing. She is laughing. "You're such an ass, Nick," she says. "You're all upset about this little stripper, but I cheat on you every chance I get."

She cackles again and then starts naming names.

"Carl at school," she says.

I put the car into gear.

"Tony at the Lucky Strike," she says.

I pull the car onto the highway and accelerate.

"Craig nailed me on his boat," she cackles.

I align the spiderweb crack in the middle of the windshield with the next light pole. I floor the pedal. Thump.

Interlude 7: Darkness

I am on my knees, wailing. I lean forward and slam my fists against the ground with all my might.

"That was worse!" I scream. "That was so much worse."

A random man springs from the crowd, grabs my hand and pulls me to my feet. The story of me murdering my wife courses through him like a current of electricity. His eyes open wide. He tries to release his grip, but he can't let go. The story culminates and he tears his hand away from me. He cowers and looks at me with revulsion.

"I'm sorry. Something told me to fight for her, like Piper!" I scream and cry. I fall to my knees again. I curl up fetal. I just re-lived the worst moment of my life twice in rapid succession and I am devastated.

The man shakes his head at me. I reach out to him and again he shakes his head no.

"You can't say no." I scream and spittle shoots from my mouth. Snot runs down my nose. "I'm sorry. I thought I was sup-posed to do better! Please show me how to do better."

He continues to deny me and walks back into the crowd.

I was lucid long enough after the crash to register the con-tents of Lori's split skull dripping onto the airbag draped across her. Her body was torn at the waist.

Another car had stopped when the driver saw our crash. A man and his wife were the first witnesses of the aftermath. "Don't come over here, Jane. Just stay over there."

"Are they OK?" Jane asked.

"No," he said.

"Oh, dear Jesus, please help them," Jane said.

I'm sure my neck was broken. My head rested at an unnatural angle and I was facing Lori. I could do nothing to escape the image of her broken, beautiful face. A crimson ooze stained the right side of her face. Her left eye protruded from the socket.

"He's alive," the medic shouted.

"Don't move him," another voice said.

"Please move me!" I tried to shout, but I could not summon my vocal cords.

The sound of machinery chewing through the steel of the car became the soundtrack to the nightmare. The drips from the meridional crack in Lori's skull had slowed and her pool of blood had darkened before they were able to extract me. They removed me from the car just in time to give Emil and Carol a full view of what I had done to their daughter. They had arrived at the scene almost as quickly as the medics. It was a small town, after all. I heard Carol shriek and wail, but nothing from Emil.

"Pick him up," I heard someone say.

"Did he hit his head on the road?" asked another.

Emil must have fainted.

"Are those her parents?" an authoritative voice asked.

"Oh my God, they can't see this," another voice said.

I was in the ambulance now. My life faded. There was a flurry of commotion as the paramedics fought to maintain some green numbers on a black screen. Eventually they either ran out of training or out of options.

"This is hopeless," one man said.

"I know," his partner said. "I wouldn't want to imagine what would be in store for him after this anyway."

I died. Again.

My purgatorial plain is now darkness. My virgin glow is gone. The folks who surrounded me earlier dispersed when they saw the revulsion on the face of the man who first helped me up after

I murdered Lori. Now strangers pounce on me in the darkness and rip my stories from me like rapists.

I had no recollection of my first death during my second-chance run with Lori, but here in limbo I am aware of every excruciating detail of falling into that canyon at Glenwood Springs. Sometimes when the rapists reach out from the darkness, I relive the last moments of my first passing. I once again feel the pain of the jagged rocks pulverizing my body as I skip along the canyon wall into the rapids below. And yet, telling that story is a relief compared to having to tell the story of my second passing.

I do my best to walk alone and contemplate the lessons I should have learned from Andres, George Cole, and Piper. Maybe I should be more practical, like Andres, or take the coward's route, like Cole. Should I embrace my sad situation, like Piper?

I see a light on the plain and run to it. If I can see the other people maybe I can avoid them. The silhouette of a small Western town emerges from the darkness. Candlelit windows and gas lamps on street corners outline the town.

I hear the bright jingle of an out-of-tune piano. There are saloons on both sides of the street. Loose women hang over the railings of an inn. There are crowds teeming inside and outside of each place. I am scared and paranoid and people can tell. I give passing strangers a wide berth. I need to find a safe place to hide.

All the other storefronts and offices along the main street are closed. The general store is dark. The barber's pole is still. The only open establishment other than the bars is the jail. I walk to the jail.

"I'm here to turn myself in," I say to the man at the desk. The tin star on his vest reads DEPUTY.

"What's your name?" he asks.

"My name is Nick Kraus." I peruse the wanted posters pinned to the wall behind him.

"Do you have any aliases?" he asks.

"Sometimes people call me Nicholas," I say. "Don't you want to know what I did?"

"OK, Nick *Nicholas* Kraus, what did you do?"

"I murdered someone."

"Fascinating. Anybody I know?"

"My wife," I say. "So yeah, maybe."

The jailer sits silently.

"Aren't you going to do something?" I ask.

"Listen, partner, I don't know who you think I am, but I know why you're here." He has his elbow on his desk. He rests his head in his palm. He smirks and then points. "Just go ahead and find yourself a spot in there."

I look to where he's pointing and see a jail cell with its gate wide open. The cell is dark, but I see three occupants as I draw closer. Two are sitting against the right wall at arm's length apart and the other is sitting across from them. I take a seat between the lone man and the pair.

I look at the two people to my left and they immediately begin to cower. They are as concerned about not touching each other as they are about my intentions, so they look back and forth between each other and me. Satisfied, they fix their stares on the man sitting across from them.

"They don't like to have any fun at all," the man to my right says. His body begins to bounce a little as he emits a low laugh.

"Me neither," I say as sternly as possible.

"What you in for?" he asks. He slides closer. I slide to my left and the pair to my left slide even farther. One of them is against the bars by now.

"Murder," I respond.

"That's it?" he laughs.

"It was someone I loved," I say. "So, imagine what I would do to you."

A threat more idle has never been cast. I am intent to exist forever without touching anyone else ever again.

"My name is Charlie." He leans forward and extends a hand. The man against the bars whimpers.

"My name is fuck OFF," I say as I point at his face.

"I love what you've done with the place," he says. "I loved Westerns when I was a kid. I bet you were a big Ponderosa fan too, huh? How about the Lone Ranger?"

I cannot grasp how he can see my details. "How are you in my world?"

"That's my reward," Charlie says.

"Reward for what?" I ask.

"For a life well lived," he says.

In a flash, he is beside me.

"Let me show you." He places his hand on my wrist and I'm gone.

Story 8: Charlie

Charlie Musgrave was a degenerate with an addiction to whores. Charlie had a fixer arrange for him to be serviced daily. While Charlie was a steady earner, a habit like his was not sustainable unless certain sacrifices were made.

"Just how fat are we talking here, Sergei? I mean, is she just sturdy or are we talking celestial?"

Most pros appreciated the chance to establish a steady client base, but no one wanted to take on Charlie more than once unless they were in dire straits. Even Sergei was sympathetic because he knew Charlie would ruin them for the night or even drive them out of the profession for good. Charlie wasn't physically abusive or sexually aggressive; it's what he said that destroyed the girls.

"Holy shit, look at you. Does your zookeeper know you're gone?" Charlie said to the girl. She had not yet closed the car door behind her. As she eased into his passenger seat, her eyes widened. She slowly reached back to close the door. Her lips tightened as she realized that he was the one she had been told about. The girls had cut her loose. Maybe they thought of it as her initiation, maybe they were just relieved that it wasn't going to have to be one of them that night.

"Are those tights or sausage casing? I might have to call Sergei. I think I'd rather slam my dick in a car door than bang you." He started his Cadillac and put it in reverse. The young pro had not yet said a word.

It was a short drive to the industrial park of Montclair. Charlie parked in a dark lot behind one of the abandoned factories, the sex industry being the only heavy industry taking place these days. Charlie gestured for her to get in back with a point of his thumb over his shoulder.

"I can tell already it was Daddy that fucked you up. It was Mama that got you fat with all her good cooking and disappointment, but Daddy was mean." He grabbed her by the hips and wheeled her backside toward his naked groin.

She tried to stay stern, but she caught a glimpse of herself in the window and winced at the reflection of what her life had become.

"Daddy knew you were a burden he was never unloading unless he beat you out of the house." He dropped her tights to her knees and began.

She had endured years of ugly insults in high school, but she didn't expect this. This was too personal.

"I bet he tried to pass you around to his friends. He was a pig, just like you," Charlie said as he thrusted.

The fissure in her armor gaped open and she went numb. She went as still as a doe on a forest floor.

"Don't think Mama didn't notice either. She knew, she just didn't care. I know I wouldn't. You turned out to be exactly the whore Daddy always said you were." He whined and wheezed as he thrusted for a minute. He put his hands behind his head, arched his back and with a final thrust he exhaled and finished. "Jesus Christ, that was like throwing a hot dog down a hallway. You must have been some kind of pig in junior high."

He zipped up and assessed the mess left on the leather seat. "Look at this shit. How the hell did this happen? Did you spring a fat leak, you fucking hog?" He dabbed the mess with his pinky and brought it near his nose. He recoiled. "That's piss! Son of a bitch that's piss!"

The young pro stared at him with bloodshot eyes.

"What are you looking at, you fucking pig?!" Charlie screamed and pointed at the mess. "You better clean this up and you better pray it doesn't stain my leather. I paid for the premium upholstery."

Having nothing else to use, she grabbed her tights and soaked up the mess. Charlie was now in the front seat and had begun driving to the bus stop. "Mop that shit up and don't you dare sit back on those seats. Kneel on the fucking floor."

He stopped at the bus stop and opened the rear driver-side door. The young pro crawled out with her tights in her hand. She stood on the pavement, shoeless and naked from the waist down. Charlie reached into the backseat to retrieve her shoes. He threw them at her feet and dropped a $20 dollar bill on the ground. He got back in his car and left.

The young pro began running down the sidewalk in the direction of an approaching bus. The driver was at full steam coming out of the prior stop when the young pro leapt toward his windshield. She never said a word. She never touched the money.

***

"You're not supposed to be here, Charlie," Officer McMichael barked at Charlie Musgrave.

"Five hundred and ten feet; I measured it out. I even left three yards to spare," Charlie said without looking up from his newspaper.

Charlie had parked his white, windowless panel van down the block from Kiwanis Park. The park ran two city blocks and it had two ball fields, a band shell, a walking path, and a playground.

"Why can't you read the paper down there on Broadway?" McMichael pointed.

"Too close to the high school. You guys won't let me near that place either, remember?" Charlie turned to the gossip page.

"It's not us, Charlie. It's the judge, remember?" he said. "That's not why I'm here anyway. Did you meet a girl named Tanya White the other night?"

"Who?"

"Tanya White?"

"What did she look like?"

"Young black girl. Pretty smile. Sturdy frame."

Charlie folded the newspaper down across his chest and pondered. "Noooo, sorry," he shrugged and brought the paper back up.

"You're sure now? Sergei said he left her with you."

"Who's Sergei? Her dad or something?" Charlie asked from behind the paper.

"OK, OK." McMichael backed off. He looked down and twisted the ball of his foot on the pavement in frustration. "You know I'm going to nail you, you friggin pederast."

"If I had a dime . . ." Charlie answered.

"What's in that bag there, by the way?"

"Wine coolers. They're all sealed and in the bag."

"Wine coolers?" McMichael raised his voice. "Give me that shit."

Charlie dropped his paper. "You can't seize my property."

"Give me the Goddamn coolers, Charlie," McMichael menaced.

"Pick your battles, Charlie, pick your battles," Charlie muttered to himself. He handed the brown bag through the window to McMichael. "They're getting warm. You may want to get them on ice before cracking them open."

McMichael checked the bag. Satisfied, he folded over the top and tucked the package under his arm. "You're mine, Charlie.

It's only a matter of time." He turned and walked to his squad car.

"Have fun tonight, Mick. Go out and get silly with the captain. Paint the town beige," Charlie yammered after him.

***

Charlie approached the counter. "You make me want to vomit," the clerk told him.

"And good morning to you too, Barbara," Charlie replied. "Has my literature arrived?"

Barbara looked around to ensure no other patrons were around and then produced a stack of magazines wrapped in brown paper and tied with a string.

"What the hell is wrong with you? Who needs this much smut?" she sneered as she stabbed her fingernail on the top.

"I'm a collector," Charlie said as he placed condoms, lubricant, and wine coolers on the counter. "Gimme a pack of those sweet little cigars, too?"

"When you're dead, your body won't be worth the hole they'll throw it in," Barbara said. She placed the items in a bag and handed it to him.

"Yeah, well how about the quarry they'll need for you?" Charlie returned. "You got some chutzpah to lecture me about portion control."

"That's $42.40," Barbara said.

"Here you are, darling." Charlie handed her his money.

"Read a book," she said as she handed him his change.

"Eat a salad," Charlie said as we walked away.

Charlie Musgrave opened his pack of cigarillos and lit one. He walked down Grand avenue to the public library. The smoke was only half finished when he arrived, so he extinguished it on the rim of the cement planter out front and put it back in the pack.

Charlie entered and asked the desk clerk for the key to Room D. He took the key and proceeded to the basement of the building. He placed the package on the table and drew the white string until the knot was released. The brown paper unfurled and revealed the cover of the latest issue of Barely Legal magazine. He admired the cover for a moment and then turned the issue to the centerfold. Charlie opened the spread and removed a yellow sticky note. The note read APPOINTMENT: NO MAN'S LAND. 8/3 AT 7PM.

He placed the note on the surface of the table and returned his attention to the centerfold. He took the other items from the bag and placed them on the table.

***

No Man's Land was a windowless tavern on Harlem Avenue and its clientele was anything but what its name would suggest. Charlie cast his eye around the bar. No patron looked his way. The bartender did not look up from the sink of glasses he was working on.

"Over here, Charlie," a low voice said from over his shoulder. Nestled in a corner booth adjacent to the door was a man with a martini glass in front of him. He plucked the toothpick piercing the olive and popped the fruit in his mouth.

"Nice choice," Charlie said.

"It's discrete," the man said. "Do you want a drink?"

"No, I'm good. What's the gig? What's the bid?" Charlie was impatient. He was uncomfortable.

"Button job. Twenty thousand."

"Twenty K? Whoa." Charlie was careful not to get too excited. He leaned closer to his contact. "Who is it? Someone's wife?"

"Jerry Sewell," the man said quickly and quietly.

"Jerry? Why?" Charlie sat back against the cushion of the seat. He was again mindful of getting excited. He leaned forward again. "He got out of that. The prosecutor refused to prosecute."

"That's just it. Prosecutors prosecute; that's what they do. They're not trying to reach an understanding, they're not seeking justice. They want to put your ass in a cage." The man stopped and sipped his martini. "They sure don't just let you go without a deal for someone else's ass."

Charlie took a deep breath. He scratched his cheek and stared at the slurry of alcohol and blue cheese awash on the rim of the man's glass.

"Take a look at this." The man slid an envelope Charlie's way.

Charlie placed his hand on the envelope. He could tell it contained two stacks of hundreds in $10,000 bundles from the way it filled his palm.

"All up front?" Charlie asked.

"We trust you."

"I've known him a long time."

"We know." The man nodded and rose. "I'm going to hit the head. If you're gone when I get back, I'll assume we have an agreement." He began to walk away.

"Hey," Charlie said.

"Yes." The man turned.

"Make sure you're holding your own dick while you're in there," Charlie said. He tucked the envelope inside of his waistband, pulled his shirt over the bulge and walked out of the bar.

***

"You're calm," Jerry said to Charlie as they walked the parking lot outside of the private club.

"Why shouldn't I be calm?" Charlie asked.

"You just won at least $5,000 dollars at the table by my count," Jerry scoffed. "That sure would have my needle in the red."

"You want to get something to eat? It's on me," Charlie offered. They arrived at the Cadillac and got in.

"Around here?" Jerry asked. He rolled down his window and lit a smoke.

"What's wrong with around here?"

"Trenton at one in the morning?"

"What do you have against Trenton? Their eggs don't fry? Their bacon don't sizzle?" Charlie asked.

"It's a depressing hellscape. An industrial dystopia filled with hoodlums and surrounded by feeble-minded trash," Jerry said.

"My mother's from Morristown, you know," Charlie said.

"Mine too," Jerry said. They both laughed at their silliness. There are no bigger critics of Jersey than people from Jersey.

"I'm hungry. Let's go to Snuffy's," Charlie said.

"Snuffy's closed down, man," Jerry said with a shake of his head.

"Get the hell out of here."

"In June."

"I'll believe it when I see it," Charlie said.

"Suit yourself." Jerry ashed his smoke with a flick of his finger. "Steak and Egger is still open, though."

"Let's just see about Snuffy's real fast," Charlie said.

"Bet you a C-note they're closed."

"Bet." Charlie extended his hand and they shook.

Jerry laughed. "Man, you sure are calm tonight."

The drive to Snuffy's took them through a campus of factories. Stacks belched toxins. The air was acrid. There were no homes or businesses surrounding the plants other than Snuffy's. They could see from blocks away that the sign was not lit, and the windows were dark.

"What are you doing?" Jerry asked.

"I want to check it out," Charlie answered.

"Dude, they're fucking closed." Jerry pointed forward with two open palms. "Pay up and let's go get some grub."

"I want to have a look," Charlie said. He got out and walked to a window. He peered in to see stools lining the long countertop of the diner. Their vinyl upholstery reflected the streetlight. The flat-top grill was left clean, as were all the booths. It looked like they could fire back up at any moment if they wanted to.

Jerry leaned over next to Charlie and peered in as well. "Am I supposed to be feeling nostalgic for a greasy spoon diner?"

"We started coming here as soon as you got your license." Charlie had his forehead against the glass.

"Because no one ever looked for us here when we skipped school." Jerry laughed and leaned his head on the glass as well.

"No one around who gave a shit." Charlie reached down and grabbed something inside his boot.

Jerry kept his head on the glass. "Now I get it."

"Get what?" Charlie took a step back.

"Why you're so calm." Jerry stared inside the diner.

"How's that?" Charlie cocked his pistol.

Jerry pulled back and stared down the barrel of Charlie's gun. "You're calm like a hitman."

"Sorry, Jerry."

Charlie shot his childhood friend in the forehead. Jerry collapsed to the ground. Charlie placed two more shots in his chest, wiped the gun and dropped it in the dusty gravel of the parking lot.

Charlie pulled out of the lot and found his way to the highway and made a call.

"Anton, it's Chuck. I'm looking for a date."

Interlude 8: Infinite Loop

Charlie's story ends and then he pulls one from me, then another of his begins, then another of mine. I am trapped in a Möbius strip of misery.

The man is guilty of rape, murder, and every manner of social indiscretion. My only breaks from the Charlie Musgrave medley of human misery are the stories he pulls from me. He takes all he wants: my deaths and my murder of Lori, every embarrassment I endured, every beating taken from a bully, every shortcoming of character, every sexual encounter. He is obsessed with my sexual experiences. He is not looking for lessons. He is a voyeur.

My eyes are open. My mouth is open. I try to speak but I am locked in Charlie's clutches. It's like holding a live electric wire. I feel it is killing me, but I cannot let go. The current running through me, destroying me, is the vile, poisonous content of the life of an irredeemable, unapologetic, misogynistic pervert. I am distraught with suffering. Charlie reads my face and laughs. He cackles, mimicking the cackles Lori made before I drove us into that pole. Finally, I produce a sound. It is a scream of anguish. Charlie laughs harder. A vision of teenaged Charlie molesting his young cousin tears through my mind.

I feel two hands grab my shoulders and I am thrown from the cell onto the floor outside. I look up and KO is eye to eye with Charlie.

"That's not your job, KO," Charlie tells him.

"Careful, Charlie. I can take you for a ride, too." KO smiles.

"Why is he here!?" I point and scream. "Is there no hell?"

One of the men cowering in the cell sticks his face between the bars and seethes. "Is this not hell to you?"

"Do you know how diamonds are made, Nick?" Charlie asks.

KO lifts me up. "Come on. You're due back home."

I look back at Charlie as he tells me, "Pressure and time, pressure and time," he says and then adds with a shout, "and heat!"

We exit past the jailer, who salutes us with a wave and nod but nary a word. We mount KO's steed.

"That man is a demon," I say as we ride. It is dawn on the western plain.

"Charlie is no more a demon than I am an angel," KO says.

"Why is he here?"

"He is here for the same reason that I am here. Because no man is supposed to stay here."

"I'm gutted, KO. Please," I beg for a clear explanation. I try my hardest to avoid contact with KO even as we ride astride the same horse. I am afraid of human touch. "No one told me there would be men like him here."

"No one told you, eh? Did you skip orientation?" KO laughs.

I hide my face and begin to cry.

"Charlie is a motivator, Nick," KO explains. "His purpose is to make sure no one gets too comfortable around here."

The creaking crank of a water pump whines from a distant ranch. It seems like dawn and the ridge line of the distant mountains peeks through a pink, purple and blue haze. The vista looks like a Monet painting.

"Why were those other men in there with him?" I ask.

"He probably had them trapped. He was getting off on torturing them when you moseyed on through the door," KO says.

"Why don't they leave? The door wasn't locked."

"Those fellas are the nearly damned," KO says. "They are tortured by the memories of their lives, but they are too scared to return to try to live them better. They are thus condemned to a life with Charlie."

"So they are hiding in jail?" I say.

KO smiles. "Your jail actually."

"Charlie's job is too suss out cowards," I realize aloud.

"That's right," KO says. "And he sees the world as they see it, so he can find where they hide. Whether it's a jail, a long fence, or a jetty."

"What about Piper, how does he get away with hanging around?" I ask.

"Piper knows how to get out of a jam," he answers.

"Oh, yeah."

We gallop to a train depot. The whistle on the steam engine blows twice and the train pulls out of the station. KO pulls the horse parallel to the tracks and jabs his spurs into the belly of animal. We accelerate to match the speed of the train. A door opens on a car and an arm reaches out to help pull me from the horse.

"Thank you, KO!" I shout.

"I hope I don't see you again," he says.

"Me, too."

The steward pulls me into the train car, all the way back to Illinois.

Story 9: Back Home

The trip to visit Lori's parents was a success. She needed the time with her mother and to blow off some steam with her friends. It was the Sunday following the Kershaw's wedding and we were recovering from the festivities when Carol and Emil returned from church.

"You could've used a dose of service today, young lady," Mrs. Muell tells her daughter. I am sitting across the kitchen table from Lori. The morning cocktail of choice is hot coffee with an iced tea chaser.

The Muells head upstairs to change out of their Sunday finery. The real lecture begins when Carol returns to the kitchen to begin fixing lunch.

"I didn't raise you to talk like that, to be disrespectful like that," Carol says. She places her cooking apron over her head. Emil takes his seat in the parlor and turns on a Sunday national news program.

Lori looks to me for help. I'm guessing she does not remember her antics at the reception. All she wanted to do was dance, between drinks of course.

"When the husband takes leave of the floor, so does his wife," Lori's mother continues. "It wasn't a debutante's ball."

"Mother . . ." Lori gestures toward me.

"I'll leave you two alone." I grab my mug and begin to rise.

"No, please stay, Nick." Carol signals for me to sit with a slow, downward push of her open palm.

"Mother," Lori repeats with an angry tone. She holds the mug in both hands and bangs it against the table like a child about to have a tantrum.

"And how dare you talk to your husband like that," Carol says as she points to me, "in public, no less." She grows louder. "In front of friends, in front of family!"

Lori bolts from the table and heads upstairs. Carol slowly undoes the knot on her apron and pulls it over her head. She places the apron on its hook on the wall. "Excuse me, Nicholas," she says and walks with slow, heavy strides toward the staircase.

This is perfect. It could not to be more perfect. I sit at the kitchen table and enjoy my coffee and tea.

The Muell's home is a Midwestern farmhouse built in the 19th century. Conversations are audible to everyone in the house, regardless of the walls and floors between us. Mrs. Muell lectures Lori until she is satisfied. Her daughter is crying in a heap, I imagine, so Mrs. Muell begins assuring her daughter with sweet, soothing platitudes.

"All marriages have rainy seasons, darling," Carol tells her.

Lori groans in response.

"He's a patient, devoted man," her mother says.

"He's not perfect," Lori replies.

"None of us is," Carol says and then jokes. "But of course, some of us get closer than others."

The ladies laugh and it breaks through the morass of the prior tension.

"Lori Lynn, you have to promise me something."

"What's that, Momma?"

"You are going to cool it with the drinking when you get back to the city," she tells her. "And you're going to find yourself a parish to join."

"We found a parish."

We had found a parish. Indeed, we passed several charming churches on the way to brunch every Sunday.

"Do you attend?" Carol asks.

"We've gone," Lori lies.

"I want you to go back and to talk to the pastor. I want you to pray together for fortitude and grace," she says. "The fortitude will help you find the discipline to quit drinking. The grace will help curb this behavior with Nick."

A breeze blows through the kitchen from the back porch. I push my mug of coffee away and grab the tea. It's a beautiful morning.

"Nick and I plan to talk to someone once we get back to the city," Lori says.

"Good. And the drinking?" she asks, with greater concern. "I'm sorry, darling, but I can't stand the thought of seeing you again like I did last night. Or what I saw when I picked you up from the shower."

Now I'm curious about what happened at the shower but also relieved I didn't pick her up myself.

"I'll go see someone about that, too." Lori is now soothing her mother. "Maybe we'll get a discount."

The girls share another laugh.

Carol sees an opening and slips in another query. "Lori, was it true what you told that girl last night about Keith Kershaw?"

"What do you mean?"

"Katie's cousin, the girl you were yelling at after the party," Carol says.

"The snobby girl from Indy?" Lori dismisses her. "I just wanted to provoke her."

"OK, well I don't really understand that, but did you really . . ." Carol pauses. She continues in a lower voice. but I still make out what she says. "Did you really have relations with Keith Kershaw?"

That is a detail that escaped me last night.

"Oh that." Lori laughs. "No, no, no. He was sweet on me in high school, but I never let anything happen, mom."

"OK good. That's what I'll say, should it come up." Carol sounds relieved.

***

"That guy's a pussy. He does yoga," Eddie tries to assure me over beers.

"He does judo," I correct him. We are seated at a corner bar on Southport.

"Same thing," he replies.

"No. No, it's not the same thing. Not at all," I correct him again and take a swig from my pint. Eddie is a hometown friend of Lori's. He found a job in the city after college and lives nearby. Also, Eddie is a dipshit.

"Why are you obsessing over guys she knew in high school? You never had a girlfriend before Lori?" Eddie asks. He wears a button-down softball jersey. It's unbuttoned and underneath he is wearing a yellowed t-shirt with a beer logo on the front.

"Sure, but I thought I knew all about her past, you know?" I say. "And lately I've been experiencing all these little revelations. There are all these little doubts adding up. I don't know what to feel certain about anymore."

Eddie has stopped paying attention. He is watching the ballgame on the set behind the bar. He's a Cardinal fan in a Cubbie bar. He reacts when something bad happens for Chicago no matter who they're playing.

"How was Oregon?" Eddie asks.

"I told you, we turned back in Colorado. Car trouble."

"Sorry, sorry, that's right, the Kershaw wedding."

"Why didn't you get invited?" I ask.

"I got invited." He feigns offense. "But I ain't burning a gorgeous Chicago weekend for a downstate wedding. Summer is too short around here, man."

"Like, everyone from your school was there. Why didn't we get an invitation in the mail?" I ponder aloud.

"Maybe she did bang him. That would definitely explain it."

Lori arrives. Eddie does not surrender his seat so she can sit next to me, so she takes the stool to his left.

"Hey, Tony, can you make me a Bloody Mary? Spicy, but not too spicy," Lori hangs her bag on the hook under the bar ledge.

"I know how you like 'em," Tony assures her in a manner that's a little too familiar for my liking.

"How did it go, honey?" I ask. Tony looks up from his duties. He looks back and forth between Lori and me and makes the connection.

"I got the room in order. The lesson plan is still blank though," she says.

"I don't know how you guys do it," Eddie says without looking away from the game. "I'd be out back pitching quarters with the hoodlums."

We had to report to our classrooms today to prepare for the coming school year. Kids were going to start next week, and teachers used this week to prepare the room and develop lesson plans.

"Was Carl cool with you coming in late?" I ask. Carl is the principal at Lori's school.

"I stayed late and made sure he was satisfied." Lori wraps her lips around the end of the straw and slurps a hearty portion of the cocktail down.

Lori was out late the night before. She wanted one last hurrah before the school year kicked off. Craig down the hall had organized a booze cruise out of Belmont Harbor and had invited us. I declined in order to get ready for today, but Lori jumped at the chance.

Eddie stood up and slapped some bills on the bar. "You guys heading out tonight?"

"Sure, why not?" Lori says. "One last hurrah."

"Did you forget where we're going tonight?" I ask her.

"I've got to jet to a game, but we'll be done by 8:30," Eddie says.

"We'll probably just catch up with you on Saturday," I say.

"Lor?" Eddie looks past me like a jerk.

Lori looks at her watch. She glances at me and frowns. "Probably not, Eddie."

"Well, the team is heading up to the Schoolyard Tap afterwards. You can meet us there if you change your mind," he says to Lori. He looks at me and waves. "See you, Nick."

***

We nod earnestly for an hour as Father Killion lays out his guidelines for a successful, fruitful marriage. For a man who has chosen a life of celibacy he is very focused on our intentions to reproduce.

"So, you are saying that it is children that resolve the friction between a man and his wife?" I ask.

"That's correct, Nick. Children fill the void that is left once the whirlwind of young love stills," says this man who may have never known the touch of a woman.

Lori and I nod. She squeezes my hand. We know that we will get great amusement from mocking this man later.

Father Killion delivers his lecture. He does not seek much input from us. He is not here to listen. He lays out a framework of processes and duties regarding procreation with a specificity that an engineer would appreciate. He takes to writing the key points on a tablet and his work culminates in a six-part flowchart.

Father Killion finishes his drawing, tears out the sheet of paper and hands it to us. Then he reaches into his folder and hands us a pamphlet. "Pastor Schneider told me to cover this as well."

TEN STEPS TO SOBRIETY the pamphlet reads across the top.
1. Stop drinking
2. Talk to your pastor
3. Apologize
4. Yearn for grace
5. Idolize your sober self6. Never indulge
7. Get help when you need it
8. Drive out temptation
9. Rid yourself of bad influences
10. Yearn for grace

"Yearn for grace is on here twice," I observe.

"Grace is important," the priest says. He reviews the pamphlet as though it's the first time he has read it. "It completes the acronym as well."

"Oh, yeah," Lori says. She traces her finger down my page. "Staying Dry. See it?"

I nod my head. "Yes, yes, very clever."

"Start with these. Meet me after 10 a.m. mass on Sunday and let me know how it's going." Father Killion stands to show us out.

I remain sitting. I am fixated on the content of the pamphlet. "Aren't there supposed to be twelve of these?"

"I think there's a copyright on those," Lori says.

"Nicholas, if you long for more than what you find here you are welcome to improve the content, as long as it leads to your personal improvement," the priest says and begins to head to the door.

Lori and I are standing out front of the church. We are laughing about the sober, sexless man whose duty it is to guide us towards a happy, child-filled, liquor-less marriage.

"Want to have a drink?" Lori asks.

"Doesn't seem right," I say.

"Want to make a baby?" she offers.

"Now you're talking."

"See, it's working already."

***

We met Eddie at the Lucky Strike the next Thursday and the next Thursday after that. So began the Thursday ritual of cocktails and counseling. We would throw back a few and then Eddie would leave for his softball game and we would head to church.

"You been going to mass, too?" Eddie asks.

Lori and I laugh sheepishly.

"Well, technically he said to meet him after mass to check in. So . . ." Lori said.

"We went the first week," I interject.

"What was that like? Big crowd?" Eddie asks.

"Mostly Mexicans," Lori says.

"Wait. What? I didn't see that," I say with surprise.

"That's what I figured," Eddie says.

"It was like a swap meet in there," Lori says with a laugh.

"Where is this coming from?" I say to Lori. There were Hispanic folks, but it's not as though they were overwhelming the place. Mass was in English.

"Mexicans are infiltrating this city, Nick. The numbers tell the whole story," he says.

Although Eddie was a dipshit, he was good at math. In fact, I considered him more so a dipshit because he would boil every debate down to numbers.

"Math don't lie," he would say. "Numbers are the only facts."

Eddie made a handsome living as a statistician working for a legal consulting firm. They were called upon to lend mathematical rigor to whatever case the lawyers needed help proving.

"The growth rate of the Mexican population in the three zip codes from Lakeview to Logan Square has been greater than that of any other group over the past ten years," Eddie began to pontificate. "And the growth rate of that growth rate has been positive too, so we're talking a convex, non-linear trend."

"OK, first of all, I know where you two are from. I've seen more diversity in a gallon of milk," I say. "You see one family move into town down there and it's a crisis."

"Bullshit," Lori says. "There are herds of brown folks in town every fall."

"Nice, Lori, nice," I say and shake my head. "And they're gone as soon as the crops are handled."

"It's a matter of protecting your way of life," Eddie says. "Take the case we're working on now. We are showing that zip codes with a higher percentage of immigrants have higher default rates."

"Mexican immigrants are getting mortgages around here?" I ask.

"Well, no, but there is a correlation between their presence and the payment habits of the local homeowners," he explains. "The mere presence of Mexicans is making people default."

I put my face in my palm. "Please tell me about this case you're working on."

"I can't go into detail of course, but there is a bank getting sued by a certain group of citizens who claim they are the victims of discriminatory lending," he says.

"So, you're going to show that the default rates in the areas where these people live are too high? That they don't deserve credit. Right?" I say.

"That's right," Eddie squeaked, delighted that I seemed to understand.

"Makes sense to me," Lori says and sips her Screwdriver.

"Meanwhile, the people actually defaulting are not the Mexicans, right?" I ask.

"No, but like I said, the numbers show that there is a high correlation between the Mexicans being there and those people defaulting." Eddie leans forward and points at me. "The Mexicans are teaching these people to have bad credit."

"That's awful," Lori says and shakes her head.

I have a blossoming realization that I am married to a racist but at the moment Eddie's perversion of logic is what disturbs me most.

"You're a professional distortionist." I turn away toward the bar and drink my beer.

"They're changing our way of life. Can't you see it?" Eddie pleads.

"I can," Lori says.

I turn around and rest my back on the edge of the bar. "You're right. In fact, I saw it for myself just this past Saturday. I went for an afternoon run on the lakefront. I made it all the way up to Montrose Park."

"Oh my God. That place is crawling with them." Lori shakes her head.

"Like a caravan of gypsies," Eddie says. "You're lucky it was daytime."

"Yes, it was startling," I continue to mock them. "I saw this whole family. Three whole generations playing on the lawn. They were grilling and listening to a baseball game on the radio. A real alien culture. This wasn't an isolated case either. There were another ten families scattered around, at least."

"I bet that was a cover. Probably a big heroin operation you stumbled on right there," Eddie says. "Are you aware of the correlation between heroin use and the increase in Mexicans over the past ten years?"

Lori looks at Eddie as though he's made some profound revelation.

"Let me guess, the Mexicans are getting the locals hooked on heroin, causing them to default. Then they head to the bank to get a loan to buy their places," I surmise.

"Now you're seeing things clearly," he says and smiles.

"Holy shit, they are taking over." Lori looks aghast.

I look at Eddie. "You're a fucking moron." I turn to Lori. "And you're a bigger fucking moron for buying into this crap."

"Don't call me a moron." Lori leans forward and points. "You're a stupid, liberal pussy with a degree in English. Eddie knows the math."

I hold my tongue.

"Did you get your permit for concealed and carry yet?" Eddie asks Lori.

"Concealed and carry what?" Lori asks.

"Handgun," Eddie says and pats his gym bag.

"Handguns are illegal in the city of Chicago," I say.

Eddie laughs. "Tell that to the gangbangers slanging H." He turns to Lori. "How often are you on the Red Line?"

"Every day." Lori sits up straight and looks alarmed.

"And you go south of Roosevelt, right?" Eddie says.

"Every day." Lori raises both hands and leans toward Eddie.

"Well, you're just being reckless if you're not carrying a weapon—in my opinion. It's the responsible thing to do, for you and those around you," Eddie says.

"Oh my God, you're right," Lori says.

"For Christ's sake, when have you ever said to yourself 'Boy, that experience would have gone a lot better if I'd only had a gun?'" I interject. "That's never happened. Not to me, not to either of you and not to anyone you know."

"Thousands of people are shot in this city every year," Eddie replies.

"Thanks to morons with guns."

"Gangbangers with guns," he says. "We are losing the arms race."

"Don't you have a game to go to?" I suggest.

"Don't dismiss him just because you can't match his point," Lori scolds.

"Please." I roll my eyes.

"Some people only want to see things one way, Lori," Eddie says.

"So stubborn." She shakes her head at me.

Eddie stands from his stool and places singles on the bar. He slings his gym bag over his shoulder. "You want to meet me at the Schoolyard later?" he asks Lori.

"Yeah, sure," she answers.

"No, we have plans," I answer.

"Sounds like she would like to go." Eddie smiles at Lori.

"You should get going to your game," I encourage him.

"All right." Eddie puts his hands up. "Maybe I'll see you there, Lor."

I'm standing now, too. "Don't end run me, you little cunt."

"Nick, cut it out. You ain't intimidating anyone." Lori smirks and waves her hand with a limp wrist.

"Finish your drink, lush," I scold her. I step closer to Eddie. I extend my arm and point out the door. My index finger is an inch from his cheek. "Go play your game, Eddie. We won't see you later."

"You trying to show me up in my bar?" Eddie whispers.

"This ain't your bar, you fucking transplant." I laugh. "Don't act like anything in this town is your birthright just because you rent a place on Sheffield."

"Please stop." Lori is standing now. She places her hand on my shoulder.

Her touch calms me. I lower my hand.

"Have a good game," I say.

"Yeah, enjoy your therapy." Eddie says and smirks. He starts to leave but can't help but to get the last word in. "Hey Lor, first round is on me later."

I push my hand against his face. My full palm grips his mouth and cheeks and I push forward and fall out the open door onto the single concrete step. I am on top of him. We engage in what passes for a fight on the North side. There's lots of grappling and headlocks.

"Nick, stop it!" Lori yells at me.

I have a weight advantage and Eddie tires. I place my full weight on his chest with my right arm wrapped behind his head and under his armpit. I grab that arm at the wrist with my other hand and squeeze Eddie's neck as hard as I can. He slaps the concrete in submission.

"Nick, he can't breathe!" Lori screams.

"He can breathe," I assure her. "He just can't talk. Thank God."

There is no bouncer at happy hour, so Tony has to make his way from his station behind the bar. He stands in the doorway behind Lori. "Guys, you need to take your little game of grab ass somewhere else."

I relent. I place my palm on the side of Eddie's face as support to help myself to my feet. He groans as I place my weight down and smash his head into the concrete.

"Gee, Eddie, I guess you let me win that round," I say. "Maybe I'll meet you at the Schoolyard Tap later for a rematch." I wink at Lori.

Satisfied that our roughhousing is over, Tony heads back in. I lord over Eddie with my hands on my waist as he struggles to his feet. He pants and wheezes.

"Don't forget your duffle," I say and point to his gym bag on the ground.

"You best remember what's in it, asshole," Eddie threatens.

"Aww, hear that, honey? The little gangbanger is going to shoot me."

"Nick, I want to go." Lori is on the edge of tears. "We need to meet Father Killion."

"That's a shame," I say. "I think he was just about to show me his little pistol."

"Keep it up," Eddie says, but I know it's an empty threat.

"Go play your little game." I grab my wife under the arm, and we cross the street towards church.

***

I unleash a bevy of resentment at Lori once we're with Father Killion. It's a jail break of emotion and I spare no details. I tell him of the verbal and physical abuse, the drinking, the suspected infidelity.

Lori is silent, stone faced.

"Let's talk about grace, Nicholas," Father Killion says.

"It's Nick, and grace ain't going to cut it, Father," I say. I turn to Lori and yell, "Let's talk about respect, and appreciation, and acting like a Goddamn lady every once in a while."

Father Killion indulges me. He turns to Lori. "Do you think your husband is justified?"

Lori shrugs like a child cornered by a parent. A single tear rolls down her cheek.

"Lori, now is your chance to respond. Nick is casting you as an aggressor in the relationship." He encourages her to engage.

She starts to talk, but her voice cracks and she places her face in her palms. Her elbows rest on her knees as she sobs. We are sitting in the basement of the church on steel folding chairs. There is a white movie screen pulled down behind us. The church uses the basement to project mass for families with children so they do not disturb the ceremony going on above. There are rows of empty steel chairs unfolded around us like we are sitting in front of a jury of ghosts.

Father Killion turns to me. "Nick, maybe we will stop here tonight."

Lori lifts her head to speak. "He always took it. He always let me get away with it," she says.

"Oh, it's my fault that you treat me like shit!" I yell and jab my finger in my chest.

"Nicholas . . ." Father Killion extends his palm my way.

"It's Nick!" I yell at the priest. "And you can't possibly swallow this crap," I say and point at her.

Father Killion maintains composure. "Nick, you made some serious accusations. She is entitled to her response."

I sit back in the chair. The metal moans as I apply my weight.

"I've always been weak. That's why I chose a profession where I am in charge of children," Lori says. "I decided I didn't want to be weak anymore. I started going to the gym. I started getting in shape. I started looking good. It was empowering."

"Does Nick make you feel weak?" he asks.

"No, not at all." She waves this idea off. "It's the opposite."

"How so?" he asks.

"He praises me. He dotes on me." She begins to choke up again. "He loves me."

"And how do you repay me?"

"I'm sorry, Nick," she says. "I took it too far. I'm sorry."

***

The power dynamic turns in my favor. I finally have my lady in check.

I decide that would is the last meeting with Father Killion. I decide that Lori will keep drinking, and I will match her shot for shot, cocktail for cocktail. And when I say the night is over, the night is over. And when I tell her to shut her mouth, she shuts her mouth. I am in charge.

We begin a new stage. We focus on our careers and we begin to take on greater responsibilities. After a few years as an assistant, Lori takes the head volleyball coach role. I help with tennis and I lead the chess club. Our circle of friends narrows. We mature.

"I feel like Italian tonight," I say.

"How about Vinnie's?" Lori shouts from the bathroom. She applies her makeup in the mirror.

"I was thinking something more authentic." I walk to the bathroom, so I don't have to shout.

"You don't think that's Italian?" she asks.

"It's spaghetti and meatballs and mandolin music," I say.

"Sounds about right to me."

"Going to Vinnie's for Italian is like going to Disney to see royalty."

"That's fine, honey, you go ahead and pick the place." She applies blush to her cheeks with a flourish. She snaps her kit shut, puckers her lips, and turns to me. "As long as they can make a stiff Negroni, it's as authentic as I need."

Conversation is lean at dinner; we weren't able to scare up another couple to join us. We resort to talk of work, then parents. Everything is fine on all counts.

"If we plan on having kids, we better start working on it," Lori says, apropos of nothing. She stirs her drink.

"I can work on it anytime you like." I drain the last of the Chianti into my glass.

"Do you want to have kids, Nick?"

"You know I do."

"You need to tell me that you do."

"Lori, I want children."

"You need to tell me that you want them now."

I reach across the table and grab her hands. I look into her eyes. "Lori, let's have a baby. Now."

I stand and try to pull her from the table and toward the bathroom. She wrenches her hand away.

"Nick, this is serious," she says. "I saw the doctor this week. If we want kids, we need to start trying. Sooner rather than later."

"Hold on. Back up." I sit back in my chair. "What is this about the doctor?"

"There's a reason I'm an only child," she says. "My mother has a condition, Nick. It's hereditary."

"If there's a reason, this is the first I'm hearing about it," I say. "Have you always known about this?"

"I had my suspicions."

"You're telling me this now?" I raise my voice. "We're almost thirty."

"I didn't want to know. I figured I'd find out when I needed to," she explains. "And since you never asked about kids, I never felt the need."

"But you suddenly felt the need this week?"

The waiter arrives. I order a Scotch, neat. Lori orders another Negroni.

"Nick, I need an operation. Not right away, but before long I need to have it," she says. "After that, no kids."

We sit in silence. The drinks arrive. Busboys clear the table. The waiter returns with dessert menus, but we wave him off.

"Nick, please say something," Lori says.

I shake my head and twirl the Chianti around the glass.

"That's not fair, Nick. I have to deal with this too," she whines.

"Fair?" I laugh. "Let's talk about fair. My wife isn't just a hussy, she's a barren hussy at that. There's a double scoop of fair right there."

Her face goes schizoid. Her lower lip quivers with sadness but her eyes sharpen to razors and her brow clenches with anger.

"That's right," I say. "That face you're making right now. That's how I've felt every day being married to you. Now we're talking fair."

She stands. She leaves. I stay and twirl my Scotch.

***

I befriend the younger teachers at work. It's no challenge to ingratiate myself to them. Every school is a maze and there's a knot of bureaucracy to untangle. They appreciate my guidance.

The young guys even tolerate me during their prowling missions at the bars after work. I join their softball team in the summer. We attend the sporting events at the high school we feed into. We hope to network our way up the ladder.

Lori joins a volleyball club. It's off-season from the school team so she helps coach the young club team when she's not practicing or traveling to play tournaments around the Midwest.

We are spending less time together. We partake in sexual relations as a matter of routine. The doctor has us on a schedule. We've been at it over a year with no success. There is no romance. It's a job.

Lori shoves me awake. "We need to do it."

I struggle to open my eyes.

"Come on. We need to do it," she says, obviously annoyed.

"It's 6 a.m.," I say.

Lori has her day planner open before her. She runs her pen along the calendar.

"Tonight," I beg.

"I have to leave for a tournament in South Bend right after work." She stands beside me, naked. She is tall and toned. Any other man would trip over himself to get to her.

"Let me brush my teeth," I say.

"You don't have to kiss me."

"Can I pee?"

"Let's go. Move it." She claps her hands.

I brush my teeth and pee. I return to the room. She lays atop the covers. Her back is on the bed. Her legs are spread and bent at the knee.

"Go." She points at her exposed union.

I engage her. She does not respond. I thrust. Her body does not reciprocate. I try to kiss her. She turns her face away.

"Just get it done, lover boy."

I close my eyes. Images of other women creep into my mind. There is the blonde in the sun dress I see on the El platform. Is she Russian? Definitely Eastern European. The new third grade teacher enters the fray. They greet each other with a kiss and digital manipulation. They invite me to join them. I begin with the Russian, but the third grade teacher pulls me atop her. I think her name is Bridget. I call her Miss Bridget; a good Irish girl. The blonde says something in my imagined Russian and I am pulled back to her. The women pull me back and forth. I begin to lose rigidity and I panic. I feign climax with three heavy thrusts and a moan.

"That's it?" Lori says as I dismount.

I shrug. "Sorry, I'm just not that into it in the morning."

"Did you finish?" she asks.

"Of course." I put my robe on and head for the shower.

"All right," she says. "I hope you made it count. We only have a narrow window each month, according to Dr. Tekla."

"You could skip your tournament," I offer.

"You could come to the tournament," she counters.

We are both so satisfied with our selfishness. I am stoked about the prospect of a full weekend of liberty with the boys and she treasures her time competing with her team. Neither of us calls the other's bluff.

***

"The Pony is the spot for sloppy hour tonight, boys," Harold says.

We're on break before the last period of the day. Harold is the gym teacher. We wait along with Scott for the kids to come out of the locker room. Scott is the teacher of the other seventh grade section in the school. His class is combined with mine for lunch and gym.

"Did you drive?" Harold asks me.

"Red Line," I answer.

"Me, too."

Harold has no lesson plan for class, owing to the fact that it's the last period on a Friday. He places four dodgeballs at mid court as a suggestion. The kids erupt from the portal from the locker room. The first boys sprint toward the balls. They pick them up, turn and pitch them at the faces of the children trailing behind them. Bedlam ensues.

All but the butchiest girls in the grade head straight to the bleachers. Three didn't even bother to change out of their school uniforms. Harold does not ask for excuse notes or any explanation.

Kyle MacIntyre emerges from the scrum. He's bleeding, having taken a ball or perhaps an elbow to the lips.

"Mr. Kellogg, am I bleeding?" the boy folds his bottom lip over to reveal a substantial cut running from his gum line up the back of his lip.

Harold leans over with his hands behind his back to peer into the boy's mouth. "Yes, son, you sure are." A fact that is evident to Scott and me from four feet away.

Harold dispatches Kyle to the nurse's office.

"I'm out for the long haul tonight boys," I say. "Lori is off to a tournament so I have shore leave for the whole weekend."

They cock their heads and snicker at me.

"What's so funny?" I ask.

"You're hyped," he says.

"You sure do cherish your bachelor time," Scott nods.

A red ball zips past my nose and bounces low off the wall.

"Sorry, Mr. Kraus," a child shouts.

"Listen, every relationship needs a little intrigue." I affect the tone of a seasoned veteran. "It keeps things fresh."

"You're a solid wing man, Kraus, I'll give you that," Harold concedes.

"Well, more like fly paper," Scott jokes.

***

The new third grade teacher, the sassy Irish girl named Bridget, makes it out for happy hour. Her hair is dark and cropped short around the back. She uses her sunglasses to hold her bangs back across the top.

"Hey, Nick." Bridget salutes from the high-top table she's sharing with a couple other teachers.

I wave her over to the bar. It's my round. "Hey there," I say to her as she draws closer.

"I was thinking about you today, Mr. Kraus," she says. I think she's flirting.

If you only knew, I think to myself. "Oh yeah, how's that?" I respond.

"Your wife plays club volleyball, right?"

"She sure does. She's away at a tournament right now, in fact." I make a flirting gesture with a nod of my head but it's poorly executed. I'm sure I look like I'm trying to swallow a belch.

"Any chance you could ask her how I might join?" she asks. She flashes a half smile and a dimple appears on the side of her face. It's obviously a look that has served her well when asking favors, but right now I'm reading it as seductive.

Bridget is stout and firm. Her quads are thick but outlined and her hamstrings trace an arc down the back of her legs to her taught calves. She's wearing leopard print flats. Her sensible black dress is hemmed high and the bottom seam cuts tight under her ass.

"Of course. Do you want to give me your number and I'll pass it along?" Blood rushes to my face as I speak.

"Sure."

The bartender arrives with three beers. I pay and ask him for a pen.

"I'm sorry. Did you want something?" I gesture toward the bar.

She looks over at her nearly empty glass. "Sure, a rum and diet please." She makes the half-smile, dimple-face again and I'm smitten.

"Did you just get her number, Kraus?" Scott asks as I return with their beers.

"Yeah, she wants to talk to my wife," I laugh. "She's interested in volleyball."

"That's a front, Kraus. You're in," Harold says.

"Totally in," Scott seconds.

"You think so?" I'm doubtful but I let the idea tickle me.

"Totally in," Harold says.

They're patronizing me but I'm titillated just the same. I enjoy my beer and ruminate on the imbalance in the ledger of my marriage. Lori's side is full of debits for abuse and drunkenness, not to mention all the flirting. My side is full of credits for being patient and understanding. It would take me more than a few demerits to bring us anywhere near parity.

"You guys want shots?" I ask.

"Line 'em up," Scott says.

***

We've passed the twilight of happy hour, skipped dinner and are now on cruise control down the Lincoln Avenue corridor of glorified college bars. We're a cavalcade of delinquents on a quest.

Our group collects and discards participants as we progress up the street. We hit a sports bar and then Harold departs to feed on a burrito. Scott meets a girl at the next spot and escapes for potential coupling. I am left with six or so random teachers and new friends at the Rusty Pickle. Bridget is there, too. My infatuation grows and my inhibitions wane with each drink.

"So, you like volleyball, huh?" I shout into her ear. The music is loud.

"Yeah, I played in college," she yells back. She strains on her toes to force her mouth near my ear.

I sit on a stool to bring us closer to eye level. She stands betwixt my spread knees. I survey our group to note any witnesses. There are two coworkers from school; both are obliterated and concentrating on one another. Neither knows Lori.

"Were you a rover?" I ask.

"Yeah, how'd you guess?" She flashes the half-smile and curtsies to highlight her short stature.

"I'd put you on my team, no matter what," I say. I make my awkward flirty face and swallow another burp.

"You've never even seen me play." Her dimple flirts back.

"You're right, how about a tryout?" I try to whisper. My mouth is in her ear and her hair drapes my face. It smells like coconuts. I peek through the black, curly drapes and see our coworkers. They are giggling at us.

I pull away. She stares at me. Her left eye goes a little lazy and drifts.

"Let's get out of here," I yell. I make the burp face.

"Sure," she says.

We get in a cab. She gives her address. We sit close. I put my arm around her waist and it's exciting. I have not embraced another woman in more than ten years. I put a demerit on the debit side of my ledger.

We don't talk. Neither of us wants to acknowledge the impropriety of what we are about to do. We stare at each other. I smile. Her left eye fades left.

"You can't come up," she says abruptly. "It's not right."

She shows her half-smile. The dimple tempts me. I close my eyes and press my lips to hers. She does not kiss me back. Her lips recede. She curls them back within her mouth. She pulls away.

"Sorry, lover boy," she giggles. The car arrives at her place and she hops out.

"Where to, lover boy?" the cabbie mocks me.

I give him my address. I put another demerit in my ledger.

***

Lori's next tournament is local. She has been away on her own for the past two monthly competitions, so I sacrifice my weekend to attend the games and support her. The ladies sweep their games on Friday and Saturday. I tag along for a team dinner on Saturday night. The semifinal match is tomorrow.

The husbands and boyfriends congregate at the bar after dinner while the ladies remain at the table having dessert. They laugh and talk over the keys plays from their two days of victory.

Lori is laughing with the girl next to her. Her name is Martina. She is tall and tan with dark hair and grey eyes. Truth be told, it's no real chore to spend time watching these women perform and I'm proud to claim one of these gorgeous specimens as my wife.

Lori looks vibrant. Her eyes flash smiles as she laughs with her friends. Some of the girls partake of a beer or two with dinner but Lori stays sober. I am oblivious to the conversations around me at the bar. I appreciate my wife from afar, not just her physical beauty but her relaxed, joyful composure. I want to partake in their revelry, but I feel forbidden. Still, I stride over and pull a chair near Lori and Martina.

"Hello, ladies," I say. "What's going on here? Are you girls like a gang or something?"

"That's right buddy," Martina plays along. "We're a biker gang slash sewing circle."

"The Knit Riders," Lori hits her mark. We giggle together.

"No drinks for you tonight, sweetie?" I twirl the Scotch in the bottom of my glass and extend it slightly toward her. Why am I being an asshole? I like her like this.

"I want to stay sharp for tomorrow." She takes no umbrage. "I don't need to drink to have fun, you know."

"She wants to go out a winner, Nick," Martina adds.

"Go out?" I am surprised. "This isn't your last tournament, is it?"

Lori holds her gaze on Martina for a moment longer than normal. Martina smiles and blushes.

Martina slaps me on the knee. "There's a new kid coming on the team, Nick."

Lori laughs. "That's right, she's taking my spot in next month's tourney."

"That's too bad," I say. "I was really starting to enjoy this."

The girls take turns teasing me for not hanging out with the other men, but I can't resist being near Lori when she is like this.

"Hey, Kraus, are we making your hubby our new waterboy?" one lady jokes.

Lori laughs along and squeezes me around my neck. She kisses the top of my head. It is genuine affection.

"I'll be your waterboy!" I declare as I rise with my empty glass in the air. "Who needs a drink?"

A couple of girls ask for beers. I help myself to another Scotch. Sensing that we're nearing curfew for the team, I order something nice from the top shelf.

"Make it a double," I tell the man.

***

We're on the Red Line home. The El car floats and sways on the tracks like a magic carpet. It's been so long since we've shared a happy, pleasant evening that I'd forgotten just how blissful Lori can make me. We sit side by side on the train. My arm is around her and she strokes the hair on the back of my head.

"I'm excited for your games tomorrow." I smile at her. Her beauty is breathtaking. I do not deserve a woman of her caliber.

"Me, too," she says. "We have a good chance of winning it all."

"I hope you go out a winner," I say. "That's too bad you're getting bumped out of the starting lineup."

"Nick, I'm not just out of the starting lineup, I'm off the team," she says. "At least for a season."

"Are you hurt?"

Lori laughs and shakes her head. "Just how many of those Scotches did you have tonight, baby?"

"No more than usual," I say. "But seriously now, is everything OK?"

"Sweetie, everything is perfect. It's never been more perfect."

The train makes a stop at Division. I ponder the matter as riders exit and enter. I don't want to reveal my compromised state. The automated bell dings signaling that the doors are about to close.

"OK, fine. Tell me what's going on," I say.

She continues stroking my hair. "The doctor says I have to lay off the athletic activities."

"But you said you were perfect . . ."

She is outright laughing at my stupid drunken state now. "I am, but in a few more weeks I'm going to be even more perfect. We don't want to risk that."

She keeps stroking my hair. I keep thinking. She clears her throat and I look at her. Her other hand is circling her belly.

"Oh my God!" I stand and shout. The other riders are startled and look my way.

"Nick, sit down," she laughs and pulls me down to the seat.

"Oh my God," I say again but in a hushed tone. I cover my open mouth with my palm to suppress the proclamations that are poised to erupt from my heart.

"For crying out loud. It took you long enough, you ding-dong," she slaps my leg.

In a flash, I am sober. The ecstasy of the moment flushes the Scotch from my mind, and I have perfect clarity. I must protect her. I must care for her. I must serve her. Every instinct in my body tells me to place this woman before all. In two stops we will exit the train and we will take a cab for the remaining two blocks of our journey. When we arrive home, I will wrap her in blankets and fetch her all the comforts she desires.

The train slows for the next stop.

"How far along are we?" I ask.

"It's early. Tekla says eight or nine weeks," she says.

The train pulls out of the Clybourne stop. "How do you feel? I place my hand on her shoulder and survey our car for potential concerns.

"I feel the same, honey. No sickness at all. Tekla says my training regimen does me well," she says.

"Well, there'll be no more of that obviously," I contend.

"Nick, relax. We don't need to change a thing," she says. "Even at twelve weeks, as long as I don't take a spike to the gut, I'm fine."

"No, no, no." I realize she has a match tomorrow, possibly two.

She shakes her head to dismiss me. "At eight weeks, it's smaller than an ant. Feel this." She places my hand on her stomach. I can feel the definition of her abdomen through her shirt. My fingertips slip into the divisions between the muscles.

"The next stop will be Fullerton. Transfer to Brown line trains at Fullerton," the train driver announces.

This is our stop. We rise and I step in front of her to clear our way. I turn back to check that she is holding the strap for support. She sees me checking on her. She smiles in appreciation.

I begin to clear the mental ledger of our marriage. I wipe the debits from her side. I struggle to remember what most of them were. The train slows to a stop and we walk to the door. I cede the path to her and block the door from closing. She walks onto the platform.

With the mathematics of the ledger alive in my mind, a single number floats to the fore. Eight weeks. The automated bell rings. "Caution. The doors are closing," the drivers says.

I feel the automated door push on my back, but I will not allow it to close.

"Nick, come on." Lori waves me toward her. She reaches for my wrist, but I pull it away.

"Eight weeks?" I ask.

"Yes. Eight, maybe nine," she says, eager to get me off the train. "Come on."

"Please clear the doors," the driver says over the PA. The door pushes on my back.

"That's the weekend you went to South Bend," I say.

She feigns exasperation. "Yes, lover, but not before we made a baby. Remember?"

I lean back into the train car and let the door close between us. The train departs. The Scotch floods back into my bloodstream. Suddenly I am tired. I take a seat and go to sleep.

Interlude 9: Let's Call Him Zeke

"Dr. Tekla had them removed; it was still early. She went home the same morning," I answer.

"Them?" Zeke asks. His full name is Ezekiel but he lets me call him Zeke. Zeke is from the future.

"There were two," I say.

We walk around the town square. Langford City Hall consumes most of the commons in the center. Streets running along each side of the commons form a perfect quad. Shops, taverns, and hotels run along the street. Wood-plank sidewalks line the way beneath shingled awnings. There are gas lamps at each corner and a pair at the front of the walkway leading to the entrance of city hall, where there are two more affixed on each side of the grand doorway. We stroll along this walkway.

I have no trouble sharing my stories anymore. I am bereft of ideas about how to relive my life. The hope for good guidance outweighs the pain I must endure in recounting my failures. I have been back several times since Lori got knocked up by that Notre Dame kid. My life ends in reckless misery again and again.

"How did you go out this time?" Zeke asks. He has a faint glow. I am encouraged.

"Motorcycle. I bought a motorcycle after her surgeries," I tell him. "I took the Oak Street curve at 80. Tried to at least. We wiped of course. My cranium kissed the barrier. I didn't have a helmet, but it wouldn't have mattered."

"We?" Zeke asks. "You and Lori?"

"No, some girl." I shake my head. "She went flying into the lake, I think. She might have made it."

The smell of hickory smoke emanates from the butcher shop. They are smoking ribs and brisket in the back. I peer down the gangway leading to the smoking yard and the walls are pitch black with soot.

We follow the heat and the smoke to its source at the end of the hallway. We see meats in various states of finish bathing in smoke within brick and steel encasements. The smoke smells delicious but it stings my eyes.

I stare at the hanging meat and talk to Zeke. "Maybe I need to hire a hit man like Charlie."

Zeke knows nothing of Charlie, but he responds immediately. "And what if there actually is a hell?"

My attention shifts to the flames. "Should I submit to the abuse, like George Cole? Accept that my fate is simply to choose the lesser of two miseries?"

"I wonder what others might pay to enjoy your miseries." Zeke cocks his head and pouts. "I've heard much sadder tales than yours. Stuff much harder to reconcile than an unfaithful spouse."

"Want to trade?" I turn to face him.

"You don't even know my story yet." He pauses.

"I'll roll the dice."

Zeke shakes off the offer as though either of us has a choice in the matter. "How did you die the time before, before the motorcycle accident?"

"Suicide." I take the bandana from around my neck and wipe my eyes. "I tried raising the little bastards with her, but my resentment was too deep. I knew it wasn't how it was supposed to go, I just knew it. I ended it before their first birthday. I walked down to the Metra tracks at Clybourne and jumped in front of the express." I wipe my eyes again and then wrap the bandana back around my neck. "How is that you're from the future, Zeke?"

"There is no future here, Nick. We are stuck in a perpetual now," he answers.

"Well time still exists on Earth and you come from a time that I have yet to live," I contend.

"And Andres, your friend from Catalonia that you told me about, he could say the same about you, no?"

I ponder Andres. "That's it. I'll sell drugs, run guns and pimp out women along the Mediterranean."

Zeke frowns at me. "You're a silly man, Nick Kraus."

Our fellow souls stroll about the commons in the period wear that I have imagined for them. Time is my personal construct for all who dwell here but even time is no more genuine than the Stetson hat I have assigned to the gentleman untying his horse from the nearby railing, neither is the horse for that matter. My feeble human mind needs time to make sense of things, but this world requires neither time nor sense.

"Will you tell me about the future, Zeke?" I ask politely. I need only squeeze and think to take whatever lesson I am entitled to.

"Don't get too excited, it's not the distant future," he says, "And, where I'm from you need a lot of time to pass before you see much difference."

Story 10: Lightning in a Box

The bishop had punished Leroy on many occasions for reading contraband books. His parents did nothing to enforce the prescribed discipline though. How could they ever punish a boy for an addiction to reading? So, when it came time for Leroy to experience the liberty of his Rumspringa, there was no doubt about where he would head. He would head to the place with the largest library he could find.

Leroy's father, Samuel King, was a master builder, as were his brothers Eli, Amos, and Jacob. Leroy took to the trade as well, but he often met the contempt of his brothers when he would abandon projects midday to seek refuge in the pages of a book. The fact that Leroy would always make improvements to their projects the next day went unnoticed or would stir further contempt.

Leroy could make joists that were both stronger and lighter. When he worked with the blacksmith, he made his fire hotter and he forged tools that were stronger. He laid out the wood in a certain order so the saws remained sharp by the end of the stack. He sharpened the saws better too.

Leroy and I were both seventeen and nearing our Rumspringa year of freedom. By community standards, I was the head of the class at school. This meant that my command of scripture and the trades was superior to others. The fact that Leroy's trade skills surpassed mine was trumped by my knowledge of the bible and my dutiful allegiance to the strictures of the Amish community.

"That boy's tastes are too exotic for Shipshewana," my father warns me over dinner.

My father's lectures are directed at me, the eldest of his four boys and the second in line of his six total children. It does not matter whose behavior may have prompted the lesson. I am expected to reinforce the lesson with my own guidance to my siblings following dinner. I might also impose discipline for minor offenses, but corporal punishments are left to father alone.

"I saw you commiserating with him, the youngest King boy," Father says to me. Tonight's chastisement is for me.

"We are peers in class, Father," I reason.

"Class is in the classroom," Father states. "You leave him be lest you fall prey to his corrupted logic."

"Yes, Father." This is not a conversation. Father declares his decree and I obey.

***

American society had peaked in the early 21st century and then saw a massive retrenchment before the turn of the 22nd. In 2050, the American economy, indeed the world economy, was dominated by a group of oligarchs that ruled all industrial production with impunity.

There were fewer than a hundred corporations controlling the production of all material goods and services. Although the American economy was pivoted in favor of the wealthy, the power held by the common man was the power to consume. As long as America held the largest store of wealth in the world, the American consumer lived well. The oligarchy catered to their desires and ensured that a minimum standard of living was maintained even for the lowest class. As productivity was outsourced and agriculture evolved into a corporate endeavor, Americans could still earn by providing essential services to the über-rich. Relative to other developed nations, the tax burden for the rich in America was a pittance. The wealthy flocked to America and paid their income taxes there, and corporations moved their headquarters there as well. The lower classes of America were buoyed by government largess made possible by these tax receipts.

America broadcast the enviable state of their society to the rest of the world via their far-reaching media outlets. Consumers in other places began to feel entitled to the things that they saw Americans boasting over. Other nations began to extend tax breaks to corporate leaders. Government leaders began to demand some representation by their citizens within any corporation that wished to do business in their sphere of influence. High-ranking management positions were created for Kenyans, Monrovians, Cambodians and folks from other faraway lands.

The highest tax bracket in America began to thin. This was a breach in the dam holding back the massive American store of wealth that would never be repaired. First the executives defected for overseas locations, then the managers of the frontline employees left as well. As the management class relocated along with their money, their new geographies claimed a higher share of the consumer market. The service sector, the last bastion of American dominance in the global economy, was raided. The cash flow that was once the exclusive entitlement of the common American began to course towards foreign lands.

Employment and tax receipts plummeted. The populace took to their leaders to demand restitution and even punitive action against the corporations. Those leaders not already owned by the corporate ruling class summoned their remaining integrity and took action, but they only made matters worse.

Congress doubled the tax rate on the highest tax brackets overnight. They bet that the American executives would never renounce their citizenship and move away. They lost their gamble twice. First the executives left, and then the lower-level managers followed their leaders to havens in Mexico, Cuba, and Venezuela. Once the corporate class left, the common American had no one left to service. They also had no trade skills, no factories, and no farmland to call their own. We Amish called this "the Great Reckoning."

The Amish began to excel in American society even before the collapse of the economy. We were the last part of society with any manufacturing skills. We also had our own farms and weren't reliant upon technology to ply our trades. Rich and poor alike came to us for real food, to tailor garments or to just get off the grid for a moment. Wise parents would send their teenagers to work for us for a summer to learn how to be self-sufficient. They were known as "Amish interns."

Following the collapse, the exotic oddity that was the Amish community became an oasis in a desert of despair. The few remaining Americans with any wealth would come to buy our food and wares. Former Amish who had abandoned the community, sometimes generations prior, pled for readmission. The English, as we called non-Amish, clamored for entrance to the community. Our communities accepted those most fit to the extent that we could support the burden, but many were turned away, so large swaths of derelict city blocks were repurposed to mimic our system in a pseudo-Amish sensation. Mocked and ridiculed by many for centuries, the Great Reckoning finally proved that the Amish way was the one true way.

The bishops and clergy took great pains to guard and preserve the Amish way of life. New blood meant new ideas and the community had survived for hundreds of years without either. With the Great Reckoning and its affirmation of the superiority of the Amish way of life, it was high time to reinforce the barriers between us and the English.

***

I come in from evening chores and father is not at the dinner table. My mother points me to the front parlor, where I find him sitting with bishop Yoder. They are speaking our language, a derivative of Swiss German. This signaled that the matter is serious.

"Sit, Ezekiel," Father tells me, still speaking our tongue. He indicates that I should take the chair beside the bishop. "Bishop Yoder has come to us with a very special vocation for you."

"Brother Ezekiel, have you given any thought to your Rumspringa?" he asks me. He has a friendly smile framed by a long grey and white beard.

"None at all, sir. I intend to use my liberty to further dedicate myself to service to our community," I answer in perfect Pennsylvania Dutch. "The English world holds nothing for my redemption. I have all I need here."

The seams of Father's mouth tighten but not enough to make a smile.

"Bless your wholesome heart, young Ezekiel," Bishop Yoder says as he pats my arm. "While what you say is true, what if I told you it was your vocation to dedicate yourself to ensuring that our way of life is preserved for generations to come? What if I told you it was your duty to help guard us from the unenlightened horde?"

An elder has never posed questions to me like this before. I am confused and unsure, so I look at Father.

"Answer the bishop," Father says.

I nod at Father then I look at Bishop Yoder and nod at him as well. "I will fulfill my duty to you and the community, whatever you say it may be."

Father nods with a quick twitch of his head. His nose moves no more than two millimeters.

"Of course." The geriatric man caresses my arm with his leathery, dry hand. "Brother Ezekiel, do you know Leroy King?"

"Yes, he is a classmate of mine." I look to Father. "But I do not commiserate with him outside of school."

"So, then, you know nothing of his plans for Rumspringa?" the bishop asks.

"Only what he says around school, sir." I say and look again at Father, hoping his face does not signal that I will be chastised later.

The bishop leans forward. His face is close to mine. A lone white hair from his beard surrenders its hold and drapes itself over my leg. "What does young Leroy say at school, son?"

"He says he wants to go learn with the English. He says he'll go to their university and find the books that he can't find here so that he can complete his project," I tell him.

"What project, son?" The bishop leans closer. Father does the same.

I blush and let out a nervous laugh. "It's silly. We mock him soundly for it."

"Answer the bishop's question," Father orders.

I snap back from my comfort zone. "Lightning in a box," I blurt out.

"Ezekiel, you will feel the leather if you choose to make humor," Father warns.

The bishop extends an arm to calm him. "What is this lightning box, Ezekiel?"

"He thinks he can capture lightning in a box. He says he'll use the lightning rods. When the lightning strikes, he'll channel the electricity and store it." I glance at Father. He is placated at the moment. "Leroy says it's the same idea as the gutters around our building that route the water to our cisterns."

"What will he do with it?" Father nearly yells.

"How will he store it?" The bishop steps over Father's question.

"I don't know. I don't think he knows either. Maybe that's why he wants to go study the English science," I say.

The bishop looks to Father and nods. Father is allowed to ask his question.

"Whatever in the world would we need with a box of lightning?" Father laughs at the silly sound of his own question.

"Leroy says . . ." I stop to correct myself. "Leroy *believes* that lightning is power delivered from God. He says that if it's OK for us to harness the power of the wind and the flowing stream, it's OK for us to take the power of the lightning."

"That is for the bishops and elders to decide!" Father yells in English.

The bishop extends his arm again. "What then, young Ezekiel? What then?" He poses the question slowly, as though from the pulpit.

I don't answer but I imagine barns lit with electric bulbs allowing me to do my chores late into the night. Perhaps I would rise earlier to read scriptures before the dawn.

"God has protected us from the vices of the English, Ezekiel. He has guided us to the one true way to prosperity and salvation," the bishop preaches. Father nods. "The trappings of modern technology have brought them discontentment, war and starvation. This has been their reward for generations. Not long ago when they would visit our markets, I would hear them ask each other how we could live like we do. They weren't curious about how we managed to be productive and thrive. They were curious about how we could tolerate living according to such austere constraints. They pitied our condition, now they envy us."

"Do you understand what the bishop is telling you, Ezekiel?" Father asks me.

"I believe so, Father," I answer. This was not a new lesson, after all. "The ways of the English lead to sadness and suffering."

"Good. But there's more, Ezekiel." The bishop lifts his hand from my arm and raises his pointer finger in the air. He raises his voice as well. "We have never been more at risk. The English threaten our way of life every day. They stand outside the gates of our community and beg for entry, but they do not beg for assimilation. Their way of life is an infection and it will spread if we do not quarantine the community."

"But haven't we accepted newcomers before, sir?" I am nervous for having asked the bishop a direct question.

"Yes, and those we have accepted have left their old lives behind," he explains. "But they still long for the comforts that they once knew. And the more newcomers we accept, the harder it will be to deny them their vices. Our brothers in Lancaster have had to hire guards to keep interlopers from entering the community to peddle their contraband."

I struggle to imagine what they could have to sell that they would want. "Do you mean the books and magazines that Leroy likes?"

The bishop chuckles and looks to Father as he says, "He is a good boy. He has been raised well."

Father smiles and looks at me, nodding his head in approval. The hairs on my arms stand at attention and a grin spreads across my face.

The bishop rubs the back of my head. "The newcomers long for the devices that connect them to their old lives. The peddlers bring these devices and exchange them for food. Soon our people will become accustomed to these devices and then they will be commonplace, just as the battery-operated radios are today."

It had never occurred to me that the radios once had no place in our community, although it seems obvious now that he points it out.

"We must protect our way of life, Ezekiel. We are at risk, now more than ever." The bishop is more serious than ever. "The elders have never feared that we would lose our way of life because of attrition. That is why we award Rumspringa, so that the youth may see that the world is empty beyond this land. Rather, the greatest fear is that we may be overrun by the unenlightened and that they would infect and pollute us with their evil ways."

"This is a valuable lesson, sir. Thank you for sharing it with me," I say.

The bishop looks at Father. They nod in unison.

"Ezekiel, your father and I need to ask you a favor," the bishop says.

"Fulfilling your requests is no favor. I see it as my duty," I say and cock my chin high.

The bishop pats my arm. He looks at me with his dark grey eyes and smiles. His sparse teeth are brown and worn. "You will accompany young Leroy King on his Rumspringa," he states.

Father nods.

I retain my posture as my resolve crumbles inside me.

***

The driverless car arrives at dawn. Technically speaking, there is a driver, but he is physically seated somewhere in South America. Nonetheless, the driver's virtual body seated in the driver's seat is plain enough for us to see.

"Good morning, gentlemen," the driver says over the speakers. The virtual face turns and smiles at us.

"*Buenos dias, señor,*" Leroy greets him. The image nods in response.

"Off to school, boys?" the driver asks.

"*Si! Si, señor!*" Leroy says. "West Lafayette, please."

"Speak your own tongue," I scold Leroy in our Dutch. "He knows where we are going, already." Our destination had been programmed when the English dispatcher ordered the car for us.

Leroy is giddy with anticipation. "I don't know what to do first. Head to the computer laboratory or the engineering laboratory."

"Orientation is scheduled to begin with a tour of campus at 10 a.m.," I tell him.

Leroy turns the dials and taps the touchscreens within the cabin of the sedan. His orientation has already begun.

"Have you chosen your area of concentration, Ezekiel?" Leroy asks. He seems willfully oblivious to the purpose of my companionship. Nothing can spoil this experience for him.

"You are my area of concentration, Leroy," I remind him. "We have the exact same schedule."

The car is underway. It will take us three hours to reach West Lafayette. I am wearing my Sunday formals for the drive, so they do not get wrinkled in the luggage. Leroy is wearing a blue work shirt with the sleeves rolled up. It is untucked over his black slacks.

I am sitting behind the virtual driver with my arms crossed and my feet flat on the floor. I hold my hat on my lap. Leroy is reaching about the cabin to expand the informational screens broadcasting every nature of media.

"It's going to be eighty-five degrees down in Lafayette to-day," he says.

"Probably the same at home. It's a warm September." I turn from him and look out my window.

"Oh my, look, Ezekiel." Leroy taps a screen. It's an electronic map. "Do you see that there? That's the Bontrager farm. Do you see the shadow of the mill?"

I see a pattern of green and maize colors across the screen. There are structures of some type interspersed but I struggle to assign any familiarity to the image. I do not recognize the markers that he points out nor do I find value in peering through a twenty-inch portal at a place I could visit in person right now if not for this vocation.

I see the exit for Goshen. This is the southwestern boundary of my known world. I peer out the window and trace the downward arch of the power lines as we pass each pole. The advertisements on the electronic billboards switch as we pass them. They are programmed to target their publicity to the occupants of the passing cars. We are greeted with ads for tombstones, flowers, and legal services. Our clothes have no chips or markers, and more importantly we have no recent purchase history. The algorithm guesses that we must be the guests of honor in a funeral procession.

The world becomes more alien the further we progress beyond Goshen. I see a white bubble rising from the horizon like a massive mushroom cap. The closer we get the more disturbed I become by this bizarre and unnatural semi-circle enclosure. Abutting the bubble is a tower. I count twenty-five stories to the top floor and the top of the bubble eclipses that. There is a crest in the highway as we get closer and I see a sea of shimmering glass panels laid out around the complex. I notice a tall, barbed wire fence running along the highway. I expand my perspective and notice that the fence line traces the perimeter of the sprawling complex. There are turrets with guards placed within rifle range of each other.

Leroy leans over and startles me. "That's Plymouth." He points to the map on one of the screens.

"Plymouth? The *excom* town?" I ask. *Excom* is our pejorative term for people who have left the community.

"They call themselves Pilgrims," Leroy says. He is leaning over me, studying their arrangement. "That tower is probably vertical horticulture. I bet they have fish tanks on the top floors. The dirty water from the tanks trickles down to sustain plants on the lower floors. They'll have pigs and chickens on the bottom floors. They'll use their poop for the fields."

"What fields?"

"That's a Greenfield system." He points to the glass panels. "Those are clear solar panels sitting about eight feet off the ground. They generate power for the community, but they also kick off heat down below. Crops grow year round."

"That's amazing."

"It's genius," Leroy says. "That's what Bishop Yoder is afraid of, by the way."

"What do you mean?"

"Yoder. He's afraid of progress." Leroy points toward Plymouth with an open palm.

"They turned their backs to God," I dismiss them and look away.

"How do you know? They probably have a church in there somewhere. There's definitely room," Leroy says. "I admire them. That could be us."

I reach into the inside pocket of my black coat and retrieve my notebook and pencil. I open it to the first page, write the date at the top and then record Leroy's statements of insolence. I write in our language. This is what Bishop Yoder instructed me to do.

"Is that your diary?"

"It's a journal," I respond.

"Well, stick this is in your journal, Ezekiel: I am going to change the world and we're all going to be better for it. Amish and English alike," Leroy says. "You see those power lines?"

I nod.

"We can cut those down forever, Ezekiel," Leroy says. "Those are the wires that entangle mankind. Those are the bane of our existence."

"Those wires do not even reach our fence line, Leroy. You are talking nonsense." I wave him off.

"Are the English not at our fence line every single day? They come for our food, they come for our shelter, they come for our way of life. Eventually we will be overrun," he says. "We can't stop them."

Leroy regains my attention. "So how will cutting their power lines help?"

"We'll make them obsolete." Leroy notices the virtual driver. He continues in our Dutch, "If we give them their precious electricity for free, they won't need us. We will give them the means to generate and store their power."

"And then they will leave us alone again?"

"We will give them the power to heat their homes, to light their lights, to run their devices, to fuel their vehicles, to operate their factories." Leroy is pleading with me to subscribe to his reasoning. "We'll give it to them for free and they won't need anything from us ever again."

"They'll still need to eat," I point out.

"How hard is it to bury a seed in the ground?"

"There is more to it than that, Leroy. One must prepare the ground, fertilize the earth and nurture the crops," I tell him. "And the livestock are harder to raise than children. That's what my father says at least."

***

We are enrolled at Mondemon - Purdue University in West Lafayette, Indiana. It is one of the greatest engineering universities in America. Purdue was formerly a public, land-grant university but it is now wholly owned and operated by the Mondemon corporation. The school exists to serve the research interests of the company. The matriculating body is made up of the wealthy scions of the world's elite class, as well as gifted students chosen and sponsored by the company. Every bit of intellectual property they produce is the sole property of Mondemon Corporation.

Students are not subjected to any core curriculum rich with lessons in the humanities and classic literature. On the contrary, *Discere faciendo* is the school's Latin motto. That's "To learn while doing" in English.

We are surrounded by information. Every wall, indeed, every surface, is an interactive, electronic interface. One need only perform a number of taps to open a portal. The exhaustive catalog of humanity's knowledge is everywhere for the taking. And if you happen to have your hands tied, you need only ask a question into thin air to receive a response.

"Prompt open prompt," Leroy says as he gazes through a microscope.

"Prompt open, Mr. King," a robotic voice answers.

"Prompt: Tell me parts per million of molybdenum in isotonic seawater. Go."

"Zero point zero one parts per million of molybdenum in isotonic seawater. Stop."

"Close prompt close." Leroy jabs a finger in my direction, and I write this information down in my notebook. I am Leroy's scribe.

We have been here for ten weeks and Leroy has a throng of disciples. At first it was just fellow students but as his genius spread, he attracted professors and then people from the industry. The Mondemon corporation assigned an engineer to shadow him at all times.

I am now convinced of Leroy's brilliance. Bishop Yoder was right to have me follow him. I had dismissed him as a crackpot, but the attention of these English scientists is affirmation that he is a prodigy.

"Mr. King, how will you attract the uranium to the ribbons?" a man asks, his name is Graham. He is the nominal professor assigned to this class, but he ceded command of the lab to Leroy by the fifth week.

"That's a function of the valence of the isotope. I can't say with precision without knowing the mixture of minerals in the solution," Leroy answers without looking up from the microscope.

This goes on for hours and the energy of some in the group begins to wane. Fellow students peel off first, followed by the professional engineers. Eventually the only remaining acolytes are the professor and me.

"What type of library do you boys have back on the farm, Ezekiel?" Professor Graham asks me as Leroy starts a centrifuge of tubes spinning.

"Nothing that would stir your mind, I'm sure," I tell him.

As an academic, he's certainly familiar with the Amish. We are the model community of modern America and thus we've attracted many scholarly types on sabbatical.

"I spent a summer in Jo Davies County not long ago and I never saw anything approaching Leroy's wealth of knowledge. I regularly visit Plymouth and there isn't anyone there with his expertise, notwithstanding their advanced level of sophistication." The professor is flummoxed. "I've spent my adult life in lecture halls and laboratories, but I can't touch young Leroy here in my mastery of this science."

"Can I ask you a question, Professor Graham?" I pose.

The professor turns to me.

"Are there churches in Plymouth?"

Professor Graham smiles. He seems satisfied that one of his students is asking for his guidance. "Yes, Ezekiel, the Pilgrims remain very pious. Their community is very much like yours I would imagine. They are dedicated to their families, they are hard-working, they are disciplined, and they are most certainly humble before their God."

A bitterness stings me. I wanted to hear that they're rotten.

"But do they have all this?" I double-tap the table and an electronic portal opens.

"Yes and no, Ezekiel." The professor looks up to contemplate the best response. He returns to me. "They can access everything we have here, but they keep it in its place. They are not distracted by it. If you walk into a home and tap on the kitchen counter there will be no portal popping up to tell you a recipe. Every building has a special room called a Sapatorium set aside to serve their information needs."

"Kind of like a bathroom?" I ask.

The professor laughs. "More like a workshop, Ezekiel."

"Are they a contented people?" I ask.

"They are a lot like you and your brother. They are calm and confident." He smiles as he looks back and forth between us. "Pleasant and generous."

I am ashamed as I recall all the nasty things we say about them after they finish their visits to Shipshewana.

"I am tired, Ezekiel." The professor watches as Leroy carefully extracts the tubes from the apparatus and places them in a rack. "Would you please secure the laboratory when you finish tonight?"

"Of course. Thank you, professor."

"Thank you for what?"

"Thank you for sharing your insights."

"It's my pleasure, young man. It's always a pleasure." The professor smiles. "Please wish Leroy a pleasant evening, and good night to you as well of course."

Leroy waves me over after the professor departs. We commence to the work of memorializing today's discoveries. Leroy dictates and I record the findings and their significance in the notebook. All my notes are written in Pennsylvania Dutch.

Our language is one of very few to have never been codified by the English machines. Moreover, my shorthand is unknown and indecipherable. Leroy and I have devised our own symbols for the periodic table of elements.

***

Leroy has befriended some Pilgrims he met on campus. I suspect he sought them out. In any event, they are eager to embrace him. Leroy is a celebrity amongst the student body.

"Leroy, come to the Phi Gamma Psi house tonight. There's a Halloween party." Abram is the protagonist of the group. He is eager to show us all the fun we are missing out on.

Leroy looks to me. The fact is that I have no orders to record any salacious behavior. Bishop Yoder was not interested in prescribing any prohibitions. In fact, it is likely that he favors Leroy getting it all out of his system.

"Look not to me for approval nor recrimination, Brother Leroy," I say. "Your hesitation stems from your heart alone."

A girl in the group named Martha speaks, but I ignore her.

"He is my voice of reason," Leroy says to her.

Another girl, Hannah, comments. I ignore her as well.

"I doubt it, but you can try," Leroy responds to her.

The Pilgrim boys laugh and Leroy joins in.

"Let's have a look, Ezekiel," Leroy says. "Think of it as a cultural exploration."

"It's a pagan ritual in a den of iniquity," I reply.

"And you can write a full report of it to Yoder to show just how righteous we are compared to these heathens." Leroy pats one of the Pilgrim boys on the back.

"You've already decided we're going. Let's dispense with the charade, shall we?"

The Pilgrims let out a cheer and turn heel toward fraternity row.

The outside of the Phi Gamma Psi house is decorated like a Catholic church. There are purple shrouds hanging from the windowsills and a banner over the front portico reads HAPPY HALLOWEEN: RAISE A TOAST TO THE HOLY GHOST.

The Pilgrims greet some fraternity brothers at the front door. They are dressed as cardinals. They rush us in. The front foyer looks like the inside of the Sistine Chapel; that is, the walls and the ceiling of the room are actual projections of the Sistine Chapel. I am enthralled by the imagery. I try to place each of the depictions to the biblical verse from which it was inspired but I am distracted by one of the Pilgrims.

"Come on." Hannah tugs at my vest. "You have to eat the body and blood."

Hannah points up the wide staircase leading to the mezzanine. There is a line of partiers heading toward a makeshift altar. A fraternity brother in priestly garb is presiding over a ceremony to dispense the sacrament.

"This is the body of Christ." He raises a toast point in the air and laughs. He places it on the tongue of the party goer. She is wearing thigh-high stockings and high heels, along with a hooded frock tied at the waist with a rope.

"Mary Magdalene. Total whore," Hannah says. There are many like her teeming about. The girls dressed as nuns are also sporting stockings and heels, as are the Catholic school girls in short, plaid skirts.

We reach the altar for our turn. I notice that there is peanut butter and jelly on the toast. Hannah takes that down and turns to the priest's assistant.

"This is the blood of Christ," he says and hands Hannah a clear plastic cup with what looks to be gelatin inside. She slurps it down in one go.

The priest character makes the sign of the cross over Hannah. "Go forth to love and serve the fraternity."

We head back down the stairs. Hannah doesn't bother to ask me to partake of the ritual. She can tell that I am awestruck by the spectacle of sacrilege taking place around me. I am no papist, but I have been taught to at least respect other faiths. This is blasphemy.

"Look, a Calvinist!" A man dressed as a Roman soldier points at me.

"I'm an Anabaptist," I try to correct him, but he's already gone.

Leroy finds me amongst the crowd. Abram follows him carrying a paper plate of peanut butter and jelly wedges. The entree is garnished with a heap of the little plastic cups of red gelatin.

"Fancy a snack?" Abram asks as he presents the plate to me.

"Don't worry, Ezekiel. They've been desanctified." Leroy laughs.

I turn my nose away like a child.

"It's just a snack. Geez," Hannah says. I can't fathom why she continues to lurk around me. I haven't responded to anything she has said since we got here.

Leroy grabs a wedge, turns to me, and jams it in his mouth. He grabs two plastic cups and empties them in his mouth too. "Relax," he tells me.

I am hungry so I grab a wedge. I place it near my nose and give it a whiff. I dab the tip of my tongue on the exposed confection. Satisfied, I pop it in my mouth. It's good.

Leroy, Abram, and the girls stare at me. They are pleased for some reason.

"It's just food. You never seen a man eat before?" I am annoyed by their attention. Leroy hands me a gelatin. I repeat my ritual and then eat it.

Hannah draws closer. She hooks a finger inside the seam of my vest and runs it up and down. I push her away.

***

I am infected. I am sure of it. I partook of the devil's banquet and I am infected with his evil.

"Leroy, how do you feel?" We are seated on plush leather couches watching bodies gyrate around the foyer. A digitized rhythm pulsates from the floor as electronic sounds emanate from the walls. I am fixated on Botticelli's Trials of Moses that is cast on the southern wall. I swear that the characters in the fresco are moving.

"I feel mellow, very mellow," Leroy says with a smile. Abram and Martha are dancing together in front of us. Leroy's foot is tapping with the beat. He seems eager to dive into the mix but can't find the courage to take the plunge.

"I feel mellow too," Hannah says to me. She is sitting on my lap. My energy is sapped. I can no longer summon the will to resist her advances.

Her eyes are brown, but her pupils are dilated so wide they seem black. Her skin is as fair as porcelain and her hair is chestnut brown just like the rest of ours.

"You remind me of my cousin." She nuzzles her nose close to my ear.

"Leroy!" I shout. "Let's dance."

I jump from the couch and Hannah topples over on to her back. I grab Leroy by the arm and pull him onto the dance floor. We begin to sway with our arms fixed at our sides. Hannah is reclining lengthwise across the couch like a model in one of those French paintings. I remind myself that those models were whores and I feel a pang of guilt for my impure thoughts.

The music escalates. Leroy loosens his arms and spins like a whirling dervish. The hypnotic noise bores into my ears and the undulating walls put me in a trance. I bend at the knees and then stand upright. I repeat the movement and snap my fingers with the rhythm. I embrace my infection. What a spectacle I must be.

I look at Hannah and she is laughing. She has her arm wrapped around her waist to constrain her rolling belly. I look at Abram and Martha and they are laughing too.

"Leroy?" I look to my companion for reassurance. He is bent over, facing the floor. When he stands his face is red and he is breathless with laughter.

I look around and it seems that everyone is laughing. The DJ is laughing, and the music has stopped. The sound of laughter is piped through the audio system. I look to the south wall. Moses is pointing and laughing while Jethro's daughters cover their open mouths with their hands.

I break for the front door and run back to my dorm room without stopping.

***

Students are no longer allowed to join us in the laboratory. The crowd of onlookers had become overbearing and none contributed anything to Leroy's research. Leroy had tolerated them for weeks, but he had them banished once he noticed how uncomfortable I was around them. I was struck by how many

Mondemon engineers were in the crown, once the students were banned.

I stood close over Leroy's shoulder and the professor stood close over mine. Ten or so of the higher-ranking engineers stood in a semicircle around us. Another ten sat above us in the loge. Our new laboratory was set up for demonstration lectures, but Leroy never spoke, except to me. He would dictate to me in our language and I would take my notes in the same manner.

"They want to know what 119 is. They keep murmuring that number between themselves," the professor whispers to us. It is a certainty that he would like to know, too.

"I'm sure Leroy will present his full dissertation when it's ready," I reply at full voice. If the technology exists to recreate the Sistine Chapel within a frat house in Indiana, I'm sure the monitors in this room are advanced enough to pick up on his whispers.

Leroy stands to address the crowd, and everyone snaps to attention. "Who is the lead engineer in this group?"

A small, old man with caramel skin points to a tall, bespectacled woman in a white coat. The other Mondemon employees nod in unison. Her expression does not change.

"My name is Doctor Ramirez," she says. "Are you in need of something?"

"I need 10,000 gallons of seawater. Can you obtain it?" Leroy asks.

"If need be," she says. "Can you tell me why?"

"What's the strongest power generator you have on campus?" Leroy ignores her question. "I need 1.5 P of power for 30 microseconds."

"You need a lightning strike," another engineer says.

"I need to pass 15 billion watts of power through 10,000 gallons of seawater with a pH of at least 8.1 and salinity of 36 PSU for 30 microseconds," Leroy says.

Doctor Ramirez taps a surface to open a portal. She enters her codes and an interface opens. She attends to her business for a minute and then turns to Leroy.

"Do you want it to arrive tomorrow?" she asks.

Leroy has his own portal open. He is reviewing the weather forecast. "Friday morning," he answers.

***

Hannah tells me she loves me every day. I feel guilty. I do not love her. I can barely tolerate her. Nonetheless, she is something familiar in an unfamiliar place even if she's an *excom*.

Abram and Leroy are close now. Abram shows an interest in Leroy's work and this engenders Leroy's attention. They spend so much time rapt in conversation that I am often left with Hannah and Martha.

The Midwestern winter is at its very nadir at the end of January, but the university recreation center is bright and warm. The facility has several large pools surrounded by beach chairs and artificial sand. Massive heat lamps beam artificial sun rays upon us.

Martha and Hannah are wearing bikinis, blue and black, respectively. They are reclined in lounge chairs and their fluffy bellies glow pink. I sit with my legs crossed in an upright chair. The lamps are hot, so I remove my hat and vest. I place them carefully beneath my chair.

"Isn't this your Rumspringa, Ezekiel?" Martha asks. She also has chestnut hair, but her eyes are a lighter shade of brown.

"Yes."

"Why do you insist on wearing those traditional clothes?" Martha asks.

"These are the only clothes I own," I tell her.

She stands fast and approaches me. She reaches out and grabs my shirt on each side of the collar and pulls. The two top fasteners open but the third rips. I am stunned silent by her behavior.

"I mean, why are you wearing them at all?" She laughs as she settles back in her recliner.

Hannah laughs, too, but then extends her mercy. "Don't fret, Ezekiel, I will mend it for you."

I see Leroy and Abram enjoying refreshments at a picnic table on the patio. I want relief from my present company, so I decide to join them. As I approach, I notice that Leroy is speaking our Dutch.

"We will execute tomorrow morning, depending on cloud cover," Leroy says.

"How do you intend to score a lightning strike in winter?" Abram asks.

I am curious about this as well.

"Doctor Ramirez will have the clouds seeded with silver," Leroy says. "The lower cloud ceiling of winter is actually quite helpful."

"That will create lightning? I can't believe it." Abram is incredulous. "How does one seed a cloud, anyway?"

"A cargo plane will fly above the clouds and drop a few hundred pounds of silver iodide." Leroy smirks. "Pretty simple."

"Such arrogance before God." I can't help myself.

"It's science, Ezekiel," Leroy tells me.

"You are buying lightning," I tell him.

Abram seems to appreciate my take on the matter. "You know he's right in his own Amish way."

"We will be in the south plots behind the football stadium. If you sneak in you could go up to the top rows and watch the whole thing," Leroy says to Abram. He downs his drink. I can smell that it contains alcohol. "Don't stand too close to the light stands though. God might throw us a freebie or two with our purchase."

***

It is cold. Cloud cover is one hundred percent. The train tankard full of seawater sits atop the trailer it was wheeled in on from the yard. A tall copper pole extends fifty feet in the air from the trailer bed. Two wires run from the finial. The first is a very heavy gauge of copper that runs into the tank of water. The second is a normal, rubber coated cable that extends to the negative pole on a large battery sitting beside the tank.

Leroy explains the configuration to me. "The battery provides the negative charge to the finial, thus attracting the lightning strike. The finial will conduct the electricity into the tank of water. The ribbons in the water will be activated and harmonized."

"The ribbons?" I hear one of the engineers ask another with a whisper.

"Is that the 119?" another asks.

"Are you ready, Mr. King?" Doctor Ramirez asks.

"Yes, where is the cover I requested?" Leroy replies. "That battery is going to explode like a bomb when the strike happens."

"We put grounded, insulated trailers in the west plots. We can view remotely from there."

The group retreats to the trailers. Doctor Ramirez opens a portal and orders the planes to seed the clouds over the coordinates she provides.

"They are already airborne. They will pass in five minutes," she reports.

Leroy asks for Professor Graham's watch. He sets the timer and we wait. When there are twenty seconds left, he draws close to the monitor. He draws me close by the elbow as well. As the final seconds tick away, all eyes shift back and forth between the digitized numbers on the dial and the monitors. The timer flips to positive. We are at +5 seconds and there is no activity. +6, +7, +8 . . . .

Flash. Boom.

We are blinded by the first strike. The sound waves roll and reverberate across the plain. The strike has destroyed a light standard in the parking lot of the stadium.

Flash. Boom.

Another strike. More reverberations. The splintered remains of an ancient oak rain down on the plots.

Flash. Boom.

Lightning strikes the rod. There is an explosion. Once our vision heals from the flash, we see that the small battery is gone but the tankard of sea water is intact. Shouts of joy fill the room. Several of the engineers are over-eager and make their way towards the exit of the trailer.

"Hold it," Leroy shouts. "I will be the first to review, but not until that field clears."

"That was nice of you," Doctor Ramirez says. "I was going to let them go out and get killed."

Everyone is abuzz. Even I can tell this is a success. I bet everyone here except Leroy expected the tankard to explode. Seeing that it didn't, it seems that the energy was conducted somewhere else. If Leroy is right, it is clinging to the metal ribbons he dropped in the water.

***

"I heard some of the engineers scoff at you, Leroy," I say. He is fixing my tie. We are wearing English clothes that we borrowed from Abram and his friends.

"Really? What did they say?" he asks.

"They said you wasted about half a million dollars of silver to make a car battery. Not to mention the cost of shipping the seawater and the property that was destroyed."

"Myopic fools," Leroy laughs. His tongue juts from the side of his mouth as he puts the finishing touches on my tie.

"Do I have to go tonight, Leroy? You know how uncomfortable I'll be," I whine.

Leroy places his hands on my shoulders and looks at me square. "You are free to do whatever you want, but your vocation is to follow me, remember?"

I nod.

Leroy continues, "And it would break sweet Hannah's heart to miss seeing you like this."

I look in the mirror hanging on the back of the closet door. I look foreign. I don't recognize myself. This disguise brings feelings of both liberty and inhibition.

There is a knock on the door. I open it. Hannah is wearing a green, sparkling dress. The seams of the dress follow the outline of her body. This new geometry is alluring.

Hannah is holding a green carnation boutonniere. She is fiddling with the needle and has not yet looked up to see me in my strange clothes. I am happy to watch her patiently.

"Ezekiel, you devil!" Hannah shrieks once she looks up. She jumps toward me and plants a kiss on my mouth. She wraps her arms around my back and plunges the needle of the boutonniere into my flesh.

I scream and writhe trying to remove the needle, but I cannot reach it. Hannah rushes to help, but I turn unexpectedly, and she plunges it in further. I scream again.

"Lay down on the bed," Leroy shouts. I do so and he straddles my back like he's mounting a horse. He removes the needle.

I jump to my feet and remove my coat, tie, and shirts. Hannah is ready with the salve and synthetic skin sealant from the first aid kit. She wipes away the blood and disinfects the hole.

"You are a clod!" I scream at her. The wound is sore and warm.

"I'm sorry, precious. I am so, so sorry. Are you OK?"

"You pierced me with a needle. It hurts."

Hannah returns to the first aid kit and finds the antidolorifica spray. She sprays it around the wound and it instantly goes numb. She keeps rubbing my naked back and shoulders.

Leroy finishes dressing himself. "You look nice, Hannah," he says.

"Oh, thank you, Leroy, but I am not concerned about me right now," she says as she rubs my shoulders. She presses her mouth near my ear and whispers, "Are you better now, sweetie? I am so sorry."

"I'm fine." I jerk away from her grip. I turn and she has a pitiful smile. She is gorgeous tonight. I decide to forgive her, but I will milk this for a little while longer.

"Wait until you see what we have in store for you, Leroy," she says. "Grace is coming all the way from Plymouth for the dance tonight. Abram must have really spoken highly of you."

Leroy reviews his visage in the mirror. "Well, I hope I don't let either of them down."

***

The Phi Gamma Psi house is unrecognizable from my last visit. Tea lights line the walkways leading to the front door. An usher in white gloves greets us as we proceed into the foyer. There is jazz music playing in an anteroom. Hannah leads me by the hand to explore the sound.

"Are they real?" I ask. There are two rows of men in tuxedos and a man playing a grand piano. They are all wearing white ties.

"Of course they are, silly," she answers.

"One never knows around here," I say. "I am not eating ANY-THING, by the way."

Hannah places her fingers beneath my lapels and then grips them with her thumbs. She smiles and then pulls my mouth to hers. She kisses me and I let her. My eyes remain wide open as I scan the band for any signs of queer behavior.

She pulls away and opens her eyes. "I won't let anything happen to you, Eazy."

"Eazy?"

"Ezekiel is such a mouthful. I like to call you Eazy." She giggles. "Do you want to get a drink?"

"No, but I'm happy to watch you pollute yourself," I say. She always laughs when I say things like this. I wonder if she doubts my sincerity.

We go to the bar on the mezzanine. Abram is in deep conversation with Leroy while Martha chats with Leroy's date, Grace.

"Does your friend have eyes?" Hannah asks.

"Excuse me?"

"Vision. Is Leroy blessed with such faculties?" she asks. "Grace is the most gorgeous girl in Plymouth. Why isn't he talking to her?"

Grace's long chestnut hair drapes over her white shoulders. Her face is sleek except for her plump, pink lips. Her head floats atop her long white neck. She is wearing a thin choker of black ribbon with a small silver pendant to accentuate this sensuous feature.

"Take it easy, Eazy. You're mine tonight." Hannah reminds me.

She draws me back to her. She is right to retrieve my attention. Hannah is beautiful and I desire her. I am conflicted. If she were common English, I would remain in good moral standing should I surrender to desires of the flesh, but she is an *excom*.

"You look distressed," she tells me.

"Kiss me," I tell her. She does so and I savor the forbidden flavor of her strawberry lip gloss.

"Would you like to dance, Hannah?"

She bounces on her toes and smiles with glee. She takes me by the hand and leads me back toward the band.

I hold her right hand high at her shoulder and I place my right hand at her waist to lead. Her firm flesh fills my palm and it excites me even through the fabric barrier of her dress. I commence to leading her through the four-pace box step. The song is upbeat and calls for more vigor, but I am cautious to mind my limitations.

She draws me close and we dance cheek to cheek. She whispers in my ear. "You will leave soon, won't you?"

"In four months." I smile. "Just four more months."

She is quiet now. We sway back and forth. The lights are dim, but I notice for the first time that the walls are lined with oak siding. I squint my eyes and imagine we are in the community hall in Shipshewana. The band finishes the tune, but we continue to sway until another begins, once again oblivious to the rhythm.

"Will you stay with me tonight?" she asks.

Someone pats my back to gain my attention. It is not aggressive, but the hand touches me precisely where the needle had pierced me earlier. I flinch and jerk forward. I turn to see Martha. Grace stands behind her with a perturbed look.

"May we cut in, Eazy?" Martha says, revealing that my new nickname predates this evening.

"No," Hannah scolds.

"Hannah, Grace wants to leave," Martha says. Grace stands behind her silently with her arms folded across her chest. She is wonderfully endowed and a petite girl. I notice the other men stealing glances as they dance about with their dates.

Hannah leans toward Grace and waves. "Bye!"

Martha loses her temper. She grabs Hannah by the wrist and draws her close. Through grit teeth she growls. "Remember your vocation, Cousin."

Hannah's shoulders slump as she looks at me with a pitiful smile. "Thank you for the dance, Ezekiel."

"I can get Leroy's attention. Is that what this is all about?" I say.

Martha is still frustrated. "He hasn't said two words to her all night." She points to Grace, who I have yet to hear speak.

"Let me break the ice, Martha," I say. "After that, may we stay a little longer?"

Hannah clasps her hands and looks to Martha. Martha looks to Grace, who shrugs.

The party on the upper floors of the fraternity house is much wilder than what is taking place below. The fraternity brothers are wearing black tuxedos with tails and white bow ties. Everyone is carrying martini glasses and their contents splash about as the boys stumble down the narrow hallways.

We reach the top floor. Hannah sees a boy and waves him over. He is excited that she notices him, and he hustles over, spilling half of his refreshment as he arrives.

"What's the plan, Hannah banana?" the sloppy youth says. No amount of formal finery can mask his uncouth manner. "You looking for a nibble?"

"Ron, I'm here with friends, Abram and another boy, Leroy. Have you seen them?" Hannah asks.

"Oh, you're looking for the king?" Ron shouts.

I was curious about how he knew Hannah, but now I am alarmed by his familiarity with Leroy.

"Yes, Leroy King. Is he in one of these rooms?" I ask. I hear shouts and music pulsing from a room down the hall behind the boy.

Ron smirks at me. He must know where Leroy is but is reluctant to take me to him. The boy notices Grace in our company and brightens.

He leads us to the party room. The door reads PENTHOUSE NORTH. Ron knocks three times, there are two knocks in return, and he returns one knock. The door opens.

The revelry ceases and conversation stops when the assembly of fraternity brothers sees me and the girls follow Ron into the room. Leroy and Abram are sitting on stools in the middle of the room. They are naked.

Without breaking his glare from Ron, the leader of the group finishes the recitation that was interrupted by our arrival. "Now rise and clothe thy selves in this brotherhood of men. Before you were naked in a world of plebes and now you will clothe yourselves for the first time as members of Phi Gamma Psi."

Ron raises his empty glass in the air to toast them. "High, high, high!" he exclaims.

"Phi Gamma Psi!" a chorus returns.

"High, high, high!" another brother shouts.

"Phi Gamma Psi!"

The back and forth continues. Leroy and Abram dress themselves and exchange salutes with their new brothers. They drink shots of liquor.

Hannah and Martha are not amused. Grace turns and leaves.

***

I was told that I would be provided something called a twin mattress with my lodging in the dormitory. Upon seeing my sleeping arrangements for the first time I figured I was either misinformed or the description was a misnomer. The name "twin" suggested sufficient space for two adults to sleep, or so I felt.

The insufficient size of the mattress had only become an issue for the first time last night. I had succumbed to Hannah's advances. Following the intercourse, she signaled an expectation that I should remain near her. The reasons for this behavior are still unclear to me. Perhaps she wanted me to comfort her from the guilt of her beastly act.

I held her until she fell asleep and then retreated to Leroy's bed to be alone in my own tortured mind. I would not sleep all night, but I knew that before engaging in relations with Hannah. I anticipated that I would need to unweave the lace of conflicting impulses in my head. Also, I waited for Leroy.

I turn my head to watch Hannah as she sleeps. I can no longer deny my attraction to her. It was becoming tortuous. I will engage with her as little as possible for our remaining months, but it is not realistic to resist her entirely. I will rectify my crisis of conscience when I return to the community.

Hannah shifts in the bed. Her arm reaches out to search for my body. She opens her eyes. Her vision clears and she sees me staring at her. She smiles. She is beautiful.

"I love you, Eazy," she says.

"Please call me Ezekiel,"

"I love you, Ezekiel," she says.

I exhale heavily. "Thank you."

"I will miss you if you leave." She clutches the covers and pulls them to her chin.

"When I leave."

"Come with us. Come back to Plymouth. Your Rumspringa lasts until September, right?" She shifts and sits up on her elbow. Her naked shoulders are exposed.

"This is not my Rumspringa. This is my vocation," I say. "Tell me, Hannah, what is your vocation? What was Martha talking about last night?"

She shifts and lies on her back. She pulls the covers back to her chin and stares at the ceiling.

"Why can't you tell me? Are you ashamed? Is it dishonorable?" I ask.

Hannah begins to cry.

"I see. You are ashamed," I say. "Well, it's time you own it. You should clear your conscience with your bishop, or whomever you *excoms* have out there under your bubble."

"I am not crying because I am ashamed. I am crying because I have failed. We have failed," she says.

I lift my upper body weight to my left elbow. "What is your failure, exactly?"

"We are here to find worthy converts," she says as a matter of fact. "Our little bubble needs a lot of sharp minds to stay functional."

Her revelation triggers a physical reaction in my body. My diaphragm flexes and my throat narrows. I try to swallow but I cannot.

"You said you loved me," I say, barely able to muster the sound.

"I do. I do love you, Ezekiel." She must realize what her revelation implies. She begins to cry again.

"I'd appreciate it if you would go. Thank you." I turn in Leroy's bed. I face the wall to hide the tears welling in my eyes. I hear her throw off her covers and she is upon me.

"We always fail, Ezekiel. No one wants to live in Plymouth. I weep because this time it also means I will lose you." She grips my shoulder and shakes it as she speaks.

"I find it hard to believe that I am your vocation, Hannah," I say. "If so, you Pilgrims have some warped ideas when it comes to carrying out the lord's duties."

Hannah explodes in laughter. A smile cracks my face and I begin to chuckle as well. The chuckle boils over into full rolling laughter.

"I know you're in there, Eazy. I know there is a boy in there who cares for me," she says.

"Perhaps," I say as sternly as possible. I cease laughing. "I need to know what Martha was talking about last night, about Grace and Leroy and your vocation."

She opens my covers and wedges her naked body next to mine. She nestles her chin on my shoulder. "We need to save Leroy from Ramirez. We need to get him, and you, out of here."

"Now there's something we can agree on," I say.

She looks at me. "I'm serious. They are going to take his research and keep it for themselves. They'll keep him, too, if they can."

"He's already been seduced," I realize aloud.

"Mondemon corporation is in the energy business, among others," Hannah explains. "They don't want any disruptive technology coming online unless they do it themselves. And they sure as hell don't want anyone giving it away."

"Language please." I wag my finger at her. "Why can't they just use what he's done so far?"

"Ezekiel," she guffaws, "Leroy created a new element! This isn't textbook research. They need the expertise."

"One nineteen is a new element?" I ponder aloud. "Is that a big deal?"

She covers her face with both palms. "Aren't you in charge of logging all of this?"

"Of course, but I simply write down whatever Leroy tells me to. He fills in the formulas," I say. "He never told me 119 was a *new* element."

"Let me see the book," she says. "I'll show you."

I extricate myself from the bed in a discreet manner. I am wearing my undergarments, but I am still conscious of my semi-nakedness.

"Ezekiel, did you know that Leroy isn't the first person to make a breakthrough like this?" she says. "I mean, he is a true genius and he is making breakthroughs but he's not the first person to develop an alternative energy solution."

I slide my leg through my black slacks. "You know where I'm from, Hannah. I know nothing of this science."

"Nolan Oder came up with something over fifty years ago. It's what our system in Plymouth is based on."

"The Greenfield system," I state. I button up my shirt and tuck it in.

"Yes." She nods and smirks with surprise. "Why do you think no one else uses it?"

"No idea. Doesn't really matter to my community." I retrieve my satchel from a hook behind the door.

"The conglomerates control the energy regulations. They forbid innovation wherever they have control. It's too costly for them to scale up globally. They make more money with the status quo," she says. "Thankfully, we are not subjected to their regulations."

"Hannah?" I say. "It's not here."

I toss open the flap on the satchel and dump the contents on my bed.

"It's not here," I repeat.

***

We meet Doctor Ramirez in the laboratory. She stands behind a team of engineers, none of whom I recognize. Up to now, only Leroy and I have been permitted in the lab.

"Congratulations Mr. King. You have discovered the 119th element. We are calling it Mondemonium," Ramirez states.

"My cousin does not appreciate this disturbance on a Sunday," Leroy states. His appearance is ghastly. He is wearing a black coat and tails over the outfit he left the dorm with last night. His chestnut hair is ratty and disheveled. His eyes are red.

"Mr. King, you and Mr. Fisher rushed in here; I did not force you to come," she says.

There are three ribbons soaking in a tank atop one of the desks. The ribbons' glow casts a greenish blue hue over our faces.

"You stole my book." I point and accuse her.

She waves me off. "Mr. Fisher, you understood the agreement when you decided to come here. All research of the students is the sole intellectual property of the Mondemon corporation."

"Where is the book?" Leroy demands.

"Actually, I'm glad you asked. We need you to take us through it." Doctor Ramirez grins. "Someone fetch Graham."

The engineers part and Ramirez walks over to us. One of the men can't restrain himself and bows at Leroy. "Congratulations, Doctor King. Amazing breakthrough."

Emboldened, another speaks. "The ribbons have been generating stable energy for hours. Zero radiation, zero decay, 7.5 kilowatts with no variance."

One of Ramirez's men escorts Professor Graham into the lab. He looks tired and sad. His head is low, but I notice him steal a glance in our direction as he proceeds toward Ramirez. He hands her our notebook along with another of his own.

"It's very cryptic," Professor Graham states.

"You told us you knew their Dutch," Ramirez challenges him.

"Much of it, but they have their own slang and shorthand. It's between them. Only they know it."

Ramirez tucks the books under her arm. She approaches Leroy slowly and smiles. "Mr. King, I hate bargaining. I'm a very direct person so I'm just going to tell you what it is we are prepared to offer you."

Leroy says nothing so I speak for us. "You have nothing to offer us," I say, "except sadness and suffering."

"To the contrary, Mr. Fisher. I've seen where you live, I've seen how you live. You have never experienced the comforts that we enjoy outside your community," she tries to explain.

"You have nothing compared to us. You are blind to the true comforts provided by God."

She focuses on Leroy. "You've more than earned your doctorate, King. We will give you your own lab." She smiles as she assesses his attire. "I understand you've made friends here as well."

"I'm expected back in my community at the end of the school year," Leroy states.

"We will shuttle you every day in the hyperloop then," Ramirez states. "I understand that might be permissible by your community's rules." She looks to Graham as she says so.

"That's not how it works," I say as I glare at Graham. "I have strict instructions to bring him home. It is my vocation. After that, you can deal with Bishop Yoder."

"Relax, Ezekiel. We are going home," Leroy says calmy, "and we are not coming back."

"Then you are guilty of theft and we will have you charged," Ramirez says with the same measured calmness. "In the least, you are guilty of defrauding the university. You promised us the fruit of your research in exchange for your education."

Professor Graham places both hands on a countertop and hangs his head. "What do we owe him for having educated us?"

Ramirez taps a surface and an interface emerges. "This is Doctor Ramirez. Please have the university constable send a security force to the Florida Avenue Laboratories. Main lab."

"You need to understand, Doctor King, it is no hardship for us to live in a world without your discoveries. Mondemon corporation will continue to thrive," she says. "But you will live the rest of your life knowing your breakthroughs sit in a desk drawer gathering dust. The world will never benefit from your genius."

Leroy wavers. "Keep the book and use it. You will eventually figure it out. Professor Graham is a brilliant man."

All eyes are on Graham. He looks up but then back to the countertop. He shakes his head.

"It's worthless without you, Leroy. Worthless." She lights a burner on one of the desks. She holds the book over the flame. There are gasps amongst the engineers. One man darts at Ramirez but his colleagues stop him.

The corner of the pages ignites, and Leroy is upon Ramirez. He swats the book from her hand and sends it twirling across the floor. It is aflame. He picks it up with a bare hand and throws it in the tank with the ribbons. It sinks just below the surface and is then suspended in an electric field. It sits entrapped in a blue-green web of energy. All are mesmerized.

Ramirez rises to her feet. She pulls the other notebook from beneath her lab coat. Groans echo around the lab and emotions stand down. Ramirez places the book flat on the desk next to the burner. The flame licks the air.

"We will keep the book, Doctor King. We will keep your work safe." Ramirez pats the book. "But there is a lesson here. We all are called by God—by our creator—to fulfill a duty in this life. A vocation, if you will, Mr. Fisher." She presses the cover of the book with her palm. "This. This is your vocation." She picks up the book and holds it in the air. The engineers squirm. She sweeps her arm in the air. "This is your workshop, Doctor King."

The security force arrives. There are five men in black body armor and helmets, visors down. There is a sixth man in formal dress. He also sports a helmet, but his visor is up. "How may we assist you, Doctor Ramirez?"

"Please escort these students to their dorm and ensure they do not leave the premises." She points to Leroy and me. "Scramble their communications. Use my personal enigma."

My vocation is at the forefront of my mind. I must fulfill my duty. Leroy may still be convinced to stay. He has made friends, he has joined a fraternity. He treasures his achievements and there is no way to repeat this research outside of this setting. Where else can one buy a bolt of lightning?

"Doctor Ramirez, I will translate the work for you," I say.

"Are you able?" she says.

"I wrote it."

"All of it?"

"No, Leroy filled in all the formulas," I say. "But that's just math. I assume you understand all of that already?"

Several engineers look at the floor but Professor Graham looks up. "I can help bridge the gap on the quantitative component."

Leroy seethes. "You are a maggot. You just want to go home to Yoder and your pigs," he tells me in our tongue.

"My vocation is to bring you home," I respond, still in Pennsylvania Dutch.

"My vocation is here," Leroy cries in English but then continues in our language. "You will ruin everything. We can just stay here. We will sneak our findings out somehow. I will figure something out."

Professor Graham must understand us. He stands stock still as though it will help him go unnoticed. While remaining face to face with Leroy, I cast my eyes toward Graham.

"My vocation is to bring you home," I repeat.

Leroy grabs me with both hands and throws me to the floor. He is upon me. His fists batter my ribs like twin hammers on a bell. A man from the security force tackles him off me.

"Take him to his dorm," Ramirez commands the security force.

Two men swing their arms beneath Leroy's armpits and lift his butt from the floor. They begin to carry him from the room. His heels dragging, Leroy releases a ferocious scream, "You will fail! You are a maggot!"

He is gone.

"Get me a fresh notebook," I tell Graham in our tongue.

***

Months pass before I can complete the work with Graham and then I am released. There is fanfare when I arrive in Plymouth, but I fear Leroy's bitterness. I want so badly to explain to him but Hannah intercepts me before I can seek him out.

"Welcome, welcome, my love." She squeezes me around my chest.

"Where is Leroy?" I look over her head and search for his face in the crowd.

"You will see him after lunch," she says. "There are so many people who want to meet you here."

"Please take me to him now," I say. A man introduces himself to me. I shake his hand without even listening to his name. I need to find Leroy. I must not fail.

"Leroy is busy in the workshop with Abram," she says.

"What kind of workshop?" I ask, assessing my surroundings. It is bright and sunny within the bubble. The grounds are very familiar. They modeled their original town perfectly.

"He is in his lab, working," she says. "We aren't outfitted as nicely as Purdue, but he's made some advances. He is so brilliant."

"I know he doesn't want to see me, Hannah, but you have to take me to him."

"Hello, maggot," Leroy says from behind me. Abram is beside him.

I am filled with relief to hear his voice. I reach out to embrace him, but he steps away.

"Leroy, it's OK. I saved your work," I gush. "I couldn't tell you because I knew they would hear."

"It's not possible," he sneers. "They would never let you smuggle it out."

"It's up here." I tap a finger on my temple.

"You memorized it?" Hannah blurts.

"I can't believe it," Leroy says.

I begin to recite the book of Esther from memory. I make it well into the second chapter before indulging their pleas to stop.

"Oh, Eazy, you did it." Hannah plants a kiss on my cheek.

I stand proud. "Leroy was always better in school except for one subject. I could memorize the scriptures better than any-one. The notebook was brief by comparison."

"Let's get him to the workshop. He can fill in all of our gaps," Abram urges Leroy.

"How long did it take to translate the book, Ezekiel?" Leroy asks.

"About a month but most of that was figuring out the math. I worked on memorizing the text while Graham sorted all that out," I tell him. "While he spent the next month conducting ex-periments to prove he had done it, I memorized the formulas."

"So, he did it?" Leroy asks.

"Well, he repeated what you did. He made 119," I say.

"It's called Reyez. I named it Reyez," Leroy says.

"OK, Reyez. He made Reyez."

"If they let you go, that means they have all they need to file the patent," Leroy states.

"Then we have to get to work and file ours first," Abram says.

"Don't be foolish. Ramirez was in the hyper loop to DC the moment she had what she needed." Leroy glares at me again. "You stupid maggot. You failed anyway."

"That's hurtful, Leroy," I tell him. "Do you really think I'm that dense?"

"Yes," he says. "And you are the bane of my existence."

"Graham promised me," I say with a smile.

"Promised you what?" he asks.

"That he would wait."

"Wait for you to file the patent?" Leroy scoffs. "Yes, Ezekiel, you really are that stupid."

"No, Leroy, that he would wait for me to get here."

Sirens blare within the bubble. An automated voice announces the cause for the alarm.

"Boundary alert. Boundary alert."

An elder brings up a security portal and live images of all four outer gates are broadcast. There is a swarm of people at the gate off the frontage road from the highway. The elder selects an image and zooms.

There is a man in a white lab coat. He is holding two notebooks and an open flame. There are men on his side of the gate trying to apprehend him, but he holds them off with his torch. He stands amidst several puddles of liquid. A metal can has been cast aside.

"It's Graham. You have to let him in," I scream to the elder.

The elder convenes with those around him. Surely, they are concerned about the swelling mass of men in body armor that will follow Professor Graham through the gate.

A tall woman in the crowd outside the gate shouts an order and the armored men rush at Graham. He drops the torch. Professor Graham and his books burst into flames. Thick black smoke billows from his writhing body and the armored men recoil from the massive, roiling fire.

Interlude 10: Eazy Does It

"What was your sin, Eazy? May I call you Eazy?" I know longer wish to call him Zeke. I want to call him Eazy, like the others.

"I only know one way, Nick. That is why I fear I am doomed to an eternity of limbo."

"But . . . you did the right thing?" I want what he did to be enough.

"Well, all Professor Graham had to do was self-immolate. But then, yes, everything ends well after that I suppose." Eazy lets out a nervous laugh. He knows it's not enough.

"What do you mean when you say you only know one way?"

"I mean that what I believe is exclusive of what others' believe. I deny myself new experiences, new relationships, because others don't believe the same things that I believe," Eazy says. "My piety is my insulation from blame for my sins."

"Find another path, my friend," I tell him. A wave of warmth rushes over me. The citizens communing in the square notice us and draw near. The street is ablaze in light.

"What other path, Nick? I have only ever been shown one path," he says.

"What about the paths you have seen from others?" I ask. "Have none of them inspired you?"

"I can't help but to see people making the same mistakes over and over again." He shakes his head. "I feel like my path is closer to righteousness than anyone else I've met."

He notices the crowd. He notices my glow and their attraction to it.

"It's the same for you, Nick. It's the exact same thing," he challenges me. "You choose a life with Lori or a life of nothingness. You do so over and over again."

"You love your path. You love your life. You want it to be the right way," I say with realization. I am aglow. My fellow souls dart and hover around me like moths.

"Of course I do," Eazy says. "Our community is joyous and untainted by the material ways of man. I want that to be the right way. I don't want it to be wrong," he pleads to no one in particular.

"That's your sin, Eazy!" I exclaim.

"Well, then it is yours, too," he tells me.

"Life isn't supposed to be perfect. It's not heaven," I say.

"My home feels like heaven."

"But it's fragile and it can be overrun. And then what would you do?"

Eazy smiles, "Even a moment in heaven is worth a lifetime in limbo."

"You must be wrong," I know I'm onto something.

My Western scene is gone. My world is now centered by a massive bonfire in a prairie. All the people encircle the fire. They are laughing and sharing their stories.

I am a tongue of fire within the circle of the bonfire.

I think of my selfless aunt, who was blessed with riches but only found joy giving it away to others. "Eazy, you need to return the love you've been offered, without question."

Eazy thinks aloud. "I want my path to be the right one. I don't want to consider anything else, like Leroy did."

"Yes, like Leroy did." I think of the many times I returned to Lori to fight for our relationship and when that was for naught, how I abandoned the gift of life.

I see Andres in the crowd speaking with Cole. I see Piper and he winks at me. Charlie Musgrave, eyes glowing red as rubies, darts around behind the crowd.

I reach out to Eazy and tell him of Jay Hustle and the curse of the answered prayer. Eazy nods but still he hesitates. I want him to understand but I can't force my epiphany on him.

The bonfire pops and I am transformed into an ember. I spiral upward in a vortex of heat. I drift higher and higher above the plane until it disappears from view.

Epilogue

Hartsel, Colorado

The Kraus compound achieved self-sufficiency by 2030 and profitability not long after that. The food produced on the property was sold in stores across western Colorado. Kraus garments were prized for their quality and were sold at a premium by specialty outfitters in Aspen. The surplus electricity generated on the premises was pumped onto the grid and helped light homes as far east as Colorado Springs. The compound was open to the public and the communal dining halls were renowned for their fare. The geothermal system that helped provide heat and hot water across the compound was also used to create hot mineral baths for the on-site spa. Some residents opened their homes to visitors for overnight lodging— sometimes for profit but often just in the spirit of brotherhood.

The residents of the compound were also its employees. That was the deal. It was a commune, but a commune that was very much capitalistic by design. Qualified applicants were welcomed to the community and provided housing and board. Children were schooled by highly qualified educators while their parents contributed to the greater economic good of the enterprise. In addition to their hourly wage, the resident/employees shared in the overall profits.

The Kraus family hosted holiday parties at their sprawling ranch house at the far southwest corner of the 1,400-acre property. All 400 residents were invited, and every holiday was a celebration of family and community. The full grandeur of this mini utopia was on display at these holiday feasts. And yet, newer residents sometimes had second thoughts, and others used these gatherings as an opportunity to approach Nick Kraus about their concerns.

Suzy Kraus steals her husband's attention from a group of friends on the back patio. "Nick, Jennifer and Dale would like to speak with you." Easter is late this year and many guests are enjoying the extra sunlight of the mid-April evening.

"Jennifer and Dale, the Conroys?" Nick asks.

"Yes, the newcomers, from California. They arrived at the end of fall."

"Of course, with their son, Alan." Nick nods. "Did they say what about?"

***

Nick meets the Conroys in the music room. The cover art of his favorite albums hangs in frames on the walls. An LP spins on a record player and table-high speakers pump Memphis soul from the corners of the room. Guests mingle about but the ambient noise is enough to shield the conversation.

Jennifer speaks first. "What a wonderful day, thank you so much for having us."

"This is just about our favorite thing to do in the world. Thank you for coming." Nick raises his glass to the couple. Suzy and the guests follow suit. "Tell me, how are you finding it here so far?"

Dale replies, "Absolutely wonderful for us, but it's been a tougher adjustment for Alan. He misses the trappings of his old life. He just turned fifteen over Christmas and he's dealing with a lot of tough transitions right now."

"We asked a lot of him in bringing him out here." Jennifer looks at the floor. "We are beginning to doubt the wisdom of our decision."

Nick and Suzy listen to their concerns. All families bring their expectations with them for the move and those expectations are always the last thing they unpack. Jennifer and Dale are talented engineers and their son displays all signs that he inherited their brilliance. He is also mature and resolute in his beliefs. They expected him to embrace his new circumstances with the same vigor they did.

Nick recalled them from their interview. The couple had met at Cal Tech. After graduation, they went to work for Pike Industries in northern California. Jennifer's specialty was nanoengineering, while Dale's focus was batteries. Pike Industries treasured the couple's contributions to the company's private space program and the company fought hard to keep them around. To have them knock at the gate of the compound was an absolute coup for the Kraus commune.

"We don't want to come across as immodest, Mr. Kraus, but we have done well for ourselves," Dale explains. "We are not here for equity or profits. We value our contribution to what goes on here. We want to be here."

"What we do here gives us purpose and satisfaction," Jennifer adds.

"But..." Dale begins.

"But you need to do what is best for your child," Nick cuts him off.

"Yes," the Conroys answer in unison.

The couples finish their wine and pour more. Nick and Suzy try to soothe the couple. They point out the other people around the room and all their various backstories. The Brewsters from Alabama, who were master horticulturists, had started their family here. Roland McMaster from Manchester, England was an author. He arrived single but eventually married a divorcée with two teenage sons. Roland was a home educator for families on the compound. He and his family were neighbors with the Rossis. The Rossis stumbled through during a cross-country camping trip. Following the trip, they returned to Virginia, sold everything, and moved to a home on the compound. Their eldest daughter recently moved into her own residence near the reservoir. She was an architect, like her parents.

"Everyone here has a story they're willing to share, I promise you," Nick assures them. "We hope you'll hear some of those stories before making your decision."

Jennifer asks the hosts, "What's your story? How did you meet?"

The Kraus's laugh and look in each other's eyes. It is a silent showdown to decide who would start. Suzy cracks first. "Our story begins at the Chalet Diner outside of Basalt."

***

Nick Kraus parks the ATV within the grounds of the solar farm. Alan Conroy jumps out of the passenger side of the vehicle. Nick holds the glass door open for his guest and they enter one of the towers. They head to a receiving room, where they put on safety gear.

"Have you ever been in here?" Nick asks his guest.

"I've been on the grounds but never in here," Alan answers.

"This was the first thing we built once we received the federal funding."

They entered the heart of the complex through an airlock from the receiving room.

"It's beautiful." Alan casts his eyes across a tangle of pipes and wires framed in cement. Any beauty to be found was in the function and not the form.

"I agree." Nick follows Alan's gaze.

"Why did you do this?" Alan asks.

"An autonomous community requires self-sufficiency with regards to energy," Nick says matter-of-factly. "First, we created the farm to feed ourselves, but then we got to work on this."

"Of course, but why did you choose to do *any* of this?" he asks.

They walk a spiral catwalk that ascends the walls of the complex at a mild grade. A gutter full of wire traces the railing of the walkway and pipes run beneath the grating below. Fans pump a vortex of cool air around the complex. Blue sky is visible through the oculus above.

"Everyone has their own definition of success, Alan, and success to me meant never having to depend on others to live freely," Nick says.

"But don't you rely upon on the labor of the residents?" Alan asks.

"Of course we do, but we have an agreement and we share our profits fairly."

The boy does not respond. He proceeds with his eyes straight ahead.

"Are you afraid your parents had you join a cult, Alan?"

"That's not the right word for it, but something like that." He is relieved that he doesn't have to explain it. "I've studied you, Mr. Kraus. You're a fascinating man. People are drawn to you. Outstanding, accomplished people walk away from their homes to live here with you. Why?"

"I think it's because I'm a good listener," Nick answers. "I wasn't always, but I learned to be."

A technician descends the walkway, forcing the two of them to cede the way.

"Why does a Nobel Laureate need you to listen to him, Mr. Kraus?" Alan asks.

"Most don't, Alan." Nick looks at the young man and smiles. "But Ben Davidson had something he wanted to share, something that he wanted to do, and I listened to his idea." He explained how he had met Dr. Ben Davidson while camping on his own in Oregon, shortly after leaving his first wife. The young physicist had big ideas about society, and he wouldn't be content publishing research for the rest of his life. Nick and Dr. Davidson became friends. They would meet again the following summer and every summer after that. Nick started the compound in Hartsel at his behest and, more importantly, thanks to his funding.

Alan shakes his head. "I really don't know what the hell I'm doing here. I don't know what I'm *supposed* to be doing here."

Nick listens to the boy. He is lonely. He misses the city and he misses his friends. He had resented the culture of consumption he found in the city, but the quasi-socialist attitudes of communal living were extreme to the point of being alien.

"Don't torture yourself, Alan. Don't force yourself to believe that this is the place for you. It very well may not be, and it doesn't matter if all the role models in your life think otherwise."

"Thank you, Mr. Kraus."

Nick escorts Alan around the entire compound. He introduces him to the experts running all the different facets of the enterprise. He has them share their stories with the boy. As suppertime draws near, they agree to head for home. Dinner will be at Nick's house tonight and the Conroy's will be their guests.

As they drive from the vertical farming complex to the residential area of the compound, Alan observes, "Mr. Kraus, I just realized there's no church or any other house of worship on the compound."

Nick looks at Mount Harvard looming before them. The descending sun beams from behind the ridge line and it casts salmon and orange hues through sparse clouds. "I never saw the need for one."

"Do you believe in God, sir?" The boy asks and blinks his eyes. He rubs them and looks again at Nick.

"Yes, I believe in God, but I would never force that on anyone else."

"Do you think God wants us to be happy?"

"Yes," Nick answers quickly.

"How can you be so sure?"

Nick stops the vehicle and looks at Alan. "Because he never gave me everything I wanted."

"I don't understand."

"Alan, my grandfather, my father's father, was a farmer. We called him Grandpa Red, which I never understood as a boy because his hair was stark white," Nick says. "I was a silly little boy and couldn't imagine a youthful version of my grandpa with bright orange hair."

"What does this have to do with God, Mr. Kraus?"

"I'll get there, I'll get there," he assures the boy. "Now, Grandpa Red was an organic farmer before there was such a thing. He was so smart. He knew which herbs to plant with the crops in the field to keep the mold away. He knew which birds would eat the bugs that would eat the corn. He knew those birds loved the shelter of certain trees, so he kept large groves all about his property. He never cut them down even though that meant fewer acres, especially when you consider the shade they would cast when they were mature."

"OK," Alan says politely.

"Here's the thing. Large groves of trees in the middle of corn fields are heaven for deer and my grandpa's farm was loaded with them. My grandpa, my dad and his brothers would cull their herd each fall and we had venison to last all winter long."

The sun has dipped below the ridge line of the mountains. The brightest stars of the early night sky begin to emerge.

"I was too young to make the association between the meat and where it came from. I loved the deer," Nick says and then clarifies, "Alive that is; I loved them alive. I would hike out to the trees every chance I got to try to find them and maybe play with them."

"Did you ever find any?" Alan asks.

"All the time," Nick answers. "But they would always run away, except for this one time."

"What happened?"

"I was staying with my grandparents for a little while one summer. My Aunt Flo was pregnant with twins, so my mom went to help her while she was on bed rest," Nick told him. "I would head out to the closest grove of trees every morning and one day I found a baby deer, a fawn, lying as still as could be behind a bush. I'll never forget her white spots and huge round eyes."

"Was she OK?" Alan asks.

"She was fine. That's their instinct when they're that little. They just stay still and hope you don't see them. I probably could have picked her up and brought her home if I weren't just a boy."

"So, what did you do?"

"I went back the next day with a pocket full of corn. I found her and laid it near her. I walked a ways away and hid. I watched her rise and eat the corn," Nick says. "I came back every day after that and looked for her. Most days I found her and I always had a treat for her. Corn or a sliced apple or a carrot. Eventually she began to trust me, and she would rise and eat right in front of me."

"Where was her mother?" Alan asks.

"Certainly not far away, but after surviving more than a few hunting seasons, she was conditioned to fear humans, even a little boy like me," Nick says. "But the fawn was young enough that I could build her trust. And I did. She started to approach me when she heard me coming or smelled my scent."

"Wow, that must have been amazing for you."

"It was, and then I started to get a little bolder. I would reach out and try to pet her. And I would get so close to touching her. Each day I would spend a longer amount of time with her and I would get closer and closer to her. One time I stayed all the way until I heard my grandma calling me for lunch."

"Did she ever let you pet her?" the boy asks.

"I would get so close and then she would always flinch away at the last moment." Nick laughs and shakes his head. "And then one day I brought a heaping pile of sugar and she couldn't resist. I put a little bit on top of a small pile of corn so she could get an idea of what it was all about. Her ears perked up when she tasted it and she looked up at me. Her little tongue darted around her little deer lips and then she licked her nose."

Alan laughs.

"I reached out to show her the pile of sticky white crystals in my palm and she walked toward me. I extended my hand further and she started licking the sugar right out of my palm." Nick smiles at the memory.

"All right, success."

"Sure, and then I slowly extended my other hand to caress her snout," Nick continues. "And she lunged with her open mouth to bite my fingers viciously before running off into the forest."

"Aw, that's too bad. Did you ever go back?" Alan asks.

"Yeah, I kept trying but she always disappointed me," Nick says.

"I see," Alan says.

"Do you?"

"I think so."

"You shouldn't have been trying to pet that deer," Alan tells him.

"That's right," Nick agrees. "Deer aren't meant to be our pets."

"So that's how you know there's a God?" Alan asks, incredulous.

"I never thought of that little deer until much later, Alan. Not until I was older and smarter, and I thought about all my unfulfilled desires," Nick says. The sun has set. It is dark. "And I realized how much happier I am without them."

Otto Frank Miller is an author, statistician and financial professional. He is also an amateur musician whose only brush with fame was playing two measures of Hoochie Coochie Man at open mic night at Rosa's Lounge in Chicago before his amp lit on fire and he had to pitch it out the back door of the club. He is a lifelong Chicagoan save for several blurry years spent in Champaign, Illinois and another five lost in New York City. He now resides in Riverside, Illinois with his wife and daughters. Otto is a Scorpio.